PUFFIN BOOKS

The Demon Headmaster
and
The Prime Minister's Brain

Gillian Cross worked in a school and a bakery before studying at Oxford and Sussex universities. She has also been a child-minder and an assistant to an MP. She has written around thirty books for children, many of them published in Puffin. In 1991 she was awarded the Carnegie Medal for *Wolf* and has won both the Smarties Prize and the Whitbread Award for *The Great Elephant Chase.*

Gillian Cross lives in Warwickshire with her husband and two of their four children. Her hobbies are orienteering and playing the piano.

The Demon Headmaster
and
The Prime Minister's Brain

Gillian Cross

PUFFIN BOOKS

PUFFIN BOOKS

Published by the Penguin Group
Penguin Books Ltd, 27 Wrights Lane, London W8 5TZ, England
Penguin Books USA Inc., 375 Hudson Street, New York, New York 10014, USA
Penguin Books Australia Ltd, Ringwood, Victoria, Australia
Penguin Books Canada Ltd, 10 Alcorn Avenue, Toronto, Ontario, Canada M4V 3B2
Penguin Books (NZ) Ltd, 182–190 Wairau Road, Auckland 10, New Zealand

Penguin Books Ltd, Registered Offices: Harmondsworth, Middlesex, England

The Demon Headmaster
First published by Oxford University Press 1982
Published in Puffin Books 1984
The Prime Minister's Brain
First published by Oxford University Press 1985
Published in Puffin Books 1987
Puffin Film and TV Tie-in edition first published 1995
1 3 5 7 9 10 8 6 4 2

Made and printed in England by Clays Ltd, St Ives plc

Contents

The Demon Headmaster

Gillian Cross

Illustrated by Gary Rees

Contents

Chapter 1

A Girl in the House

'Our last moments of freedom,' Lloyd said darkly. He glowered round the battered walls of the playroom, at the motorbike posters peeling off the wallpaper and Harvey's model aeroplanes neatly ranged on top of the bookcase. 'She'll be sticking up pictures of flowers and ballet dancers when she comes, I bet.'

He mooched about gloomily, kicking at the furniture. '"Take care of her," Mum said. What does she expect us to do? Hold her hand and tell her bedtime stories?'

Harvey, curled in his chair, stolidly went on reading *The Aeromodeller*.

'H!' Lloyd banged him crossly on the shoulder. 'Why don't you say something?'

Harvey looked up and grinned. 'You've gone all red in the face.'

That only made Lloyd angrier. 'Red in the face? I should just think I have. Purple pancakes! Don't you realize how awful it'll be? Having a girl come to live here!'

'But you've known for ages,' Harvey said mildly. 'Mum's always wanted to have someone to foster.'

'I thought she meant a baby,' Lloyd spluttered. 'That would have been OK. Just a bit of screaming at night. But a girl! A wretched girl, as old as me! She'll never be out of our hair. We'll have to take her to *school* with us.'

'So?' Harvey shrugged. 'Might be a good thing. She might be on our side. Another Normal.'

Lloyd looked at him scornfully. 'Is it likely? I ask you. There's only five of us in the whole school. No, she'll be one of *them*. And what about the others? What will they say?'

'Have to wait and see, won't we?' Harvey picked up his magazine again. Enraged, Lloyd leaped across and knocked it out of his hands. 'Harvey Hunter, you're an *idiot*! Can't you see what it means? We'll have a little goody-goody about the place all the time, going on about how wonderful school is, and how marvellous the Headmaster is. I can't bear it. It'll be like having a spy in the house.'

For a moment, Harvey looked troubled. Then he brightened. 'Might not be as bad as that. If she watches us, we could watch her too.' A distant expression came over his face. 'You never know. We might actually be able to discover something. Find out what's going on.'

Lloyd stopped pacing the room and stared coldly at him. 'I've told you a hundred times,' he hissed, 'that's crazy. It'll just get us into trouble. We've worked out a good system for having a quiet life. I don't want anyone interfering with it.'

'But don't you ever *wonder*?' Harvey said dreamily. 'I do. In the afternoons. I sit and stare across at the Hall and wonder what the rest of them are doing, and why they're so –'

'Shut up!' Lloyd caught him by the shoulder and shook him hard. 'I've managed to keep you out of real trouble ever since you came to the school. And jolly difficult it's

12

been. Four years of watching and being careful. I won't have you mucking everything up now. You just behave yourself and –'

'OK, OK.' Scarlet in the face from the shaking, Harvey held up a hand to push Lloyd away. 'Keep your hair on. You don't want to be looking like a raging demon when she gets here.' Coolly he picked up his magazine and started to read again. Lloyd stared at him in disgust.

'Just wish I *did* look like a demon. That might frighten her away.' And he resumed his restless, furious pacing round the room.

'They're such a nice, *normal* family,' Miss Wilberforce said encouragingly, as the car jerked to a stop at the traffic lights. 'I'm sure you'll like living with them, Dinah. Lloyd and Harvey, the two boys, are very sensible and ordinary. It's a pity you couldn't meet them beforehand, but I'm sure you'll get on.'

'Yes, Miss Wilberforce,' Dinah said woodenly.

'Of course, it's hard on you, having to change schools. I hope you won't find the work too difficult. You'll just have to put your back into it.'

'Yes, Miss Wilberforce.'

Miss Wilberforce sighed and looked round at her, taking one hand off the steering wheel. 'You don't seem very relaxed, dear. Are you, perhaps, just a teeny bit afraid? Mmm?'

'No, Miss Wilberforce.'

Miss Wilberforce sighed again. 'Hmm. Oh well, we're here now.' She steered the car in towards the kerb. 'Let's go in and meet them all.'

13

'Yes, Miss Wilberforce.' Dinah climbed out and stood stiffly on the pavement while Miss Wilberforce got her case out of the boot. Then the two of them marched up the front path of the Hunters' house and Miss Wilberforce rang the doorbell.

'Don't worry if you feel a bit strange at first,' she whispered. 'They'll do their best to make you at home.'

The door opened.

'Dinah, dear, how nice to see you again,' Mrs Hunter said. She held out her arms and gave Dinah a friendly hug and kiss. Dinah's body stayed quite stiff.

'Hallo, Mrs Hunter. Hallo, Mr Hunter,' she said, without expression.

'Come in and take your coat off. The boys are dying to meet you.'

'Oh,' said Dinah.

'I'm sure Dinah's looking forward to meeting them, too,' Miss Wilberforce put in quickly. 'But she's bound to be a bit shy, aren't you, dear?'

'No,' said Dinah.

Mr Hunter grinned at her. 'At least you know your own mind. Go into the living room. I'll call the boys.'

Dinah went in and sat on the edge of the sofa, with her knees pressed together. Her eyes flicked from side to side of the room. It was just what she had expected. Three piece suite. Television. A shelf of ornaments. A very ordinary room. She sighed softly. Then she sat up straighter as everyone else came in.

'Here they are,' Mrs Hunter said proudly. 'Lloyd's the big one, and Harvey's the little fat one.'

'Cheek!' Harvey protested amiably.

Dinah looked them up and down. Lloyd was taller than she was, with a mop of wild hair and a cocky look. Harvey was roly-poly and cheerful. There did not seem to be anything special about either of them. She held out a cold, rigid hand.

'Hallo,' she said unenthusiastically.

Chapter 2

Not a Good Beginning

'Hallo,' Lloyd said back, just as unenthusiastically.

He stared down at her hand, but he did not take it. She was even worse than he had expected. A pale, pinched face and two stringy plaits. Crimson cabbages, she looked just like a wooden doll.

She gazed awkwardly at the two of them, and they gazed back.

'I'll tell you what,' Mrs Hunter said briskly. 'I'm sure you'll get on better without a lot of grown-ups breathing down your necks. Why don't you boys grab some tea from the kitchen and take Dinah into the playroom? Then you can get to know each other properly. Off you go.'

With excessive politeness, Lloyd held the door open for Dinah while Harvey went out to the kitchen for some food. A few moments later, the three of them were sitting round the playroom table silently eating sandwiches.

'Have another cheese sandwich, Dinah?' Lloyd held out the plate.

'No thank you.'

'How about peanut butter?' Harvey said helpfully.

'No thank you.'

'Another glass of coke?' Lloyd picked up the bottle.

'No thank you.'

16

With a sudden snort, Lloyd exploded. 'That's all you've said so far. "Yes please". "No thank you". What are you? A robot?'

'Perhaps she's shy,' Harvey said kindly.

'Well?' Lloyd looked at her. 'Are you shy?'

'No,' Dinah said.

'Go on then.' Lloyd prodded her. '*Say* something. Tell us about yourself.'

Dinah drew a breath. 'My name is Dinah Glass. I'm eleven. My mother and father died when I was one. I've lived in the Children's Home for ten years.' Her mouth snapped shut again.

'Suffering crumpets!' Lloyd made another clutch at his chaotic hair. 'She *is* a robot.'

Harvey smiled at her encouragingly. 'No she's not. Go on, Dinah. Say some more. Aren't there any questions you want to ask us?'

Dinah sat for a moment, frowning slightly while she considered. Then she said, 'Tell me about the school.'

'I told you, H, I *told* you!' Lloyd rolled his eyes dramatically upwards and banged the table. 'That's all she's interested in. Rotten school! It's going to be terrible.'

Dinah looked at him coldly. 'What's the matter?'

'What's the matter?' Lloyd jumped up, knocking his chair sideways. 'What's the *matter*? Scarlet sausages, why should I want to talk about school when I'm not there? You'd think anyone would be glad to escape for a day or two and not have to think about –' He paused, panting for breath.

'He doesn't like our school,' Harvey said.

'So I see,' Dinah said. 'Why not?'

Lloyd looked craftily at her. 'Guess. What's the worst thing you can imagine in a school?'

With one finger, Dinah rubbed the end of her nose thoughtfully. 'Chaos. Children running round shouting everywhere, and nobody keeping any order.'

Lloyd gave a loud bellow of laughter and Harvey grinned and shook his head. 'Nothing like that. Try again.'

Dinah frowned. 'Vandalism? Kids smashing everything up?'

Harvey giggled, and Lloyd looked scornfully at her. 'You haven't got a clue. Not a clue. Just you wait until Monday. It won't be at all the way you expect.' He reached forward and switched on the television.

'You're not going to tell?' Dinah said.

'Nope,' Lloyd said annoyingly. 'Don't want to go on talking about school for ever, do I? Anyway, can't you see what time it is?'

Dinah glanced round at the clock. 'Six o'clock. But what does that –'

'Don't know what six o'clock on Friday means?' Lloyd sniffed. 'Didn't they watch the Eddy Hair Show at your Children's Home then?'

'Oh. Yes.' Dinah shrugged. 'I just forgot.'

'Good thing Lloyd remembered,' Harvey said. 'We don't want to miss the Great School Quiz at the end of the programme, because – OUCH!'

Lloyd had given him a sharp kick. 'Will you *shut up* about school, H!'

'So I can't even ask *him* about it?' Dinah said stiffly.

With an irritating grin, Lloyd wagged his finger at her. 'Got you guessing? *That's* how I like it!'

18

The television screen flickered and then a picture swam into focus. A man with long purple hair and a purple-painted face was standing on his head, waggling his feet at the camera. 'Got you guessing?' he said chirpily. *'That's how I like it.'*

Dinah pulled a face at the screen. 'I think Eddy Hair's stupid. And you're even more stupid, Lloyd Hunter. I'll find out about your daft school on Monday.'

For the rest of the weekend, Dinah avoided Lloyd and Harvey even harder than they avoided her. Whenever Mrs Hunter sent them up to play with her, she was curled on her bed, reading a book and not wanting to be disturbed. They hardly spoke to her again until Monday morning. Then, when they clattered down the stairs, late for breakfast, she was already sitting at the table, neat and prim in a white blouse and a blue skirt and jumper. Lloyd stared at her.

'What's that you're wearing?'

'School uniform.' She smoothed her skirt. 'From my old school.'

Harvey was looking worried. 'The Headmaster won't like it.' He sat down and heaped sugar on to his porridge. 'All green, he likes. We all have to be green.'

'Or else,' Lloyd said with relish.

Dinah ate her last spoonful of porridge and folded her napkin precisely. 'Or else what?'

'You'll see,' Lloyd muttered darkly. 'Pass the sugar, H. We don't want to be late.'

'Or else?' said Dinah sweetly. She looked at them over her cup as she drank her tea. 'Scared?'

19

'I'm not scared of anyone,' Lloyd blustered. 'Not even the Headmaster.'

'Bet you are,' Dinah said.

'Bet I'm not.'

Dinah smiled annoyingly.

'*I* am,' Harvey said calmly. 'I'd be a fool if I wasn't. He –'

'Shut up!' Lloyd said sharply. 'Don't tell her a thing. Let her find it all out for herself.' He went on eating his porridge.

Harvey spooned his breakfast quickly into his mouth. He still had not finished when Mrs Hunter bustled in.

'Hurry up, hurry up.' She flapped round the room. 'You'll all be late if you don't go in five minutes. I wish I could come with you, Dinah dear, but the gas man's coming and I daren't go out. We'll freeze to death if we don't get the central heating mended soon.'

'That's all right,' Dinah said politely.

'I've written a letter to the Headmaster, and the boys will take care of you. They know – oh Harvey, do get your coat on!'

Shoving and nagging, she pushed them out of the front door and they walked up the road in an awkward threesome. Dinah was on the outside so that she had to step into the gutter, trailing her feet through frosty leaves, whenever they passed anyone. Lloyd kept as far away from her as he could and watched her carefully out of the corner of his eye.

As they approached the school, they began to see groups of children, all neatly dressed in green with white shirts and striped ties. They walked sedately along the pavement, without laughing or joking, and Dinah looked at them curiously.

'Funny,' she said. 'Don't they play or fight or anything on the way to school?'

'Never,' Lloyd said shortly. As the school came in sight, he and Harvey fell into step, marching with their eyes straight ahead.

'Faster,' Harvey said anxiously. 'I've got to take the registers round. Remember? The Headmaster told me on Friday.'

Lloyd groaned. 'Why didn't you say, you idiot? You'll be late.'

'We could run,' murmured Dinah.

'No we couldn't,' snapped Lloyd. 'No one runs.'

She opened her mouth to say something and then shut it again as they reached the school gates. Without any comment, all the children had stopped. Taking combs out of their pockets, they combed their hair neatly, put their hats straight and smoothed their ties. Dinah stared. Lloyd was dragging a comb through his unruly curls and Harvey twitched nervously at the lapels of his blazer.

'Will I do? He won't complain?'

'You're fine.' Lloyd clapped him on the back. 'Perfect. And I think you've just got enough time for the registers. Go in and do it as quietly as you can, so no one notices you started late.'

With a nod, Harvey plodded round to the playground, behind the school, and began to walk up the steps into the building. Dinah glanced at him as she and Lloyd followed.

'Why was he worried? I thought he was quite tidy *before* he combed his hair.'

'You would,' muttered Lloyd. 'You don't understand. I just hope he gets the registers out without trouble.'

'Why should there be any *trouble* about *registers*?' Dinah sniffed. 'That's silly.'

Lloyd opened his mouth to answer her, but before he could say anything a tall, fair-haired boy came slouching across the playground towards them. He did not seem in any hurry, but as soon as he was close to Lloyd he whispered, with great urgency, 'Quick! What was Harvey doing, going into school? I tried to catch his eye, but he didn't see me.'

'That's OK, Ian,' Lloyd said. 'He's gone in to do registers.'

'Registers?' Ian's face did not change from its casual, cheerful expression, but his voice sounded horrified. 'No he's not. Rose came out and told Sharon to do them, because it was so late. She said the Headmaster wouldn't have anyone else in there before school started.'

'Oh no!' Lloyd gasped. 'Orange onions with silver skins! I'd

better go in and try to get him out before anyone sees him.'

'It won't matter, surely,' Dinah said. 'If anyone sees him, they'll just send him out again.'

Lloyd and Ian looked contemptuously at her. 'You'll see,' Lloyd said. 'Here.' He fished his mother's letter out of his pocket. 'Take this. I've got to go and look for Harvey.'

Without another word he was off, hurrying up the steps into the school. Ian turned away and Dinah was left standing all alone in the playground, shivering in the bitter, wintry wind. She looked thoughtfully up at the school. At one window, she could see a motionless figure, in a green blazer with a large white P sewn on to one pocket. It was gazing through the window, but not at her. Its eyes were fixed on the steps up which Harvey and then Lloyd had just hurried. Dinah stared at it for a moment and then, with a shrug, turned back to the playground.

Chapter 3

The Headmaster

It was a big playground, full of groups of strange children. No one so much as glanced at Dinah and she felt very awkward. But she was not a person who showed her feelings. Her pinched mouth did not relax for a moment. She looked round, wondering if there were any games she could join in. She thought there would be football, skipping and He. And lots of people shouting and telling the latest crazy jokes from Friday night's Eddy Hair Show.

But it was not like that at all. All the children were standing in small neat circles in different parts of the playground, muttering. Carefully Dinah sidled up to the first circle, trying to catch what the voices were saying. When she heard, she could hardly believe it.

'Nine twenty-ones are a hundred and eighty-nine,

Ten twenty-ones are two hundred and ten,

Eleven twenty-ones are two hundred and thirty-one ...'

Extraordinary! She left them to it and moved across to another group, wondering if they were doing something more interesting. But they seemed to be reciting too. Only what they were saying was different.

'William the First 1066 to 1087,

William the Second 1087 to 1100,

Henry the First 1100 to 1135 ...'

She stood beside them for some time, but they did not waver or look round at her. They just went on chanting, their faces earnest. Behind her she could hear a third group. There, the children were muttering the names of the capitals of different countries.

'The capital of France is Paris,
The capital of Spain is Madrid,
The capital of the United States is –'

'New York,' said a little girl's voice.

'Lucy!' A bigger girl took her by the shoulder and shook her. 'You know that's not right. Come on, quickly. What is it?'

'I can't – I can't remember,' Lucy said in a scared voice. 'You know I was away yesterday. Tell me. Please, Julie.'

'You know we're not supposed to tell you if you haven't learnt it,' Julie said crossly. 'Now come on. The capital of the United States is –'

25

Miserably, Lucy chewed at her bottom lip and shook her head from side to side. 'I can't remember.'

The whole circle of children was looking accusingly at her and Dinah was suddenly annoyed with them for being so smug. Stepping forwards, she whispered in Lucy's ear, 'It's Washington DC.'

'The capital of the United States is Washington DC,' Lucy gabbled, with a quick, grateful smile.

From the rest of the circle, cold, disapproving eyes glared at Dinah. *Never be too clever*, she thought. *I should've known that.* Her face pinched up tight again as she stepped back and heard them start up once more. 'The capital of the USSR is Moscow. The capital of Brazil is –'

Woodenly, Dinah walked on round the playground, waiting for the bell to ring or the whistle to go.

But there was no bell. No whistle. Nothing. Instead, quite abruptly, all sounds in the playground stopped and the children turned round to stare at the school.

There on the steps stood a row of six children, three boys and three girls. They were all tall and heavily built and they were marked out from the others by a large white P sewn on to their blazer pockets. Without smiling, the tallest girl took a pace forwards.

'Form – rows!' she yelled into the silence.

'Yes, Rose,' all the children said, in perfect unison. As quietly and steadily as marching soldiers, they walked together, forming neat straight lines which ran the length of the playground. Each child stood exactly a foot behind the one in front. Each line was exactly three feet from the one next to it. Not quite sure what to do, Dinah stood by herself, a blotch of blue among the green.

The tallest boy on the steps walked forwards.

'Lead – in!' he bellowed.

'Yes, Jeff,' chorused the children.

Still in total silence, they began to march forward, row by row, up the steps and through the door into the school, their eyes fixed straight ahead and their feet moving in step. There was no giggling or whispering or pushing. The whole thing was utterly orderly, the only sound being the steady tramping of feet.

Dinah continued to stand still, watching, until the playground was almost clear. As the last line marched off, she tacked herself on to the end of it and walked towards the school. When she got to the top of the steps, Rose stuck out an arm, barring her way.

'Name?' she said briskly.

'Dinah Glass,' Dinah said. 'I'm new, and –'

'Just answer the questions,' Jeff interrupted her. 'What's that you're wearing?'

'It's my old school uniform. I –'

'Just answer the question,' he said again. There was no friendliness in his voice and as he spoke he looked not at Dinah but over her shoulder. 'It is not satisfactory. All pupils here shall wear correct green uniform. Kindly see to it.'

He looked so haughty and spoke so stiffly that Dinah was irritated.

'I don't know why you're being so bossy,' she said coldly. 'Anyone'd think you were one of the teachers, instead of a measly kid like anyone else.'

'All pupils shall obey the prefects,' chanted Rose, in the same stiff voice. 'The prefects are the voice of the Headmaster.'

27

Dinah felt puzzled, but she was determined not to show it. She thrust her chin up and looked straight at them. 'Well, I think you should take me to see the Headmaster. I've got a letter for him.'

The prefects looked doubtfully at each other. Then Jeff vanished inside the school, while the others stood barring Dinah's way. It had grown colder and the icy wind was turning her fingers blue. She lifted them to blow on them.

'Hands by your sides,' Rose rapped out instantly. 'Good deportment is the sign of an orderly mind.'

Stubbornly, Dinah went on blowing. At once, Rose said, 'Sarah! Simon!'

Dinah's hands were instantly seized by two of the other prefects, who forced them down to her sides and stood holding them like that until Jeff reappeared.

'The Headmaster will see you,' he said. 'Follow me.'

Thoroughly bewildered now, Dinah walked into the school after him and along a straight corridor. At her old school, all the walls had been covered with pictures and drawings done by the pupils, but these walls were completely blank, except for a framed notice hung halfway along. Dinah swivelled her head to read it as she passed.

The man who can keep order can rule the world.

Frowning slightly, she went on following Jeff until he came to a stop in front of a door which had the single word HEADMASTER painted on it.

He knocked.

'Come in.'

Jeff pushed the door open and waved Dinah inside, pulling it shut behind her.

As she stepped through, Dinah glanced quickly round the

room. It was the tidiest office she had ever seen. There were no papers, no files, no pictures on the walls. Just a large, empty-topped desk, a filing cabinet and a bookcase with a neat row of books.

She took it all in in one second and then forgot it as her eyes fell on the man standing by the window. He was tall and thin, dressed in an immaculate black suit. From his shoulders, a long, black teacher's gown hung in heavy folds, like wings, giving him the appearance of a huge crow. Only his head was startlingly white. Fair hair, almost as colourless as snow, lay round a face with paper-white skin and pallid lips. His eyes were hidden behind dark glasses, like two black holes in the middle of all the whiteness.

She cleared her throat. 'Hallo. I'm Dinah Glass and I –'

He raised a long, ivory-coloured hand. 'Please do not speak until you are asked. Idle chatter is an inefficient waste of energy.'

Unnervingly, he went on staring at her for a moment or two without saying anything else. Dinah wished she could see the eyes behind the dark lenses. With his eyes hidden, his expression was unreadable.

Finally, he waved a hand towards an upright chair, pulled round to face the desk. 'Sit down.' He sat down himself, facing her, and pulled a sheet of paper out of a drawer.

'Dinah Glass,' he said crisply, writing it down in neat, precise script. 'You are being fostered by Mrs Hunter?'

Dinah nodded.

'Answer properly, please.'

'Yes, sir.'

'And why is she not here, to introduce you?'

'She couldn't come, but she's sent you a letter.'

29

Reaching across the desk, the Headmaster twitched it out of her hand and slit the envelope with a small steel paper knife. As he read the letter, Dinah settled herself more comfortably, expecting to be asked a string of questions.

But there were no questions. Instead, he pushed a sheet of paper across the desk towards her. 'This is a test,' he said. 'It is given to all new pupils.'

'Haven't you got a report on me?' Dinah said. 'From my other school?'

'No one else's reports are of any use to me,' said the Headmaster. 'Please be quiet and do the test.'

His voice was low, but somehow rather frightening. Dinah took a pen out of her pocket and looked down at the paper.

The questions were fairly hard. Mostly sums, with a bit of English thrown in and one or two brain-teasers. She knew that most children would have found them difficult to answer and she paused for a moment, working out where she was going to make her deliberate mistakes. Not too many. Just enough to avoid trouble.

Then she picked up the pen and began to write. As she scribbled, she could feel him watching her and every time she glanced up he was the same. Pale and motionless, with two black circles where his eyes should have been. She was so nervous that she stumbled once or twice, getting some of the answers right where she had meant to make mistakes. To keep the balance, she had to botch up all the last three questions. Not very good. It did not look as convincing as it should have done. Her hand trembled slightly as she passed the paper back across the table.

The Headmaster scanned it carefully for a moment, then looked up at her.

'You are an intelligent girl.'

Dinah's heart sank, but, with an effort, she kept her face calm, meeting the Headmaster's gaze steadily. At last, he said, 'But you make too many mistakes. I wonder –' He chewed for a moment on his bottom lip. Then he shrugged. 'It doesn't matter. I dare say we shall find out all about you in due course.'

She looked down to the floor, trying not to seem too relieved, and waiting to be told which class she should go to. But the Headmaster did not seem in any hurry to get rid of her. He crumpled the test paper in his hand and dropped it into the rubbish bin. Then, slowly, he reached up a hand to take off his glasses.

Dinah found herself shivering. Ridiculously, she expected him to have pink eyes, because the rest of his face was so colourless. Or perhaps no eyes at all ...

But his eyes were not pink. They were large and luminous, and a peculiar sea-green colour. She had never seen eyes like them before, and she found herself staring into them. Staring and staring.

'Funny you should be so tired,' he said, softly. 'So early in the morning.'

She opened her mouth to say that she was not tired, but, to her surprise, she yawned instead.

'So tired,' crooned the Headmaster, his huge, extraordinary eyes fixed on her face. 'You can hardly move your arms and legs. You are so tired, so tired. You feel your head begin to nod and slowly, slowly your eyes are starting to close. So tired and sleepy.'

He's mad, Dinah thought muzzily. The whole school's raving mad. But she felt her eyes start to close, in spite of all she

31

could do. She was drifting, drifting ... All she could see was two pools, deep green like the sea, and she seemed to sink into them as she drifted off and off ...

She opened her eyes again and gave a nervous laugh. 'I'm sorry. What did you say?'

'You fell asleep,' the Headmaster said coldly. 'You have been asleep for a long time.' He put his glasses on again.

'Asleep?' Dinah stared.

'For the whole morning.'

She looked at him in bewilderment and then glanced round at the clock on the wall. To her amazement, the hands pointed to twelve o'clock. 'But I don't understand.'

'Perhaps you should go to bed earlier,' he said, with a strange smile. 'Now go and have some dinner. The dining hall is at the end of this corridor. After dinner, you will go into the Hall with Class One.'

Still puzzled, Dinah nodded.

The Headmaster looked disagreeably at her. 'Your uniform,' he said, 'is not what I require.'

'It's what I had for my other school. When I was at the Children's Home.'

His lips narrowed. 'I dislike argument. It serves no useful purpose. You will appear in the correct school uniform by next Monday. I am sending a list to Mrs Hunter to ensure that she buys the proper items. I like to see all my pupils dressed in an orderly manner.' His voice rose a tone. 'I will not *endure* disorder. It is inefficient. Now go and have some dinner.'

Shakily, Dinah stood up and made for the door. As she

32

reached out her hand for the handle, the Headmaster spoke again.

'I have put you in the same class as Lloyd Hunter, but I wish you to have as little as possible to do with Lloyd and Harvey. They are not a good example. They do not fit in at this school.'

'That –' Dinah had been going to say that it would be difficult. But just in time she remembered that he did not like argument. Better to be quiet and obey. Until she had had time to think everything over, to try and work out why the school was so strange. 'Yes sir,' she murmured.

As she went out and shut the door, her head was humming with thoughts. Asleep? All the morning? It did not make sense. And had the Headmaster simply sat and stared at her all that time, without trying to wake her up? She shuddered and put a finger into her mouth to suck it thoughtfully.

Something made her take the finger out again and look at it. It was sore. There was a small red patch at one end, as if a pin had been driven into it. But she did not remember having pricked her finger. Frowning, she walked along the corridor towards the dining hall.

Chapter 4

'The Best School
I've Ever Been To'

At the door of the dining hall, Dinah stopped. She must be too early. There was no sound coming from inside, none of the hubbub of chatter that she associated with dinner time. But when she pushed the door open she saw that the room was full. Table after table of demure children in green uniforms eating platefuls of sausages and chips. Going to the counter, she collected a tray and looked round for Lloyd and Harvey.

It was easy to see them. Although the dining hall was crowded, the table they sat at was half empty. The two of them were sharing it with Ian and two girls, one tall and red-haired and the other short and chubby. The remaining five seats were vacant. Dinah walked across and sat down in one of them.

No one spoke to her. Harvey gave a shy smile, but Lloyd scowled and looked away and the others all stared at her, in a hostile way. Dinah chewed calmly for a moment before she said anything. Then she turned to Lloyd.

'I'm in your class.'

'Oh good,' Lloyd said sarcastically. 'Where've you been all the morning, then?'

'Went to see the Headmaster.' She finished off her first sausage.

Lloyd and Harvey exchanged glances and Ian looked at her curiously. 'What do you think of him?' he said.

Dinah opened her mouth to say that she thought he was creepy and peculiar. Instead, she heard her voice say, 'He is a marvellous man and this is the best school I've ever been to.' She put her knife and fork down.

'Ah ha!' said the chubby little girl savagely. The red-haired girl prodded her.

'Be quiet, Ingrid.'

'But Mandy –'

'Be quiet.'

The five of them went on eating stolidly, while Dinah studied their faces. But she could not guess anything from them. They were determinedly blank. After a moment or two, Mandy said casually, as if the question had not been asked already, 'What do you think of the Headmaster?'

Automatically, Dinah found herself repeating the same words. 'He is a marvellous man and this is the best school I've ever been to.'

'Ah *ha*!' said Ingrid again, unrepentantly. The others simply snorted and went on eating their dinner.

'But I don't understand.' Dinah looked round at them.

'They all say that.' Lloyd shrugged. 'All of *them*.' He waved a hand round at the rest of the dining hall. 'Try asking them some time. They think he's just as marvellous as you do. I can see you're going to fit in beautifully.'

Dinah looked over her shoulder at the green-uniformed children. Then she looked back at the hostile faces opposite her. She could not understand what was going on. She was not used to not understanding things. And she did not like it at all.

'I bet he said you were to go into the Hall after dinner,' Ingrid said sneeringly.

'Well, yes, he did. Doesn't everyone?'

'No,' Mandy said quietly. 'We don't. Everyone else does.'

Ian gave a languid, amused smile. '*We* have extra work. With one of the prefects to watch over us.'

'And you needn't go thinking we're thick or anything.' Lloyd slurped up the rest of his semolina, the noise sounding disastrously loud in the quiet canteen. 'It's not that at all. We just aren't like the others.'

'Oh,' said Dinah. She still did not understand anything, but she made up her mind not to say so. She would just watch and wait.

Lloyd got to his feet. 'Mind you're not late to the Hall,' he said nastily. 'You don't want to get into trouble on your first day, do you?'

He turned away, and the others followed him. Harvey, going last, whispered 'Good luck,' and then hurried after, as if he were afraid the others might have heard him. As the five of them passed down the long canteen, two hundred pairs of eyes watched them expressionlessly, while two hundred sets of teeth chewed in rhythm.

Ten minutes later, as if at a signal, everyone stood up. As Dinah was beginning to expect, the children formed a neat crocodile, without any pushing, and began to file silently out of the canteen.

Waiting until nearly everyone had gone, Dinah found herself walking behind Lucy, the little girl who had not known the capital of the United States. She reached out and touched her on the arm. Lucy turned round with a jerk and then smiled timidly.

36

'Thank you,' she whispered. 'For what you did in the playground.'

''S all right.' Dinah smiled back. 'Can't think why the others wouldn't tell you.'

Lucy shrugged and started to turn away again, but Dinah had had an idea.

'Have you been at this school a long time?' she murmured.

'Since I was five,' Lucy whispered. 'Ssh! We're not supposed to talk.' She looked nervously over her shoulder.

'There's no one there,' Dinah said encouragingly. 'We're the last. Do you like the school?'

She had half expected the answer, but it was still a shock when she heard it. Lucy turned to look at her and said in a rather mechanical voice, 'The Headmaster is a marvellous man, and this is the best school I've ever been to.'

'It's the *only* school you've ever been to,' Dinah said.

But Lucy only looked puzzled and put her finger to her lips. Dinah walked on quietly, her thin face wrinkled with concentration. There was something very queer here. Something not like a school at all. Perhaps she would understand it better after she had seen what the Assembly in the Hall was like.

Following Lucy in, she sat down in a chair at the back of the Hall. It was full of children, and teachers were seated on chairs round the edge, as silent and stony-faced as their pupils. After a moment, the Headmaster appeared. He stalked up the aisle between the chairs, his long gown flapping behind him, seeming even taller than Dinah had remembered. Slowly he climbed the steps up to the stage and turned to look down on the crowded hall below him. There was no need for him to call for silence. Everyone, teachers and

37

children alike, was gazing at him. With a thin smile, he reached up and took off his glasses and his huge green eyes stared out at them.

Dinah felt that he was looking directly at her. She could not move her eyes away from his steady green stare. Then he began to speak.

'Funny,' he said gently, 'that you should all be so tired. So early in the afternoon.'

But that's what he said before, Dinah thought, with a jerk of surprise. *When I was in his office. It's peculiar.*

Her amazement had jolted her out of the dreamy vagueness that his voice was producing in the others. All of a sudden, she felt grimly stubborn. She had had enough peculiar happenings for one day. She tried to turn her attention away from the tall black figure on the stage, so that she could think. But it was very difficult. There seemed to be no escaping those eyes. Then, all at once, like a light, she had a little flicker of understanding.

That's it! She thought triumphantly. *When he takes his glasses off – when I see his eyes – I want to go to sleep. And that's when things get peculiar.*

With an almost gleeful feeling, she shut her own eyes tightly, blacking out the Hall, the rows of yawning children and the compelling green stare. This time she would not get caught.

'You all look very tired,' said the Headmaster's hissing voice.

No I don't, Dinah said rebelliously, inside her head, behind her closed eyes.

'*So* tired,' he went on. 'Your hands and feet are heavy, and your eyelids are like lead.'

39

No they're not, Dinah thought ferociously. She turned her head sideways and, with great caution, opened one eye. All around her, she could see heads starting to nod. Children were rubbing their eyes. Teachers were giving huge, uncontrollable yawns. Then, gradually, the eyelids closed. Dinah shut her own eyes again and listened.

'You are asleep,' the Headmaster hissed down the Hall.

Ha ha! No I'm not, Dinah's inside voice said rudely and triumphantly. She was going to do it. She was going to get the better of him.

'When you wake up,' his voice went on silkily, 'you will remember that you saw a film about ants. If anyone asks, you will say, "It was a film about ants. It was very interesting. We saw how they build their nests and look after their eggs and how their queen lives." If you are asked any more questions, you will say, "I don't remember." Now, repeat that, please. What did you do in Assembly today?'

'It was a film about ants ...' the children started, their voices wooden, in perfect unison. Dinah joined in, trying to sound as lifeless as the rest of them, but all the time she was gloating, because *she* knew that what she was saying was a lie. Even if she did not understand why she was supposed to be lying.

As the children stopped speaking, there was a pause and, unable to resist the urge, Dinah opened her eyes a fraction to glance at the rows and rows of apparently sleeping children, their faces turned to the front and their hands clasped in their lap. There was something sinister about the sight and, before she could stop herself, she shuddered. Instantly, she closed her eyes tightly and dropped her head forward, imitating theirs, but it was too late. From the front of the Hall she heard heavy footsteps coming down the aisle towards her.

'Dinah Glass, open your eyes,' said the Headmaster's voice softly.

Mechanically, she opened them, letting her gaze settle on a distant point, way past the Headmaster, hoping that he would think she was asleep. She could not see his face, but for a moment she thought that she had succeeded in deceiving him. He stood perfectly still, watching her.

Then she heard him say, 'Your left arm is completely numb. You can feel nothing.'

Oh yes I can, her mind said obstinately – a split second before she realized what he was going to do.

He leaned forward and she felt a sharp pain, darting into her left forearm. Unable to stop herself, she winced, looking down to see him pull out the pin with which he had pricked her.

'As I thought,' he said sharply. 'Pretending, Look at me, Dinah, when I'm speaking to you.'

She went on looking stubbornly at the floor.

'Look at me!' This time his voice was loud and threatening. Frightened in spite of herself, Dinah looked up.

He was staring straight at her, a lock of pale hair falling over his forehead and his green eyes wide and translucent.

'I can see that you are not yet accustomed to our ways,' he said, more quietly. 'I hope you are not going to be a person who won't cooperate with me.'

'It depends what you want,' Dinah said coldly.

'But it's not what *I* want.' He sounded almost amused. 'It's what *you* want.'

'What I want?'

41

'Yes,' he crooned. 'What you want. You want to go to sleep. Because you're so tired. So very, very tired.'

Too late, she realized that she had let herself get caught off guard. This time, try as she would, she could not close her eyes or turn them away from those great pools of green that seemed to swim closer and closer . . .

'You are so sleepy,' murmured the Headmaster, 'You feel you have to go to sleep . . .'

I'll forget it all, Dinah thought frantically. *I'll forget everything I've discovered. What a waste.*

As her eyelids began to droop, she gathered all her energies together, to try and fix something in her mind.

Remember it, remember it, hypnotism, hypnotism, HYPNOTISM. Grimly, she struggled to concentrate. *Remember it, remember it, hypnotism, hypno-, hyp- . . .*

But the words in her head drifted off into silence and floated away on a great tide of sleep as she slumped slowly forwards in her chair.

This time she did not feel a thing when the Headmaster stuck the pin into her arm.

Chapter 5

Assembly – Keep Out

Harvey looked up from his page of sums and stared out of the window, fidgeting. All around him, the others were working hard. Ian was writing steadily, in his elegant, sloping script, Mandy was frowning over a difficult problem, and Ingrid was running her hands through her untidy hair and chewing the end of her pencil. Even Lloyd was not paying him any attention. But Harvey could not concentrate. Because Dinah had made him think about Assembly again. What *did* go on in the Hall when they were all in here?

'Harvey!' said Rose sharply, looking up from the book she was reading. 'Why aren't you working?'

'I'm just thinking for a moment.' That was true enough, anyway. He waited until Rose was bent over her book again and then prodded Lloyd. 'What d'you think they're doing?' he mouthed noiselessly, pointing towards the Hall.

Lloyd frowned at him and mouthed back. 'Films, of course. Get on with your work.'

Harvey looked across at the Hall and frowned. The blackout curtains were certainly drawn, as if for a film. But all round the edges of the curtains he could see thin streaks of light. And it was always like that. Every day. He often looked across while he was supposed to be working, and he had never seen the lights go out. Not once. So they could not really be watching films. What *were* they doing? He wriggled in his chair with frustrated curiosity.

'Harvey Hunter, *will* you sit still and get on!' Rose was really irritated now. Harvey could see that he would have to be careful, or something nasty would happen. He was just about to go back to his sums when he suddenly had an idea.

'But I can't concentrate, Rose,' he said, making his voice into a whine. 'I want to go to the toilet.'

Rose looked even more annoyed. 'You should learn not to be so disorganized.'

'*Please*, Rose.' He knew he sounded stupid, but he could not bear it any longer. He *had* to go and have a look in the Hall. 'Please. I can't wait till the end of school.'

She looked rattled for a moment, as the prefects always did when you asked them something unexpected. Then she nodded reluctantly. 'Oh, all right. But be as quick as you can.'

As he jumped up, he saw the others looking at him. Mandy's gentle face was worried. She had guessed he was up to something. He slipped quickly out of the door before she could mouth a question at him and ran along the corridor on tiptoe, until he reached the Hall doors.

The double doors had glass panels at the top, with heavy curtains drawn across. By stretching up and peering, he could see through a narrow gap at one side, and he stood there looking.

There was no screen on the stage, no projector, no sign at all of anyone getting ready to show a film. Instead, everyone in the Hall, teachers and children, were staring fixedly at the stage.

44

On the stage stood the Headmaster, stooped forward like a giant vulture. Harvey saw, with amazement, that he had taken off his dark glasses. *But I've never seen him like that*, Harvey thought. *Except on the first day I came here.* He leaned further forwards, pressing his nose against the glass in an effort to try and find out what was going on.

The Headmaster seemed to be reading aloud from a book that he held in his hands. As Harvey watched he stopped, then glanced up and spoke a few words. Immediately, all the people in the Hall started to chant in a regular monotone, as if they were repeating back, from memory, what he had read. It must have been pages long, because the voices went on and on and on. But, struggle as he might, Harvey could not make out more than a few words. He caught '... system

'...' several times and, once, a number '... minus twenty-six point nine ...', but none of it made any sense. And still the voices went tirelessly on.

It was tempting to stay, to try to find out more, but just in time Harvey remembered that he would spoil his excuse if he did not get back quickly. Gnawing his bottom lip, he hurried away along the corridor.

He did not look back. If he had, he would have seen Jeff slide out from behind a tall bookcase beyond the Hall doors and stare after him with a gloating smile on his face. But it never occurred to him to glance over his shoulder. He was too busy getting back to the classroom.

As he let himself in, Rose scowled at him.

'You were too long.'

'Sorry.' He slid into his chair. Better write hard for a bit, until she had stopped watching him. He scratched away industriously, keeping an eye on her under his eyelids. When he was certain that she was deep in her book, he scrawled a message on a spare piece of paper.

They weren't watching films, so sucks. They were listening to the Headmaster.

With great care, he flicked it across on to Lloyd's desk. Lloyd gave him a disapproving frown, but when he had read the note he raised his eyebrows and a few moments later another note landed on Harvey's desk.

We'll ask Dinah when we get home.

As they sat over their tea, Dinah was even quieter than usual. She gazed into her cup, watching the brown liquid swirl round, and Mrs Hunter had to ask her three times whether she wanted another piece of cake.

46

'Sorry.' She looked up at last.

'Thinking about school?' Mrs Hunter smiled. 'I was going to ask if you had a nice day. What did you think of it?'

'I think,' Dinah said steadily, 'that the Headmaster is a marvellous man and this is the best school I've ever been to.'

Harvey sniffed scornfully and looked at Lloyd, but Lloyd was watching Dinah. Her face had gone white, almost as if she were frightened by what she had said. The next instant, she had lowered her eyes and began to munch her piece of cake.

'Let's all go in the playroom,' Lloyd said suddenly. 'Come on, H. You coming, Dinah?'

Dinah swallowed her mouthful of cake. 'If you like,' she said carefully.

She followed them through and sat down as Lloyd closed the door.

'Now,' he said, 'suppose you tell us what you were all doing in the Hall this afternoon.'

Dinah said mechanically, 'We saw a film.'

Lloyd looked knowingly at Harvey. 'Oh yes? What was it about?'

Dinah took a deep breath and began to talk as if she were reciting. 'It was a film about ants. It was very interesting. We saw how they build their nests and look after their eggs and how their queen lives.' She stopped abruptly.

'What else was it about?' Lloyd said.

'I don't remember.'

'Did the Headmaster talk to you about it afterwards?'

47

'I don't remember.'

'Rubber ravioli!' Lloyd burst out, 'don't you remember anything? You're a proper dunce, aren't you?'

Harvey giggled suddenly. 'She'll never be on Eddy Hair's Great School Quiz.'

'Oh, shut up about stupid Eddy Hair,' snapped Dinah. 'What's all this about, anyway?'

'Oh, nothing,' Lloyd said airily. 'We just wanted to know what happened, that's all. But if you're too thick to remember anything . . .'

'I *always* remember things,' Dinah said slowly. 'Always. I don't quite understand.' For a moment she looked as if she were going to go on. Then her face snapped shut and she shook her head. 'I've told you what I can. I can't tell you any more.'

'But I can tell you something,' Harvey said.

'Be quiet, you idiot.' Lloyd gave him a shove.

'No.' Harvey looked obstinate. 'It's not fair to ask her questions and then not tell her. Besides, I want to hear what she's got to say.' He turned back to Dinah. 'I sneaked out of our room and had a look through the Hall door. I didn't see any sign of a film.'

Dinah stared at him and he nodded.

'That's right. Nothing. No screen or projector or anything. And I was watching from across the playground all the rest of the time. The lights in the Hall didn't go out once. So you can't have seen a film. You're lying.'

'What did you see?' Dinah said hesitantly.

'I saw you all sitting looking at the Headmaster on the stage. He read something long out of a book and you all

48

repeated it back. I don't know what it was, but you must know. You all said it from memory.'

Dinah frowned harder and shook her head. 'I don't remember anything like that happening.'

'Huh!' Lloyd sat down and stretched his legs out. 'What did happen then?'

'I told you. We saw a film. It was a film about ants.' She was talking in that steady, reciting voice again. 'It was very interesting. We saw how they build their nests and look after their eggs and how their queen lives.'

'That's what you said before.' Harvey bounced up. 'It's *exactly* what you said before.'

'And it's not true.' Lloyd banged his hand down on the table. 'So why do you keep saying it?'

'I – I don't know.' For a moment, Dinah looked bewildered. Then her face pinched. 'I don't want to talk about it. Why do you keep going on about it?'

'Because it's ridiculous,' Lloyd snapped. 'You heard what Harvey saw.'

Dinah was beginning to look annoyed. A faint pink flush ran along her cheekbones, and the tip of her nose turned white.

'You hadn't got any business to be seeing anything,' she said crossly. 'What did you think you were doing, snooping around like that?'

'I thought there was something peculiar going on,' Harvey said mildly. 'And I was right, wasn't I?'

'You don't know anything about it,' Dinah muttered. 'And if you go on nosing, you'll get into trouble.'

'I told you not to tell her anything, H!' Lloyd burst out.

49

'Bright green baked beans! Suppose she goes off and tells the Headmaster what you said?'

Harvey turned pale. 'Oh, but she wouldn't do that. Would you, Di?'

'Of course not,' Dinah started to say. Then she stopped and looked craftily at Lloyd. 'At least, I might be tempted to. If you don't leave me alone.'

'Don't you dare!' Lloyd jumped to his feet. 'Harvey hasn't done anything wrong.'

'Oh no?' Dinah said triumphantly. 'Then why is he looking so scared?'

She was right. Harvey's round face had crumpled with fright, and he was twitching nervously at the edge of his jumper.

'He was silly, that's all,' Lloyd said. 'I've told him a hundred times not to get involved with things. But he didn't do anything *wrong*.'

'Can't he speak for himself?' Dinah said scornfully. 'Look at him. He's shaking like a jelly. He's nothing but a baby. Running round the school and peering in at windows. It's so childish.'

'That's all you know.' Lloyd had gone red in the face. 'It was a silly thing to do, but it was very brave. Only I don't suppose you would understand.'

'Why not?' Suddenly, Dinah went very quiet. She stopped looking at Lloyd and turned to Harvey. 'Why don't you explain to me? I know *he* doesn't like me –' she waved a hand towards Lloyd '– but you've been quite nice really. And I want to understand. Why was it so brave of you to look in at the Hall?'

'Don't tell her a thing,' Lloyd said sharply.

'Go on,' Dinah said in a soft voice. 'Tell me, Harvey. What's going on in that school? Why is everyone so well behaved? And what do you think happens in Assembly?'

'I – I don't know,' Harvey stuttered, 'but –'

Suddenly, Lloyd darted at Dinah, pushing her through the door and into the hall, with one gigantic shove. Slamming the door shut, he leaned against it and glared at Harvey.

'Haven't you got any sense at all, H? Can't you get it into your thick head that she's one of *them*? If you tell her anything – anything at all – she'll probably go off and repeat it all to the Headmaster. And then you'll get me and all the others into trouble as well.'

Harvey went even paler. 'I don't think she would. Not really. Would she?'

'I don't know,' Lloyd said grimly. 'We'll just have to wait and see, won't we?'

Harvey chewed nervously at the end of his finger.

From outside in the hall came the sound of voices. Mr Hunter had come in and he was saying to Dinah, 'How did you get on at school, then? What do you think of it?'

Dinah's mechanical voice came clearly through the door.

'I think the Headmaster is a marvellous man and this is the best school I've ever been to.'

Chapter 6
Snow

Dinah sat up in bed for a long time that night, a stiff little figure in a white nightdress, hugging her knees. She knew that there was something wrong about the school, with its well-behaved children, all doing the right thing at the right moment, but she could not understand what it was. And she knew that she did not like the Headmaster at all. She could not understand why she kept saying how wonderful he was. She hated not understanding things.

In the end, she did what she always did when things baffled her. Slipping quietly out of bed, she pulled back the curtains so that the room was lit by moonlight from outside. Then she went to stand in front of the mirror. Pale and prim, her reflection stared back at her, the eyes thoughtful and the mouth pursed up, considering.

'Well?' she murmured, 'What's wrong? Why is the school so peculiar?'

Gazing into her own eyes, she suddenly knew the answer. *Fear. It's because they're all afraid.*

She nodded briskly. Yes, that was the right answer. 'But what are they afraid of?'

The reflection stared back, unwinking, and she heard the reply in her head. *That's what you'll have to find out.*

'How?' But she hardly needed to ask. The answer to that one was obvious.

You'll have to be naughty, and see what happens to you.

Her hands, clasped on top of the dressing table, began to shake slightly, but the face that looked back at her out of the mirror was amused.

See? You're afraid yourself, and you don't know why.

Defiantly, she stuck her chin up and pulled a face into the mirror. 'I don't care if I am scared,' she said out loud. 'I want to know, and if that's the only way to find out, that's what I'll do.'

With a determined hand, she closed the curtains and climbed back into bed, feeling as though she had settled something. Curling up under the covers, she fell asleep trying to think of something bad she could do.

When the morning came, she was still considering. She did not expect Lloyd and Harvey to speak to her after their quarrel the day before, and she came down to breakfast in a proud silence, not saying anything even to Mrs Hunter. But things were a bit different. Something had happened that she had not counted on.

It had finally snowed. Outside in the garden, a white, unbroken sheet stretched across the grass, gleaming in the crisp, clear light. And Harvey was so excited that he had forgotten about everything else. He wriggled delightedly in his chair.

'Oh, I *wish* we didn't have to go to school today. Don't you, Di?'

'Sky-blue sandwiches!' snorted Lloyd, his mouth full of porridge, 'd'you ever want to go to school?'

'No, but it's different today,' Harvey said earnestly. 'If we stayed at home, we could build a snowman and have a snowball fight and – oh, Mum, couldn't we?'

'Don't be silly, dear,' Mrs Hunter said placidly. 'There's no point in asking questions like that. Just make sure you wrap up warmly. You know the cold's bad for your chest.'

She hovered over them while they dressed, insisting on bundling Harvey up in extra scarves and gloves, until he looked like a little round parcel. And all the time he was hopping up and down, peering longingly out of the window at the snow. When she finally let them go, Harvey ran joyfully outside and kicked his boots about, scattering a fine dust of snow.

'Oh, it's beautiful! It's lovely! Don't you think it's gorgeous, Di?'

'Yes, I like snow,' she said dreamily. 'We used to have terrific snowball fights at the Children's Home. The sort where you pick sides and build up great stocks of snowballs before you start.'

'Oh, fantastic!' Harvey reached down for a handful of snow.

'Come on!' Lloyd said crossly. 'We'll be late for school.'

Harvey's face drooped. Still deep in her own thoughts, Dinah said, 'We could always have a snowball fight in the playground. In morning playtime.'

She was so busy thinking of her own plans for the day that she did not notice how Harvey brightened and started to whistle. All she could think of was that she had found a good way to be naughty.

She was so busy thinking, in fact, that she walked into school and into her classroom in a daze. It was not until

54

she was sitting in her desk that she realized that she had automatically moved into line and marched in with the others, as if she had been told what to do. But she did not remember anyone having told her.

Before she had time to work that one out, however, she had another surprise. Mr Venables, the class teacher, was giving out pieces of paper.

'This morning,' he said, as he moved round the room, 'I want you to write down everything you know about the solar system.'

As it happened, Dinah knew a great deal about the solar system. But she had no intention of writing it all down. That would be asking for trouble. She settled down to consider what she could safely say. But before she had thought about it at all, she found herself writing, in strange, stiff little sentences.

'The planets of the solar system are Mercury, Venus, Earth, Mars, Jupiter, Saturn, Uranus, Neptune and Pluto.

The Sun is the star of the solar system.

The Earth is 0.137 light-hours from the sun.

The magnitude of the sun is −29.6.'

She stopped, with an effort, and stared at the last sentence she had written. *But I didn't know that*, she thought. She never remembered seeing that particular piece of information before. Yet there it was, confidently written down on her piece of paper, as though someone had slipped it into her head without her knowing.

Cautiously, she leaned sideways, to glance at the paper on the desk next to her. The boy beside her had just written, 'The magnitude of the sun is −29.6.'

Although the classroom was warm, she found herself

shivering. Everyone in the room was scribbling busily, and she was suddenly sure that they had all just written, 'The magnitude of the sun is -29.6.' Thirty little robots, all obediently writing down the same things, things that had been put into their heads for them. The only person who was not writing was Lloyd. He was chewing the end of his pencil, as if he did not know very much about the solar system. Dinah let herself feel a little quiver of mean pleasure that he was in trouble. Then she started to write again, and the information went on pouring out. Most of it she knew, but every now and again came a little bit she did not.

And as she wrote, she pursed her lips together determinedly. Things were getting queerer and queerer. And she would find out why. She *would*.

At playtime, she put on her hat and coat and marched out into the playground, ready to carry out her plan. Without speaking to anyone, she knelt down and began to make a heap of snowballs, intending to throw them when she had a pile of ten.

But she had reckoned without Harvey. When she was only halfway through, he came bounding across to her, past all the groups of children chanting tables and dates.

'Oh Di! You remembered!'

'What?' She looked up, vaguely.

'You remembered. We really *are* going to have a snowball fight!'

Suddenly she realized what she had done. 'No, Harvey! I didn't mean you.'

'Don't be a spoilsport.' He bent down and picked up two of the snowballs she had made.

Almost at once, Lloyd was there. He came bounding across the playground at top speed. 'H! What are you doing?'

'We're going to have a snowball fight,' Harvey said cheerfully. 'It's Di's idea.'

'Don't be an idiot.' Lloyd knocked the snowballs out of his hands. 'Let her get into trouble if she wants to, but don't you get mixed up with it.'

'That's right,' Dinah said. She did not realize how odd it sounded until she saw Lloyd staring at her. She stared back defiantly, and while the two of them were distracted, Harvey stooped down and picked up two more snowballs.

'I think you're both rotten!' he shouted. 'And I *will* have a snowball fight. The snow might be all gone, by tomorrow.'

His yell sounded eerily loud among the mutters in the playground. As he drew his right arm back to throw, Lloyd shouted warningly, 'H! No!' And from the other side of the playground came the sound of Ian's voice, calling, 'Watch out, you lot!'

But it was too late. As total silence fell over the playground, the two snowballs flew from Harvey's gloved hands and spattered messily, one on Lloyd's coat and one on Dinah's.

'Lloyd and Harvey Hunter! Dinah Glass! Come here!' bellowed a voice from the steps.

Ranged on the steps, the prefects were staring at them, a row of six stern faces. Slowly, Lloyd, Harvey and Dinah walked to the foot of the steps and stood looking up.

'Wait there!' Rose said curtly. 'We'll deal with you when the others have gone inside.'

Chapter 7

The Punishment

As Rose began to call out orders, the neat rows of children formed and filed into the building, Lloyd, Harvey and Dinah stood awkwardly, not looking at each other, until the whole playground was empty and they were alone, gazing up at the prefects, who stood like a row of iron statues.

Jeff stared down at them and chanted, 'It is forbidden to waste time by playing in the playground.'

'It is forbidden,' Rose went on, 'to make a mess of your school uniform.'

'You must be punished,' Sarah said.

'In a suitable manner,' finished off Simon, smiling slightly.

Drawing together, the prefects whispered for a moment and then Rose turned to them again. 'Go inside,' she rapped out. 'Take off your hats and coats and gloves. Then come back here.'

As they walked towards the cloakroom, Dinah whispered to Lloyd, 'What will happen? What will they do?'

'I don't know,' he said sourly. 'But whatever it is, it'll be all your fault. I wish you'd never come.'

'No, it's my fault,' Harvey said in a miserable voice. 'I threw the snowballs. And whatever they do, it'll be *terrible*.'

When they came out of the door again, four of the prefects had gone. Rose was standing looking out over the playground, with a pleased smile on her face, and Jeff was by her side, holding three long-handled brooms.

'Now,' he said in a silky voice, 'you're very lucky. We've decided to be kind to you.'

Lloyd and Harvey looked uneasily at each other.

'Yes.' Rose's smile broadened. 'Because you're so fond of playing with the snow, we're going to let you have some more of it.'

Jeff held out the brooms. 'You will each take one of these, and you will sweep all the snow from the playground into a heap. Then,' he looked at Rose, with a grin, 'you will make the whole heap into a pile of snowballs.'

For a second, Harvey looked perplexed, but Lloyd burst out, 'Aren't you going to let us put on our coats and things?'

Rose went on smiling. 'Certainly not.'

'But you can't do that! Harvey's got a weak chest. He could be ill. He –'

'Silence!'

'Suppose we say no?' asked Dinah, in a stiff voice.

Rose and Jeff looked at her as if she had said something unbelievably stupid. Together, they chanted, 'The prefects are the voice of the Headmaster. They must be obeyed.'

Then Jeff thrust the brooms at them. 'Get sweeping!'

Resigned, Lloyd and Harvey trailed off down the steps, dragging their brooms after them. Dinah lingered rebelliously for a second or two, then joined them at the far end of the playground.

'Let's do it as quickly as we can,' she said. 'Perhaps that'll keep us warm.'

'Huh!' Lloyd snorted. 'Don't know why you're so cheerful.

None of this would have happened if you hadn't started talking about snowball fights.'

He banged his broom crossly into the snow and began to sweep, pushing it into a great white mound in front of him.

For the first ten minutes or so, it was not too bad. The exercise kept them fairly warm. But then the wind started to blow, scattering the snow as they swept it and freezing their fingers.

'I'm so cold,' Harvey said plaintively. 'And we're only halfway across. We'll never get it all swept.'

'Don't give up yet,' Lloyd said grimly. 'This is the easy part. Just you wait until we start on the snowballs.'

Dinah shuddered at the thought, as the wind whipped through her thin school shirt. Then she found that she could not stop shivering. Her whole body was shaking, and her teeth were clattering together uncontrollably. She put down her broom for a moment to clap her arms round herself, for a bit of warmth.

Instantly, from the building behind them, came an irate rapping. Turning, she saw Rose gesturing furiously at her through the window. She picked up her broom again and began to sweep harder, trying to ignore the shaking.

At last the snow was piled into a single heap, almost as tall as Harvey. The three of them laid their brooms down at one side and stared at it.

'I don't think I can do it,' Harvey said woefully. 'My hands are *hurting*.'

Lloyd watched him anxiously. His face had a bluish tinge and he was starting to breathe wheezily.

'Why don't you stop?' Dinah said. 'Tell them you won't do it. I don't suppose the Headmaster would really be angry. He must see –' Then her teeth rattled together so hard that she could not go on speaking.

Lloyd and Harvey said nothing. Just looked at her as though she were completely idiotic and bent down to start making snowballs.

'Oh, all right,' she said crossly. 'Be like that. I bet I can make snowballs faster than you.'

As soon as she touched the snow, she knew that it was going to be a nightmare. Her hands were already painfully cold, but at least they had been dry up to now. The snow made them wet, and the cold wind, whipping across, stung them so that they felt almost as if they were burning. Anxiously, she wondered how long it would take before she got frostbite and her fingers started to turn black and drop off.

It would not have been quite so bad if Lloyd and Harvey had been sympathetic, but neither of them spoke to her. Lloyd was making snowballs in a frenzy, trying to get through the huge heap as quickly as possible. If he looked at her at all, it was only to pull a disgusted face. And Harvey had started to cry. Without stopping work, he was sobbing with pain, his face growing red and raw now as the wind scoured the tears from his round cheeks.

I can't, murmured a voice in Dinah's head. *I can't, I can't, I can't.* But all the time, mechanically, she went on making snowballs, until it seemed that she would never stop, as if she would go on until the end of the world, stooping, seizing a handful of snow, squashing it together in her agonized hands and dropping it on to the pile.

They seemed to have been there for about a hundred years when Lloyd said suddenly, 'Two or three more each and we've finished.' Glancing sideways at his watch, Dinah saw that it was not yet twelve o'clock. Gritting her teeth, she scrunched together the last couple of handfuls of snow and flung them triumphantly on top of the pile.

'That's it. We've finished! Let's go inside and get warm.'

'Not yet,' Lloyd said bitterly. 'Look. They're coming to inspect us.'

Sure enough, the prefects, all six of them, were trooping down the steps from the school, marching in perfect time. They walked across the playground and stood in a half-circle round Lloyd, Harvey and Dinah.

'Not a very tidy heap of snowballs,' Rose said grudgingly. She looked sideways at Jeff, and his spotty face suddenly creased into a leering smile.

'But you must have enjoyed yourselves,' he said softly. 'Since you're so *fond* of snow. Do you think they've had enough snow yet, Rose?'

She leered back at him. 'Surely not. Not when they like it so much.'

Without warning, the line of prefects surged forwards, in unison, their hands outstretched. Lloyd, Harvey and Dinah were each seized by two prefects who spun them round and knocked them forwards, face down in the snow.

As Dinah's face crashed down into the hard, balled snow, her first feeling was one of despair. Snow slammed up her nose, into her eyes and all down her front, soaking her clothes. It seemed like the last straw, and she nearly burst into tears. But by the time she stood up, she was furious.

Furious and incredulous. Leaping to her feet, she began to yell at the prefects.

'That's too much! You can't do that! I shall go and tell the Headmaster. He'll punish you. You've got no right to treat us like that.'

Very softly, Jeff started to laugh and Rose, shaking with merriment, pointed a finger towards the school, where the window of the Headmaster's office faced them.

At the window was a pale face, its eyes hidden behind dark glasses. It stared out over the playground, apparently without expression.

'So he knows, does he?' Dinah said quietly. Her mouth set stubbornly. 'Well, I'm not scared of him, even if the rest of you are. I shall go and tell him just what I think of him for letting something like this happen to a boy as little as Harvey.'

Her feet sounding loud on the cleared tarmac, she stamped across the playground and into the school, carried along by the force of her cold rage. Without stopping to consider what she was doing, she marched up to the door of the Headmaster's office and hammered on it with both fists.

Nothing happened.

Crossly, she caught at the handle and rattled it, but the door was locked, and so heavy that it hardly moved.

'I know you're in there!' she shouted. 'I saw you at the window. And I think it's disgusting. Fancy letting the prefects bully a little boy like Harvey. It might make him *ill*. You're inhuman.'

She paused. No sound came from behind the door and, for a second, she felt completely helpless. Then, at last, her brain began to work. She smiled triumphantly, and went on speaking in a quieter voice.

'Anyway, you won't get away with this. Even Headmasters aren't allowed to do things like that. When we get home, we'll all tell Mr and Mrs Hunter, and there'll be a scandal. You'll be prosecuted.'

There was still no sound, but she did not care now that she had worked out what to do next. Her fingers were starting to hurt as the warmth of the building reached them, so, with a final thump on the door, she began to run down the corridor, towards the cloakrooms. If only she could wash them in warm water, she would feel better. And if there was something hot for lunch, even Harvey might be all right.

She was making so much noise, that she did not hear the office door open behind her. She did not look over her shoulder and see the pale face which stared after her. If she had, she would have been puzzled. Because the face was smiling.

'So, Miss Clever Glass,' murmured the Headmaster, 'you have a soft spot for Harvey Hunter, have you? You're ready to protect him? Well, that might come in very useful. Yes, indeed. I must think about that.' His smile broadened. 'After this afternoon's Assembly.' And as he turned away, he laughed, softly and evilly.

Lloyd burst in through the back door of the kitchen, a hundred yards ahead of Harvey and Dinah. 'Mum! Mum! Where are you?'

Mrs Hunter emerged from the hall. 'Goodness me, what a fuss. The end of the world at least, I should think. Whatever is the matter?'

65

'It's what happened at school today.' Lloyd slumped down into a chair. 'It was simply terrible.'

Mrs Hunter suddenly stopped looking sympathetic. 'Now, Lloyd, I hope this isn't going to be another one of your silly stories. You know what trouble we've had in the past, with your lies.'

'It's different this time,' Lloyd said triumphantly. '*Dinah* will tell you that it's true. And you'll believe her, won't you?' He turned round and waved a hand at Harvey and Dinah, who were coming through the door.

'Well, Dinah certainly looks calmer than you do,' Mrs Hunter said.

'But she knows too,' Lloyd yelled. 'She'll tell you.'

'Don't shout, dear.'

'Oh, why don't you *ask* her?'

'Yes,' said Harvey excitedly. 'Ask Dinah what happened at school today.'

'You'll believe *her*,' Lloyd said bitterly.

Dinah was frowning, looking at the three of them in bewilderment.

'Well, dear?' Mrs Hunter said gently. 'Tell me. What happened at school today?'

In a perfectly calm, even voice, Dinah said, 'At school this morning, Harvey made snowballs and we all had a snowball fight. It was super. The Headmaster made sure we all dressed up warmly in our hats and coats and gloves. And he gave us drinks of hot blackcurrant when we came inside.'

'*What?*' Lloyd stared at her.

Harvey looked appalled. '*Dinah!*'

Mrs Hunter smiled comfortably. 'It all sounds very nice.'

'But you don't understand!' Lloyd exploded. 'It's not true. It wasn't like that at all. We –'

'Be quiet!' All at once, Mrs Hunter was very angry. 'It's always the same, Lloyd. You and Harvey come back from school with silly, unbelievable stories and whenever I ask any of the other children I find it's all lies. I'm *not* going to make a fool of myself by complaining again. I don't think it's funny, even if you do.'

'It's not *meant* to be funny!' Lloyd glared at Dinah. 'She knows that. She's a filthy, foul traitor! *She's* the one who's telling lies, and –'

'That's enough!' Mrs Hunter banged her hand on the table. 'I don't blame Dinah for not wanting to join in with your silly games. You've been unpleasant to her ever since

67

she came, I won't have it. This is her home now, as well as yours, and you'll just have to get used to it.'

'But –'

'Not another word!'

'It doesn't matter, L,' Harvey said miserably. 'We ought to have known it would be like this. It's always like this. Two hundred people to say we're lying, whatever we say. We can't do anything about it.'

'We can refuse to speak to traitors,' Lloyd said hotly. 'Come on, H. Let's go to the playroom. There's a bad smell in this kitchen.'

He stamped out. Harvey stood in the doorway for a moment, looking at Dinah.

'How *could* you?' he said reproachfully. 'When you know what it was like?'

Chapter 8

Prefects' Meeting

'We won't speak to her,' Lloyd said. 'Not ever again. Understand, H?' He pulled on his sock with such ferocity that his big toe came through the end. With a shout of rage, he flung the sock into the wastepaper basket and took a clean one out of the drawer.

'But how can we not?' Harvey said miserably. 'She doesn't know anyone except us. If *we* don't talk to her –'

'Black bananas! Think I care about that? After the way she's treated us? You're too soft, H, that's what's wrong with you. Well, just watch it. If I catch you speaking to her, I won't look after you any more. And I'll tell the others not to look after you, either. Then you'll be in trouble.' Ramming his shoes on, Lloyd stamped off downstairs and a moment later an unhappy Harvey followed him.

They sat hunched over their plates of porridge, turned away from Dinah and talking only to each other. From time to time, Lloyd glanced at her, to see what effect they were having, but it was impossible to tell. She went on eating her breakfast without speaking, her cold, pale face gazing off into the distance.

When the time came to leave, she followed them out into the hall and left the house with them, but they marched along the road ten yards ahead of her, not looking over their shoulders.

'Just let her *dare* try to catch us up!' Lloyd muttered.

'She won't do that,' Harvey said. 'She's too proud. She –'

'Oh shut up! I don't want you going on about her all day. She's not here. She doesn't exist. Understand?'

Lloyd strode faster up the road and swept into the playground, his eyes searching about. 'We must find Ian and Mandy and Ingrid and warn them about her. Tell them not to talk to her either. Then she'll only have the goody-goodies and she won't get much fun out of them.'

He saw the other three in a corner and marched across to them, followed by Harvey. But before he could say anything, silence fell over the playground and everyone turned to look at the prefects.

There seemed to be something odd about them today. They were smirking at each other and hunting round the playground with their eyes, as if they were looking for somebody. Suddenly Ian poked Lloyd in the ribs.

'Hey,' he mouthed soundlessly, 'why are they all looking at Harvey?'

It was true. Six pairs of eyes had fixed on Harvey's chubby figure and six smiles had grown wider. Harvey started to shake. Mandy reached out and gripped his hand comfortingly. 'Don't worry,' she mouthed. 'It might not be as bad as you think.'

But Harvey was already worried. As the prefects rapped out their orders and the children started to move into lines, he caught at Lloyd's sleeve. 'Don't leave me alone, L.'

'OK.' Lloyd patted his shoulder. 'We'll stick together.'

As they moved across the playground, he avoided his usual place and went to stand in Harvey's line instead, immediately behind him. He saw Dinah glance quickly across at him, but he ignored her.

'Lead – in!' Jeff shouted.

As the lines began to move, Lloyd put a steadying hand on Harvey's arm and the two of them walked together up the steps. When they were nearly at the top, Rose stuck out a hand, blocking Harvey's way.

'Harvey Hunter,' she intoned, 'you are summoned to appear before the Prefects' Council at ten o'clock.'

'Why?' Harvey said plaintively. 'I haven't done anything.'

'That's right,' Lloyd blustered. 'Leave him alone.'

Rose gave him an icy stare. 'You are in the wrong line, Lloyd Hunter.'

'That's because I'm sticking by Harvey. I don't know what you're plotting, but I'm coming too.' He saw Rose open her mouth to protest and he said quickly, 'Even in the courts, people are allowed to have lawyers to speak for them.'

Rather to his surprise, Rose shrugged. 'Please yourself. You can be Harvey's lawyer. It won't do any good. Ten o'clock.'

For an hour, Lloyd sat in his classroom, chewing the end of his pencil. All around him, people were scribbling industriously, writing facts about the British Constitution. Lloyd did not know the facts – as usual – but this morning he did not even care. All he could think of was the minute hand on the clock on the wall. It seemed to be racing round towards ten o'clock at twice its normal speed.

71

At five to ten, he stuck his hand up.

'Yes?' barked Mr Venables, looking startled. People hardly ever put their hands up. It was not encouraged.

'Please, sir, I've got to go to the Prefects' Council.'

Mr Venables frowned. 'I was not informed. This is most disorderly.'

'I've got to go,' Lloyd insisted. Without even waiting for an answer, he bounded out of his seat and made for the door. He could see Dinah watching him and he almost pulled a face at her. Then he remembered. No communication.

Outside the door of the prefects' room, Harvey was standing shivering. 'Oh, what do you think is going on? What are they going to do to me now?'

'Dunno. We'll have to go in and find out.' Lloyd slapped him encouragingly on the back. 'Cheer up. At least the snow's melted. They can't make us do that again, anyway.'

Boldly he hammered on the door and heard Jeff's voice say, 'Come in.'

The prefects were sitting in a line behind a long table, their faces grave and their uniforms immaculate. Each of them had a pen clipped neatly into the top blazer pocket, at precisely the same angle, and their hands were folded on the table in front of them in a straight row. Six doubled fists.

'Sit down,' said Rose, pointing at two chairs, drawn up on the other side of the table.

'What's this all about?' Lloyd muttered. 'What's going on?'

'Sit down!' Rose said again, more curtly. 'And don't speak unless we ask you questions.'

Lloyd and Harvey took the two chairs and sat facing the

72

row of accusing eyes. Slowly, Jeff reached out for a grey folder which lay on the table. A neat label on the front said *Harvey Hunter*. Opening it, he pulled out a piece of paper.

'Harvey Hunter,' he began, 'we have called you before us, on the instructions of the Headmaster, to deal with your disobedient and disorderly behaviour this week. He has been most displeased with you.'

Rose nodded. 'You are a disruptive influence in the school.'

'That's nonsense,' Lloyd burst out. 'He's never influenced anybody.'

'Please be quiet,' said Jeff, 'and listen to the charges.' He looked down at the piece of paper. 'You are accused of three things. First, on Monday, you came into school before you were called in by us, although you know it's against the rules to come in early. Have you anything to say?'

73

'I was going to do the registers,' Harvey faltered. 'The Headmaster told me to.'

Jeff shook his head and ran a finger down the paper. 'Clearly rubbish. My information is that Sharon Mandeville did the registers on Monday.'

'It was a mistake,' Lloyd said quietly. 'The Headmaster changed his mind.'

'The Headmaster never changes his mind,' Rose said crushingly. 'Indecision is disorder.'

'Second,' Jeff went on relentlessly, 'later the same day, in the afternoon, you left your classroom, telling Rose that you wanted to go to the toilet. Instead, you went up to the Hall, to spy on the Assembly – which you are not permitted to attend.'

Harvey gasped and turned to look at Lloyd, but this time Lloyd could only shrug.

'Third,' Jeff said, 'yesterday, in the playground, you threw two snowballs, although you knew that playing anywhere on school premises is most strictly forbidden.'

'But that's not fair!' Lloyd shouted. 'He's already been punished for that.'

'The prefects took such action as they saw fit,' Rose said crushingly, 'but the matter has not yet been dealt with by the Headmaster. We are now acting under his instructions.'

'I don't believe you,' Lloyd said. 'If the Headmaster wants to deal with Harvey, why doesn't he see him himself?'

But even as he spoke the words, he knew they were stupid. Simultaneously, the figures round the table chanted, 'The prefects are the voice of the Headmaster. They must be obeyed.'

'Well,' said Lloyd desperately, 'if you're the voice of the

Headmaster, then when you punished Harvey yesterday, that *was* a punishment from the Headmaster. And it *isn't* fair to give him another one.'

Harvey twisted his hands together wretchedly. 'Oh, L, what's the use? This isn't really like a court. They're not going to let me off whatever you say. Why don't we just shut up and hear what they're going to do to me?'

Rose gave a patronizing smile. 'I'm glad to see that one of you has some sense. Especially since the Headmaster has decided to be merciful.'

'He has?' Harvey looked disbelieving.

Rose nodded. 'He will give you a chance to redeem yourself.' She reached into the file and drew out a long white envelope with Harvey's name written on the front. 'He has set you a paper of sums to do. If you get them all right, your offences will be forgotten. This time. But if you get any of them wrong, the Headmaster will deal with you himself. Most severely.'

Harvey gulped. 'Is that all? Can I go?'

Jeff nodded. 'Go straight back to your classrooms and get on with your work. The sums are not to be done until you get home.' He smiled sarcastically. 'You never know. If you do them well enough, you might land up on Eddy Hair's Great School Quiz.'

Lloyd snorted. 'I can just see *us* being the Headmaster's blue-eyed boys.'

Ignoring Jeff's frown, he made for the door. As soon as he and Harvey were safely outside, he exploded.

'Of all the stupid, trumped-up, unfair charges –'

Harvey looked sideways at him, his eyes scared. 'But how did they *know*, L? About me going into school early and

75

going to look at the Assembly? No one knew about both things. Only me and you.'

Lloyd stopped in the middle of the corridor. 'Yes,' he said softly. 'Exploding eggshells! There *was* someone else who knew. Dinah saw you go into school early. And you told her that you watched the Assembly.'

'But she wouldn't have told. Would she?'

Lloyd pulled a face. 'Of course she would. It's all her fault you're in trouble. Like yesterday. That was her fault too.' Then he saw Harvey start to look upset and he put an arm round his shoulders. 'Never mind. It could be worse. They've only given you sums to do. And you're quite good at sums.'

'I expect they're hard,' Harvey faltered.

'Let's have a look.'

Harvey ripped open the envelope and pulled out three sheets of paper folded together. He glanced at them briefly and then said, in a horrified voice, 'L, I'll never work out the answers. I can't even understand the questions.'

'Let me see.' Lloyd snatched the papers out of his hand. 'I can always help you.'

He began to read with scornful confidence, but a moment later he, too, was looking completely baffled.

'You see?' Harvey said. 'We can't. Oh, what am I going to *do*?'

Lloyd took the envelope and pushed the papers back into it. 'We'll let Mandy have a look. She's quite good at sums. And if that doesn't work, we'll show them to Mum when we get home. She'll help you if she can. And if she can't –' all at once he looked pleased '– she'll see they're much too difficult for you. Then even she will have to admit there's something peculiar going on.'

When they got home, Mrs Hunter was sitting in the kitchen having a cup of tea with Dinah. Lloyd walked straight past Dinah without even looking at her.

'Mum, we want to talk to you.'

'Well, of course.' Mrs Hunter smiled. 'Have a cup of tea?'

Lloyd flicked his fingers impatiently. 'No. We want to talk to you alone.'

At once, his mother stiffened. 'I've told you about that before. Dinah's a member of the family and you must treat her like one. If you've got anything to say, you can say it with her here.'

'But you don't understand –' Lloyd began sulkily.

'Please, L,' Harvey broke in, 'don't waste time. Let's just show her the sums.' He pulled the papers out of the envelope and threw them on the table.

'The Headmaster gave them to him,' Lloyd said, 'and they're terrible. You must help him.'

Mrs Hunter shook her head. 'Now, you know you mustn't cheat. If the Headmaster gave them to Harvey, he means him to do them by himself.'

'But Mum, I can't,' Harvey said pathetically. 'They're awful. You look.'

Mrs Hunter picked up the paper and scanned it. Then she gave a little laugh. 'It's no use. It doesn't mean anything to me. I don't understand any of this New Maths you all do.'

'It's not New Maths!' Harvey shouted. 'It's just incredibly difficult.'

'Now, now, dear,' Mrs Hunter said, a little sharply, 'calm down. Let me give you a cup of tea. Then you can go away quietly by yourself and look at it. I'm sure you'll find it's all right when you think about it. The Headmaster wouldn't be unreasonable.'

'That's what you think,' Lloyd said bitterly. 'He's a maniac.'

'Don't be silly,' Mrs Hunter said. 'I'm sure he's not a maniac. Is he, Dinah?'

With an expression of utter misery on her face, Dinah said, 'The Headmaster is a marvellous man, and this is the best school I've ever been to.'

'It's no good asking *her*!' Lloyd shouted. 'It's all her fault. She's the one who got Harvey into trouble.'

'Me?' Dinah said.

'Yes, you!' He glared at her, and she stared back, looking completely baffled.

'Oh, what's the use of quarrelling?' Harvey said desperately. 'What does it matter? All that matters is that I've got these sums to do and *I can't do them*. And nobody can help me. It's going to be *awful*.' He snatched up the papers and ran out of the room, banging the door behind him.

'See what you've done?' Lloyd shouted at Dinah. 'Oh, I wish you'd never come!'

He ran after Harvey, banging the door again, and found him in the playroom, huddled in a chair. His shoulders were shaking and he was beginning to sob fiercely.

'Oh H, do stop it. That won't help.'

'Nothing will help,' said Harvey, in a totally wretched

78

voice. 'I shan't be able to do the sums and tomorrow I'll have to go and see the Headmaster, and it will be frightful and – oh!' With a loud wail, he buried himself deep in the cushions.

At that moment, the playroom door opened again.

'Please may I see the sums?' said a stiff little voice from the doorway.

Chapter 9

Dinah's Secret

Dinah had not expected them to be nice to her. It had cost her quite a lot to push the door open. But at the sight of Harvey sobbing among the cushions, she was sure she had done the right thing.

'Please may I see the sums?'

'No you may not!' Lloyd snapped. 'You only want to gloat, don't you? You're just a mean, horrible –'

Harvey raised a tear-stained face from the cushions. 'Oh, let her,' he said wearily. 'What difference can it make? *I* don't think she's horrible enough to gloat, even if you do. There you are, Di. There are the beastly sums. On the floor.'

Dinah bent down and picked up the pieces of paper. Her cheeks had turned red and her heart was thudding uncomfortably. *Be quiet!* a voice in her head was saying. *Don't be too clever. Don't give yourself away.* She looked at Harvey and then at Lloyd's wretched, worried face. And then at the sums.

'Aren't they impossible?' Lloyd said.

Dinah took a deep breath. 'There's no way either of you could do them.'

'Ha, ha,' Lloyd sneered. 'And I suppose you could, clever clogs.'

'Yes,' Dinah said slowly. 'Yes, I can.'

Lloyd stared at her.

'It's all right, Harvey,' said Dinah. *'I can do your sums.'*

There was total silence. Harvey's mouth fell open and Lloyd went on staring.

'I can do them,' Dinah said again.

Harvey sat up, blinking at them. His hair flopped over his eyes and his cheeks were red.

'Honest?'

'Honest,' said Dinah reluctantly. 'Give me a pen and some paper and I'll do them now.'

She felt their eyes watching her as she sat down at the table and read the first sum.

'You need to use Probability Theory for that one,' she said briskly. Her eye travelled on down the page. 'And Spherical Geometry for that one. And this one – phew!' She whistled. 'You need Tensor Calculus for that. He *really* didn't mean you to do them, did he?'

'But *you* can do them?' Harvey said anxiously.

'I told you.' Her pen started to move across the paper and, behind her, she heard Lloyd gasp in disbelief. Taking no notice, she plunged into the sums, completely absorbed. One or two of the problems were so difficult that she had to think hard and she began to hum softly, enjoying herself. By the time she had finished, the two boys were staring at her with awed curiosity.

'How – how on earth did you do them?' Lloyd said awkwardly.

Dinah sat back in her chair. 'I'm clever.'

Lloyd's mouth twitched, as if he were going to jeer, and she laughed suddenly. 'No, I'm not boasting. I'm *really* clever. At sums and all sorts of things like that.'

'Nobody told us,' Lloyd said sulkily.

'Nobody knows.' Dinah pulled a face. 'Can't you imagine how other children would treat me? They'd be *beastly*. I found that out when I was about five. So – I decided to play stupid. I kept quiet and I just went on finding out about things by myself, at the library and so on. And no one's ever guessed. Nobody's known about me. Until now.'

Lloyd still looked dubious, but Harvey gave a sudden crow of delight. 'So you've done the rotten sums. Whoopee!' He jumped to his feet and did a little jig. 'I'm starving!'

'Should just think you are,' Lloyd said gruffly. 'After all that stupid fuss you made. Here – have this.' He pulled a Mars bar out of his pocket and tossed it over. Tearing off the paper, Harvey began to cram it into his mouth greedily, but Lloyd was still staring at Dinah.

'You didn't want anyone to know you were clever,' he

said slowly, 'You've hidden it all these years. But you've told us now. Why?'

Dinah looked down at her fingers, feeling embarrassed. 'I couldn't let Harvey – well, I was sorry for him.'

'But we've been foul to you!'

She grinned wryly. '*You've* been foul to me. Harvey's been quite nice.'

Lloyd frowned. 'But it doesn't make any sense. You've just got Harvey out of trouble. But it was you that got him into it. It must have been you that told about him going into school early and spying on the Assembly. No one else knew.'

Dinah shook her head. 'It wasn't me that told. Anyway, Rose saw him going in for the registers. She was watching through the window. Perhaps someone saw him outside the Hall as well.'

'But you lied about the snowballs, and you keep saying how marvellous the school is, and telling about the films you see in Assembly. And it's all lies. You know it is. I can't understand you at all.'

Dinah put her face in her hands. 'It's worse than that,' she said slowly. Then she paused for a moment. Somehow, talking about it made it seem realer, more frightening. But if she did not talk about it now, she never would. She forced herself to go on. '*I* don't understand me. All those things you've described – they come out mechanically. Before I've decided what I'm going to say. And when I say how marvellous the school is – I know what I really think, but I can't say it.'

'But that's ridiculous.' Lloyd began to march up and down the room. 'Why should you say things you don't want to?'

Harvey had finished eating the Mars bar and was watching them both with quiet interest. All of a sudden, he said, 'Assembly.'

'What?' Lloyd stopped pacing and looked at him. 'What do you mean?'

Harvey wiped his chocolate-covered fingers on the arm of the chair. 'It must be something to do with Assembly. It's the only place Dinah goes where neither of us does. What happened in Assembly today, Di?'

'In Assembly this afternoon,' Dinah chanted, 'we saw a film about coal-mines and –' She clapped a hand over her mouth and, with a visible effort, stopped speaking.

'That's right,' Harvey said. 'You didn't. I felt so rotten this afternoon I hardly did any work. Just looked out of the window. And the lights never went out.'

Dinah looked distressed. 'Don't you see?' she said urgently. 'It's the same thing again. I've said that something happened. A long explanation that came reeling out before I could think about it. And you say it's not true. Just like you said about the snowball fight.'

'And we're right,' insisted Lloyd.

Slowly, Dinah nodded. 'I think you might be. But why should I say these things? And if we don't see films in Assembly – what happens?' Her eyes were big and worried.

'You must remember, Di,' Harvey said. 'If you were there, you must remember it somehow, with some part of your brain. Go on. Remember it, remember it.'

'Say that again,' Dinah muttered, in an odd voice.

Harvey was puzzled. 'I just said – go on, remember it, remember it.'

84

'Go *on*,' Dinah said. 'Don't stop. It's coming.'

'Remember it, remember it, remember it,' chanted Harvey.

Dinah's forehead creased, as if she were making a mammoth effort.

'Remember it, remember it, remember it.'

As if she were in a daze, she started to mumble and stutter. 'Hyp –, hyp –, hypno –'

Then her face flooded with joyful excitement. 'Hypnotism!' she yelled, banging her fist down on the table. 'That's it! Hypnotism.'

Lloyd looked at her doubtfully.

'That's it!' she said again, her eyes glowing. 'The first day, when I went into Assembly, I didn't look at the Headmaster's eyes when the others did. I closed mine. And I heard him hypnotize everyone else. But then he caught me. I just had time to think *remember it, remember it* – and then I was hypnotized and I forgot. Until Harvey brought it back. *The Headmaster hypnotizes everyone in Assembly.*' She stared round triumphantly at them.

'But why?' Harvey said dubiously. 'What's the point?'

Dinah shrugged. 'It's a good way to keep everyone in order. And you know how he likes order. While they're hypnotized, he tells them what to do when they wake up. And they can't help doing it. Like me saying those things. And I think –' she paused, considering '– I think he probably makes us learn things, parrot-fashion, while we're hypnotized. Then, when we're awake, we can remember them and write them down.'

'A quick way to produce a school full of geniuses,' Lloyd said sourly. But Dinah shook her head.

85

'We're not learning to *think*. We're just learning to repeat things. Like robots. It looks good, but it's no use at all.'

Harvey shuddered. 'It's horrible.'

'It's all right for you,' Dinah said. 'He doesn't do it to you. I wonder why not.'

'He can't,' Harvey said. 'We're invulnerable.'

He was only joking, but Dinah looked serious. 'I think you might be right. Some people can't be hypnotized. Has he ever tried it with you? Gazed into your eyes and told you you were tired?'

'Yes,' Lloyd said slowly. 'He did once. When I first came to the school. He took off his glasses and stared at me and said, "Lloyd, you are very tired. You are very, very sleepy."'

'And what happened?'

'Nothing much. I just said, "No, sir, I'm fine, thank you."'

'So did I,' put in Harvey. 'He did it to me, too. I just thought he was being silly.'

'Oh no,' Dinah said slowly, 'I don't think he's silly at all. He's cruel and terrifying, and he's got an obsession with tidiness, but he's not silly. He's very, very clever. He's got a whole school full of children who will do precisely what he wants. He must feel very powerful.' Her voice was awed. 'Very powerful,' she said again. 'If I were him, I don't think I'd be satisfied with having one measly school in my power!'

'What do you mean?' Harvey said.

She looked round at them. 'Think of it. He's got a whole army of people – people like me – who'll do and say exactly what he wants. Why should he stop there? Sooner or later, he's going to want to do something with his army.'

There was a long, tense pause. Then Harvey said, 'L, don't you think – we should bring the others in on this?'

Lloyd looked carefully at Dinah. 'Think she can be trusted?'

'Of course,' Harvey said impatiently. 'Look what she's just done for me.' He flapped the paper with the sums on. 'We'll swear her to secrecy. Tomorrow. After school.'

Chapter 10

SPLAT

'We always go in separately,' Lloyd said in a mysterious voice. 'Just in case anyone's watching. You go first, H. I'll bring Dinah in a moment.'

Harvey nodded and slipped away down an alley between the houses opposite. Lloyd prodded Dinah. 'Go on. Keep staring in the shop window. As if you're interested.'

'In baths and basins?' Dinah said lightly. 'Who'd believe that? Go on, Lloyd. Tell me what's happening.'

'Wait and see.' Lloyd looked even more mysterious. 'You'll find out soon enough.'

He went on examining a purple soap dish with every appearance of enthusiasm for a couple more minutes. Then he glanced at his watch and looked up and down the road. 'OK. I think it's all right now. Come on.'

He led the way, with elaborate casualness, down the alley. At the bottom was a gate into a garden. He pushed it open and they were facing a little wooden shed. He rapped on the door.

'The man who can keep order can rule the world,' said a voice from inside.

Beside him, Lloyd felt Dinah start with surprise, and he grinned. 'But the man who can bear disorder is truly free,' he answered.

The wooden door opened. 'Pass, friend.'

He slid through, motioning Dinah to follow him. She bent her head sideways, to avoid the garden tools hanging round the opening, and walked in, to find herself confronting four pairs of eyes. Ian, Mandy and Ingrid looked frankly hostile. Only Harvey gave her an encouraging smile.

'Have a box.' He pushed one towards her, and she sat down, like the others, squashed uncomfortably close in the confined space. The shed was dark and dusty, and the box creaked perilously underneath her.

Ian looked at her, raising one elegant, fair eyebrow. 'Well, well, Lloyd,' he murmured. 'Who have you brought with you, then? I hope you have a good excuse.'

'He'd better have,' little Ingrid said hotly. 'He's broken all the rules and put us all in danger.'

Mandy smiled gently. 'Suppose we hear what he's got to say. Lloyd doesn't usually do things without a good reason.'

Lloyd nodded. 'I'm glad Mandy said that. I didn't really want to bring Dinah, but I think she's got some important information to give you.'

'But she's one of Them,' Ingrid said crossly. 'One of the Headmaster's goody-goodies. Why should we believe anything she says?'

'You will when you've heard it,' Harvey broke in. 'Oh, go on, Di. Tell them.'

'Wait a minute.' Dinah had sat quietly, listening to them arguing. Now she sat up straighter. 'You want to know that I won't get you into trouble. That's fair enough. But how do I know that you won't get me into trouble? What is all this, and why do you meet here, in secret?'

89

Ingrid bridled again, but Ian said, 'It's a fair enough question. Why don't you explain, Mr Chairman? Now she's seen this much, it can't do any more harm.'

'All right,' Lloyd said. 'If no one minds.' He turned to Dinah. 'This is the Society for the Protection of our Lives Against Them.'

'SPLAT for short,' Harvey put in.

'Us against the Headmaster and the teachers and all the goody-goodies,' Ingrid said with relish. She frowned. 'And we're Us and you're one of Them, so I can't think what you're doing here.'

'But what do you *do*?' Dinah said.

Ian grinned. 'Ah, the crucial question. Well, we all keep an eye out for the prefects, so we can warn each other, and we swap details of all the new rules the Headmaster invents, so that we don't get caught out.'

'And Mandy helps us with our sums and things,' Ingrid added.

Mandy blushed. 'It's not just that, though. Mostly it's to keep our spirits up. So we don't feel we're all alone in the horrible school, with no one to help us.'

'I see.' Dinah nodded. 'Well, I think you'll feel better when you've heard what I want to say. You see –'

'Wait a moment.' Ian held up his hand. 'I think you should take the oath first. Mr Chairman?'

'Yes, of course,' Lloyd said shortly, annoyed that he had not thought of it himself. 'Dinah Glass, do you swear to honour the secrecy of SPLAT, to protect its members and never willingly to reveal anything about any of Us to any of Them?'

'I do,' Dinah said solemnly.

90

'Right,' said Lloyd. 'Now tell them.'

'It's about Assembly,' Dinah began. 'You see . . .'

She leaned forwards eagerly and began to explain, answering their questions clearly and briefly. Lloyd watched her. He supposed she could be trusted, but somehow he had not expected the others to believe her so quickly. If he had had to put in a good word for her, to plead for her to be heard, he would have felt more friendly towards her. But the others seemed to be on her side straight away. Rather crossly, he studied them.

Ian was looking at her with cool approval and Mandy was grinning her shy, pleasant grin. Even Ingrid had been convinced. She was still raging, but now her rage was all directed at the Headmaster. She bounced up and down on her box and banged her fist into the palm of her hand.

'He's *evil*! *Wicked*! Do you mean all the others are victims really? It's him that makes them behave like that? Oh, it's fiendish, it's –'

'Calm – down – Ingrid.' Ian patted her annoyingly on the back. 'Think how pleased the Headmaster will be if you choke to death.'

She stopped abruptly and everyone laughed. Lloyd decided that it was time he took charge of the meeting again. After all, he was the Chairman. But before he could say anything, Harvey burst out, 'But you haven't heard the most important part yet – what Dinah thinks.'

'She has important thoughts, does she?' Ian said teasingly.

Mandy gave a reproachful look. 'Of course she does. You heard Harvey say how clever she was. Come on, Di. What is it?'

'Well, I'm worried about what's going to happen next.'

Earnestly, Dinah began to explain her fears about the Headmaster's plans.

Lloyd chewed irritably at the end of his finger. He had meant to do this bit himself. Get them all organized, the way he usually did. But it was no use interrupting yet. He waited until Dinah had finished and then rapped smartly on the floor to call the meeting to order.

'Right now, you've all heard what Dinah has to say. There's no evidence for it, of course, but it makes sense. The question is – what are we going to do about it?'

Mandy looked thoughtful. 'We really need a way of finding out what actually happens in Assembly. Apart from the hypnotism, I mean. If the Headmaster's going to use the children for anything, that'll be where he tells them all about it.'

'Can't you stay awake somehow, Di?' Ingrid said.

Dinah sighed. 'I told you. I've tried that. But he can tell.' She looked at them, one by one. 'But he can't hypnotize any of you. Couldn't one of you sneak into the Hall and hide?'

Ian shook his head. 'Not a chance. We always have a prefect watching us. They treat us as if we were criminals. I don't suppose they'll even let us go to the toilet. Not now they know what Harvey did.'

'Anyway,' Harvey said quickly, 'there's nowhere to hide in the Hall. You know what it's like.'

Dinah nodded silently and there was a long pause. Lloyd was straining to think of a good idea. He was usually the one with the brainwaves. He had taught the others to mouth, so that they could talk in secret when no one was looking. And he was the one who had started the Register of Rules and persuaded the others to copy bits out of encyclopaedias so that they could keep up with the goody-goodies at school. But now his mind felt like a piece of soggy cottonwool.

'It's a pity we can't bug the Hall,' he said at last, in a flippant voice.

'Lloyd – that's it!' Dinah bounced on her seat, looking unusually excited for her. Her cheeks were very faintly pink. 'We can't bug the Hall very easily, but we can bug *me*! Has anyone got a little tape-recorder? A battery one?'

'Yes,' Ian and Mandy said together.

'Well then, it's easy. I'll put it in my blazer pocket and turn it on when I go into the Hall. It won't record very well in there, but it'll probably pick up enough to tell us . . .'

She launched into a long discussion with Ian about the best way to do it. Mandy put in a suggestion from time to time and Harvey and Ingrid were nodding away in agreement.

Lloyd watched them all, totally disgusted. He might have known how it would be. He had told Harvey that there would never be any peace and quiet again if a girl came to live with them, and he had been right, for all she looked so meek and docile. There had been nothing but trouble ever since she walked into the house.

And now she had walked into her first SPLAT meeting – where she had no business to be anyway – and taken it over. No one would guess *he* was the Chairman, or that bugging the Hall had been *his* idea. He sat hunched over on his box, sulking.

Suddenly, Ingrid prodded him. 'Hey, wake up, Lloyd. We're taking a decision.' She turned to Dinah. 'It's one of our rules. Everything we do has to be agreed by all of us. Other-

93

wise we don't do it. There are so few of us that we can't afford to argue.'

Grumpily, Lloyd looked round at them. 'Right, let's take a vote. The proposal is that Dinah should take a tape-recorder into Assembly. Ian? Harvey? Mandy? Ingrid?' All four of them nodded.

'And Dinah,' Harvey said. 'You've forgotten her. She's a sworn-in member too.'

'Dinah?' Lloyd said reluctantly.

Dinah nodded slowly, watching Lloyd's face. 'What about you?' she murmured. 'You haven't said anything yet.'

'I'm not sure I do agree,' Lloyd said. 'It's a very dangerous plan, and we've always tried to keep out of danger. That's what this society's for, not for solving mysteries. What happens if something goes wrong?'

'I'm the only one who'll be in danger then,' Dinah said mildly. 'If I'm not afraid, why should you be? I won't tell on the rest of you. I swore. Remember?'

94

'But how do we know you'll keep your promise?'

'Oh L!' Harvey said impatiently.

Lloyd could see the others growing annoyed with him as well. He would have to give in. 'All right, all right,' he said with bad grace. 'We'll try it. Tomorrow. And we'll all meet at our house afterwards, to listen to the tape. But I bet we don't find out anything useful.' Ingrid glared at him, and he banged on the floor again before she could say anything. 'Meeting dissolved.'

He stamped home at high speed, trying to leave Dinah behind. But Harvey chose to walk with her and chat, instead of catching up, and that did not improve Lloyd's temper one little bit.

Chapter 11

Dinah the Spy

As Dinah swallowed her last mouthful of cheese flan, she felt more lonely than she had ever felt in her life before. All the other members of SPLAT were sitting together, on their usual isolated table in the dining hall, but they had decided that it would seem suspicious if she sat with them. So she was next to Lucy, on a table full of good, well-behaved pupils, all of them munching their way through the same-sized platefuls of cheese flan, watery cabbage and lumpy mashed potato. Chop, scrape, lift, chop, scrape, lift, went the knives and forks, in regular rhythm. No one complained about the terrible food. No one asked to leave any. No one spoke at all. Even Lucy was chewing stolidly.

Her stomach fluttering nervously, Dinah reached out for her dish of rice pudding. As she did so, she slipped her other hand into her pocket, feeling the shape of the little cassette recorder underneath the cover of her handkerchief.

'Dinah Glass!' said Rose's voice over her shoulder.

Dinah froze, rigid.

'Well?' Rose snapped.

'Well what?' muttered Dinah guiltily.

'Your knife and fork!'

Glancing at her empty plate, Dinah saw that she had left the knife and fork lying untidily askew. Trying not to

96

look too relieved, she twitched them straight, so that they lay at the same neat angle as everyone else's. Then she ate her rice pudding quickly, feeling, with every mouthful, that she might choke with fright. The tape-recorder seemed to be making a gigantic bulge in her pocket, visible to anyone.

Ten minutes later, as if at a signal, everyone on her table stood up, ready to walk off to Assembly. Lloyd, Harvey and the others were still finishing their puddings. As Dinah passed their table, she glanced quickly sideways. Not one of them looked at her. But each of them had a hand on the table and, momentarily, they all crossed their fingers. Even Lloyd. Slightly comforted, Dinah marched out of the dining room and into the Hall and sat down beside Lucy, who gave her a cautious smile.

'Hello,' Dinah whispered. 'How are things?'

Lucy smiled again and shrugged. Then, greatly daring, she whispered back. 'How are you getting on?'

'Good question.' Dinah glanced round at Them, at the children and teachers, all of whom would give her away if they knew what she had in her pocket. She grinned wryly. 'I feel like Winston Smith.'

'Winston Smith?' whispered Lucy, puzzled.

'He was a man who was spied on all the time. In a book called *Nineteen Eighty-Four*.'

'Oh.' Lucy still looked bewildered. 'Funny name for a book.'

'It means –' Dinah started, but Lucy nudged her sharply.

'Ssh! Here he comes.'

The Headmaster was walking slowly up the middle of the Hall, his long gown swirling and his head erect. He looked neither to right nor to left, but as he passed all fidgeting stopped. Children sat up straighter in their chairs and

97

faced the front. While he climbed the steps of the stage, the men teachers pulled their ties smooth and the women patted their hair.

'Good afternoon, school,' he said.

'Good afternoon, sir,' replied everyone, voices perfectly together.

He looked gravely down on the rows of heads in front of him and reached up to take off his glasses. Dinah felt a sudden spurt of revulsion at the thought of letting herself be hypnotized again. But there was nothing she could do. It had to happen if the plan was to succeed. Her finger, in her blazer pocket, twitched once, turning on the tape-recorder, and then the voice began.

'I'm pleased to learn that you have all been working very hard this morning. You have done well, but now you must be weary. Weary and sleepy ...'

Crossing her fingers hard in her pockets, Dinah shut her eyes and felt the heavy, inexorable tide of sleep start to wash over her.

She was already unconscious when the Headmaster gave his first orders, so she never knew quite what happened next. She was not aware of the Headmaster's steady voice, nor of her own, repeating what they were all told to repeat. She could not even feel the shape of the tape-recorder, clutched tightly in her fingers, inside her pocket.

'Right!' said the Headmaster suddenly. 'Now move to the groups I divided you into yesterday and prepare to receive instructions.'

Their eyes open but glazed, two hundred children rose to their feet, completely silently except for the shuffling of chairs, and started to move along the rows like robots, rearranging themselves into six groups in different parts of the Hall.

Dinah's feet took her mechanically up on to the stage. As she walked across it, she passed the Headmaster, but although her eyes passed over his face she was not aware of the irritable way it twitched.

'Dinah Glass – stop.'

Obediently, she stood to attention.

'You look slovenly. Take your hand out of your pocket at once.'

Without any hesitation, she drew out her hand, still tightly clutching the tape-recorder. The Headmaster had begun to turn away, but out of the corner of his eye he caught sight of it. He whirled back.

'Give me what you have in your hand.'

Her face blank and calm, Dinah held out the tape-recorder

and he took it from her. For a moment or two, he turned it over thoughtfully in his hands.

'Well, well,' he said softly, 'so that's the way the wind blows, is it? I can see I shall have to deal with you at once, and not leave it until next week.' Briefly his fingers moved, pressing switches. Then he said in a louder voice, 'Mr Venables. Come here.'

Automatically, Mr Venables marched up on to the stage and, with an expression of careful calculation on his face, the Headmaster began to whisper in his ear.

When Dinah opened her eyes again, blinking, she had a second of complete, distracted panic. She was not quite sure where she was. Somehow, she had expected to be somewhere else ... Then, gradually, the pieces of the room swam into place and she realized that she was sitting in her own classroom. It was totally empty, except for Mr Venables, who was at his desk, facing her.

'Good afternoon, Dinah,' he said briskly.

She blinked again. 'What – what am I doing here?'

'You are here because I have something to say to you. Come up to my desk.'

Still dazed, she stood up and walked towards him. It was only when she was standing beside the desk that she noticed what was lying on top of it. Three sheets of paper covered with sums worked in her own tiny figures. Very difficult sums. She was too controlled to catch her breath, but her face became completely wooden.

Mr Venables tapped the papers with one finger. 'You did these sums. Didn't you?'

'They were Harvey's sums, not mine,' Dinah said carefully. Mr Venables gave an impatient sigh.

'There was never any chance that Harvey could do them. They were set to see if you would do them to help him. If you *could* do them. And he will be punished for letting you help him unless –'

'But that's not fair!' Dinah broke in. 'He would have been punished if they weren't done and now he's going to be punished because they *are* done. He never had any chance.'

'Fairness is an illusion, designed to create disorder,' Mr Venables said calmly. 'Besides, I did not say that he would be punished. Only that he would be punished unless – unless you decide to help him by cooperating.'

Dinah stood stubborn and silent. Mr Venables looked at her.

'You are a clever girl, Dinah, however much you may have tried to hide it. You must see that you have no choice.'

'What do you want me to do?' she said stiffly.

Briskly, Mr Venables began to explain, and Dinah stared at him, completely amazed.

She walked home alone, in a dream, so wrapped up in what she was thinking that she did not see anything around her. When she pushed open the kitchen door, Mrs Hunter smiled at her.

'The others are all in the playroom. They wondered what had happened to you.'

'The others?' Dinah said, still vague. Mrs Hunter looked at her.

'Are you all right, dear?'

'What? Oh yes.' Suddenly, Dinah remembered what was supposed to be happening. She slid her fingers into her pocket and felt the solid shape of the cassette recorder. 'I just walked home rather slowly, that's all.'

'Do you want something to eat?'

'No. No thanks. I'd better go and talk to them.'

As she reached the playroom door, a voice from inside said, 'The man who can keep order can rule the world.'

For one moment she could not drag the right reply out of her memory. Then it came. 'But the man who can endure disorder is truly free.'

Ingrid wrenched open the door excitedly. 'Hallo, Brains. What happened? Hey, you look terrible.'

Silently, Dinah walked in and put the tape-recorder down on the table. Mandy touched her hand gently.

'What's the matter? Did you get caught?'

'No. I mean, I don't know.'

'You don't know?' Lloyd spluttered. 'Christmas puddings! Don't be silly. You must know.'

'No she mustn't,' Ian said. 'She's been hypnotized. Remember? Let's listen to the tape.'

Dinah nodded. Best to get that over first. Then she could talk properly.

Ian reached for the switch, and they all sat watching the tape run through for two or three minutes. Then he pressed another switch and ran it on a bit and they listened again.

There was no sound.

'You didn't switch it on!' Lloyd said accusingly. 'You forgot.'

'No I didn't. I remember doing it. I don't remember anything after that, but I did switch it on.'

'Perhaps it didn't pick up anything,' Mandy said soothingly. 'It was in her pocket, after all.'

Lloyd looked stubborn. '*I* think she mucked it up.'

'Oh, leave her alone!' Harvey thumped him. 'You're
always getting at her, Lloyd. Look, you've upset her.'

'No,' Dinah murmured. 'No, it's not that. I don't know
why the recording didn't work. But something else
happened.'

Suddenly they were all looking at her curiously.

'Come on,' Ingrid urged. 'Don't spin it out. Tell us.'

Dinah took a deep breath.

'Why,' she said quietly, 'didn't anyone tell me that the
school was going to be on the Eddy Hair Show next week?
In the Great School Quiz?'

Chapter 12

'Got You Guessing?'

'Oh *that*?' Lloyd shrugged. 'Didn't you know about that? Why should we get excited about it? It only means more glory for the Headmaster. And none of *us* is going to be in the team. What's that got to do with anything?'

Typical of a girl, he thought. She was just trying to distract them, because she'd messed up the business with the tape-recorder.

But Dinah was staring at him as if he were an idiot. 'Can't you see how peculiar it is?' she said softly. 'Think what the Eddy Hair Show's like. Mess. Chaos. They fling things all over the place. Flour, soot, chickens – all sorts of things. Sometimes they even break windows.'

'I expect they pay for them afterwards,' Ian said.

'But look.' Dinah leaned forwards, anxious that they should see things her way. 'Think what the school's like. If you put your knife and fork down out of line, someone's on to you. If you throw snow at someone, the whole place goes mad. Why should the Headmaster have *invited* the Eddy Hair Show to come? Because he must have done.'

'You're right,' Mandy said slowly. 'I never thought of it like that before. It is odd.'

Lloyd banged the table. 'What does it matter if it's odd? It's got nothing to do with what we're talking about.'

'I'm not so sure,' Dinah said softly. 'You see – the Head-master knows it was me that did those sums for Harvey.' Harvey gasped and she smiled at him reassuringly. 'No, it's all right. They were a trap. I was meant to do them. But so that you don't get into trouble for it – I've got to be in the Quiz team for the Eddy Hair Show.'

'So?' Lloyd said disagreeably. 'That just goes to prove what I've said all along. You're one of Them, not one of Us.'

'Oh, do be quiet!' For once, Ian was roused out of his usual lethargy, positively snarling at Lloyd. 'Can't you see Dinah's got more to say? And if she thinks it's important it must be worth listening to.'

Lloyd subsided, sulking, and Dinah went on, choosing her words carefully.

'It was Mr Venables who told me about being in the team. And the really odd thing was that he kept saying, "You must see to it that the team wins. The Headmaster says that the team *must* win. Otherwise, there'll be trouble for Harvey Hunter."'

'You can do it, can't you?' Harvey said, in a worried voice. 'You are clever enough, Di?'

'Oh, I expect so,' Dinah said vaguely. 'But that's not the point. The point is – why is the Headmaster so desperate for us to win? Why should it be important to him?'

Lloyd snorted. 'More honour and glory for his precious school.'

Dinah shook her head, frowning. 'No, I don't think that's it. It doesn't seem to fit, somehow. There's something else. Something at the back of my mind that makes it all make sense. But I can't catch hold of it.'

'Look,' Ian said suddenly. 'It's Friday today, isn't it? Well, the Eddy Hair Show's on at six o'clock. We'll watch it and see if that helps.'

'Oh, good-oh!' Ingrid chirped. 'I love it. Especially the Great School Quiz. The questions are so hard, I can never do any of them.'

'That's because we're all taught parrot-fashion,' said Dinah. 'The questions in the Quiz are puzzles, and no one in our school's encouraged to think. It's quite the wrong quiz for our sort of school. So why did the Headmaster get us into it?'

'It's just the fame he wants,' Lloyd said. 'I told you. You know what they say about the Eddy Hair Show. Everyone in the country switches on at six o'clock on a Friday to watch it.'

'But –' began Dinah. Lloyd flung his hands up in despair, ready to argue with her.

'Let's forget it for now,' Mandy said hastily. 'Who's for a game of I-Spy?'

The television set flickered briefly and then the picture swelled into colour. Six girls, apparently with no heads, danced across the screen, chased by a large gorilla.

'Yes, folks,' said a cheerful voice from nowhere, 'It's what you've all been waiting for. Your weekly dose of craziness in a sane, sad world. The Great, the Magnificent, the *only* – EDDY HAIR SHOW!'

The gorilla jumped into a dustbin. Then it reached up and pulled its head off, revealing Eddy Hair's purple-painted face.

'It's all rubbish,' he said severely. 'Only idiots watch this

show. Tests prove that ninety-nine point nine per cent of our viewers have no heads.'

Bounding from the dustbin, he waggled his purple hair at the audience. 'And just you wait till you see what a vintage load of rubbish is on the show today. If you had any sense, you'd switch off now. Got you guessing? *That's* how I like it!'

At manic speed, the show swung into its usual succession of gags, sketches and disasters. Some of it was pre-recorded, like the piece where Eddy Hair swung from a helicopter, dropping balloons shaped like fat ladies over a Beauty Contest. But most of it was live, and one or two of the disasters were obviously completely unexpected. Whatever happened, Eddy Hair laughed his raucous laugh and all over the country people fell about, clutching their sides helplessly.

Only in the Hunters' sitting room was there total, grim silence. All the members of SPLAT were watching the show like detectives, trying to see why the Headmaster was interested in it. And the more they watched, the more baffled they became.

At last, there was a fanfare of trumpets, accompanied by wild grunts from a pig.

'At last!' bellowed Eddy Hair. 'Now you'll see that the people round here are not only mad but stupid. It's – the Great School Quiz.'

Immediately, the cameras panned round the school hall where the show was taking place. Two teams, each of three children, were sitting facing each other and beside each, on a throne, sat a cheerful-looking Head Teacher. Eddy Hair walked across the stage with his knees knocking dramatically.

'Can't stand teachers!' he whispered at the camera. 'They terrify me.'

Then, with a grin, he was squatting on top of a barrel, reaching for the first question.

'Right. It's a question for the Manor Junior School. You have thirty seconds to think, and anyone can answer – *if* you're not all too thick to work it out. Here goes. "I want to buy roller skates for my chickens. Twelve per cent of them have only one leg, and half the rest refuse to wear roller skates. So how many skates do I need to buy?"'

'That's impossible,' Mandy said. 'He hasn't said how many chickens there are.'

'It's the same number of skates as the number of chickens,' Dinah said calmly. 'It works out to one leg each.'

Almost thirty seconds later, a brainy-looking boy with glasses faltered, 'The same as the number of chickens?'

Eddy Hair beamed at him. 'Watch you don't burn your mind out, genius. Thinking's bad for your football, remember. Now, the next question . . .'

As the Quiz went on, the questions grew harder and harder, but Dinah answered them all, hardly pausing to think. And the more she answered, the crosser Lloyd grew.

'Oh, shut up!' he yelled, as the last question was asked. 'We know you've got brains the size of the Eiffel Tower. No need to rub it in. I vote we turn off this stupid programme.'

'Not yet,' wailed Ingrid. 'It's just getting to my favourite bit. With the Head Teachers. Let's watch that.'

On the screen, Eddy Hair was waggling a finger at the Headmaster of Shillingstone Street School.

'Your lot,' he said cheerfully, 'are the Dimmest School of the Week. Prepare to receive your reward.'

In a flash, a giant panda appeared behind the Headmaster's chair and tipped a bucketful of flour over his head. As he emerged from the white cloud, brushing it from his beard, his pupils cheered wildly.

'I can just see our Headmaster liking that,' Ian said with relish. 'Perhaps the whole thing will be fun.'

'No,' murmured Mandy. 'We're going to win. Remember?'

'That's even better,' chuckled Ingrid. 'Do listen. What's the other Headmaster going to say?'

For Eddy Hair was now pointing at the Headmaster of the winning school.

'You seem to have a crowd of geniuses,' he said sourly. 'Suppose you tell us how you do it.'

This Headmaster was a large, cheerful man with a red face. The camera panned in on him, so that his face filled the whole screen.

'Doughnuts,' he said, perfectly gravely. 'We fill them full of doughnuts every morning before school. Good for the brain. You should try some, Eddy. And if anyone refuses to eat the doughnuts, we ...'

He went on for a full minute, with the camera to himself, explaining the magical qualities of doughnuts, before the panda reappeared and jammed three doughnuts into his open mouth.

Lloyd reached forward and switched off the set. 'You see?' he said contemptuously. 'There's nothing for us to go on. It's just a red herring that Dinah's dreamed up.'

'Wait.' Dinah had gone white, and she was still staring at the empty screen, with her mouth open. Then, as if she were being strangled, she said, 'It's always like that, isn't it? The Headmaster of the winning team gets a whole minute to talk. To say whatever rubbish comes into his head. With most of the people in the country watching.'

Ian nodded.

'Well.' Dinah gulped. 'Think what our Headmaster could do with that.'

Mandy gasped.

'Would a minute be enough?' Harvey said.

'Probably.' Dinah considered. 'I don't think it took him nearly as long as a minute to hypnotize me the first time.'

'But that's *devilish*!' spluttered Ingrid. 'He'd have the whole country in his power. Do you think that's really what he's planning?'

110

'I don't see how he could resist it,' Dinah said miserably. 'Do you, Lloyd?'

Lloyd would dearly have liked to say she was wrong. Just to show her up. But the more he thought about it, the more certain it seemed. 'I think you've got it,' he said grudgingly.

'But *why?*' Dinah chewed her bottom lip.

Lloyd jumped to his feet. 'That's obvious! Don't be so dumb, Dinah. He'll be able to make his fortune. All he has to do is to tell everyone to send him a hundred pounds, or go out and rob a bank, or something. He'll be the richest man in the world.'

'Of course!' said Ian and Harvey together.

But Dinah looked doubtful. 'I'm not sure. It doesn't seem quite –'

'Oh, you!' Lloyd said bitterly. 'You want to have all the inspirations. Just because I thought of this one –'

Mandy interrupted him, ready to make peace as always. 'I can't see that it matters why he's doing it. The important thing is – what are we going to do about it?'

'Couldn't Dinah just lose the Quiz?' Ingrid said helpfully.

'No!' Harvey went white. And Dinah shook her head as well.

'That's too dangerous. He planned all this before I came, so he must have some scheme even if the team loses. No, the only safe thing is to stop the Eddy Hair Show coming to the school at all.'

'Right.' Lloyd decided that they had all listened to her for long enough. His head was suddenly bursting with ideas, and he was determined to take charge. 'I'm the Chairman, and I'm going to make the plans.' Everyone looked round at him and he grew more confident. This was better. Like before Dinah came. Everyone waiting for him to tell them what to do. 'We'll keep quiet for a week. So that no one suspects anything. Then, on the day of the show, this is what will happen ...'

Chapter 13

SPLAT
Goes into Action

When Lloyd, Harvey and Dinah arrived at school the next Friday morning, there was something slightly different about the atmosphere in the playground. A feeling of suppressed excitement. No one pranced about, or did imitations of Eddy Hair, or boasted about being in the Quiz team. The children were standing in their usual circles, chanting away. But the chant was a bit faster and, from time to time, people looked at each other, breathlessly. It was plain what they were thinking. At six o'clock that evening they would be sitting in the Hall and they would be on television.

The members of SPLAT kept well away from each other. There was no need to speak. They knew what they had to do. For a whole week, they had been going over it at their meetings until the arrangements were perfect. This morning there were only five of them in the playground. Ian had hidden on the way to school, ready to carry out the first part of Lloyd's plan, and Mandy carried a note, forged by Dinah, which said that Ian would not be at school that day because he had a cold.

As the prefects gathered on the steps and the children started to move into line, Lloyd glanced round quickly to check that Mandy and Ingrid were there. As he glanced at them, they crossed their fingers quickly and moved off.

Lloyd drew a deep breath. Nothing must go wrong. He only hoped that he had thought of everything.

The big outside-broadcast lorries trundled through the town, carrying the equipment needed to set up that evening's Eddy Hair Show. Inside, the drivers and technicians were laughing and chatting to each other. This was the easy part of their job. Once the show started, they were tense, not knowing what was going to happen from one moment to the next. Whatever Eddy Hair sprang on them, they had to cope with, somehow. But if they got the cameras and lights and microphones set up in good time, they could cope with anything.

At the traffic lights in the middle of the town, the first driver paused and pulled out a map. 'Right,' he said. 'We turn left here, and –'

He stopped suddenly. A tall, fair-haired boy in immaculate school uniform was jumping up and down beside his cab, trying to attract his attention. He wound the window down and leaned out. 'Yes, sonny?'

Ian put on his most virtuous and reliable expression. 'Are you the television people? Coming to do the Eddy Hair Show at our school?'

'Yes, that's right. You looking for us?'

Ian nodded. 'The Headmaster sent me. He asked if you would take the lorries round the back way. You go left here, right up the little lane, over the bridge and – Here, would you like me to come along and show you? I've got to go back to school anyway.'

'Sure. Hop up.' The driver grinned at him. 'Nice to come to a school where we get looked after so well.'

Ian climbed up into the cab and began to direct. Behind, he heard the other lorries start up and his mouth went dry. If only it worked. If only they did not suspect anything.

'Left here,' he said, his voice completely calm. 'Then right.'

'You're sure you've got it straight, sonny?' As the man beside him swung the wheel, he glanced sideways, doubtfully. 'I don't see any sign of a school.'

'That's all right,' Ian said airily. 'You can't see it from here. Go through those gates, and I'll hop out and tell the Headmaster you've come. Then you can bring the lorries up to the door one by one.'

Still frowning, the driver turned the wheel again. Slowly the lorry crunched through a pair of tall gates into the disused quarry. In front of them, tall cliffs of chalk stretched up on every side, cutting off any view. Ian threw the door open and slipped down, out of the cab.

'Wait here. Won't be a moment.'

As he ran back to the entrance, the other two lorries were rolling through the gates. He waved cheerfully at the drivers and waited until they were clear, then began to shove at the heavy gates. For one panicky moment, he thought they were not going to move, but they swung together suddenly, with a clang, and he pulled out of his pocket the two big padlocks that Lloyd had given him. Quickly, he clipped them shut.

'Hey!' said a voice from inside the quarry. 'What're you doing?'

Not waiting to hear any more, Ian ran off down the road. Mission One was safely completed. Now came the tricky bit. He found the bush where he had hidden a bottle of cooking oil, pulled it out and set off towards the school. Somehow, he had to sneak in and out again, without being seen.

Mandy and Ingrid were not feeling so cheerful. Their part of the plan was next, but they had to wait until the end of the afternoon to start it, and they were not at all sure that it would work. They sat in their separate classrooms, biting their nails, and when they met at lunchtime, Mandy whispered, 'I'm scared. Suppose it all goes wrong?'

Ingrid glanced round to see if anyone was watching, then thumped her crossly. 'It had better not go wrong. You know what Lloyd said. We must get all possible enemies out of the way. Now shut up about it. I'll see you outside the staff-room at four o'clock.'

Mandy fretted her way through the afternoon, but at four o'clock she was standing bravely in the corridor outside the staffroom when Ingrid appeared.

'There's a terrible racket going on in the Headmaster's office,' Ingrid whispered. 'He's on the phone to the television headquarters, wanting to know why the cameras and things haven't arrived. I could hear him right through the door.'

Mandy grinned. 'At least Ian's first bit went OK. Let's hope the second bit did too, or we might be in trouble. All the teachers are in the staffroom. I've been watching them go in. Give me a couple of minutes to get down to the swimming pool and then knock on the door.'

She ran off, and a minute or two later, Ingrid rapped sharply on the staffroom door, panting as if she had been hurrying. When Mr Venables opened it, she began to speak quickly.

'Please, sir, I've got a message from the Headmaster. Eddy Hair wants to talk to all the teachers in the swimming pool building.'

'The swimming pool?' Mr Venables raised his eyebrows.

'It's a stunt he's got planned.' Ingrid gave her most innocent, frightened smile. 'He wants you all to join in, and the Headmaster's sounding rather cross and –'

Her lip trembled, from genuine nervousness, and that appeared to convince Mr Venables. He called over his shoulder, 'Come on, everyone. We've got to go down to the swimming pool. Some mad stunt of Eddy Hair's.'

Groaning wearily, the teachers began to emerge from the staffroom. They trooped out of the building and across the playground, towards the single-storey block where the swimming pool was housed. When they were halfway there, Ingrid said anxiously, 'Oh, do please hurry. *Run*. The Headmaster was *so* impatient!'

The group of teachers broke into a trot, making for the open door of the swimming pool. As the first few of them hurried through the door, their feet slipped on the oil which Ian had spread carefully all over the tiles. Slithering towards the water, they began to yell, but this only brought the other teachers running faster. As the last of them slipped through the door, the splashes began. One after another, they fell into the swimming pool, skidding uncontrollably over the edge.

Immediately, Mandy appeared from her hiding place round one corner, waving the swimming pool key. As Ingrid pushed the doors shut, she slid it into the lock. The shouting, splashing teachers had still not realized that they were not involved in one of Eddy Hair's crazy pranks. It would be some time before they discovered that they were prisoners. Ingrid winked at Mandy. 'That should keep them busy. Let's get out of here.'

At the same moment, Lloyd and Dinah were crouching round the corner from the prefects' room, quarrelling in whispers.

'They're not all there,' Dinah was saying. 'Rose and Jeff are still around the school somewhere. If we don't get them, it could be very dangerous.'

'Don't be so bossy.' Lloyd frowned. 'All the other four are there, but they might come out once they've eaten their sandwiches. And if we don't lock them in and get down to the Hall, someone's going to notice that we're not eating ours. We'll just have to do without Rose and Jeff.'

'But they're the worst.'

'Oh, shut up!' Lloyd knew she was right really, but it

118

did not make him better tempered. 'You're always inter-fering.'

Dinah shut her mouth tight. No use saying she had only been trying to help. She knew what Lloyd was like now. He wanted to be in charge all the time. Well, let him. She did not really think trapping the prefects would make any difference anyway.

'Go on, then,' she said quietly. 'Let's get it over with.'

Like a shadow, Lloyd stepped forwards and locked the door of the prefects' room. Then he put his ear to it.

'Hey,' he mouthed, 'They're saying something.'

Dinah came up beside him. Through the wood of the door, she heard Simon's voice reciting, as if he had learnt it by heart, 'And I take charge of transport. With twenty children to help me. According to Master Plan, Section C.'

Lloyd frowned. 'What are they on about?' he said noise-lessly.

Dinah put a finger to her lips and leaned closer, hearing Sarah's voice now.

'I'm in charge of work camps. Master Plan, Section F. With fifty children to help. All people to be split up accord-ing to age. Museums and public buildings to be used for housing them and –'

'Oh, come on.' Lloyd pulled Dinah's sleeve. 'I don't know what they're up to, but it doesn't sound as though it's got anything to do with today. Let's go and eat our sandwiches. Then we can sneak off again and see how Harvey's doing.'

Dinah dragged her ear away from the door, feeling frustrated. She was sure she was missing something very important, but Lloyd was right. They could not risk being seen with their ears to the door.

'OK,' she said. 'They sound as though they'll go on talking for hours. And I don't suppose it'll matter about Rose and Jeff.'

'Of course it won't matter,' Lloyd said angrily. But he was not very happy as they crept off down the corridor. It was the first thing that had gone wrong.

Back in the middle of the town again, Ian was beginning to grow restless. Perhaps he had missed Eddy Hair. He might have been looking for the wrong sort of person. Perhaps the purple curls were just a wig and the crazy clothes were only for wearing on television. In that case, Eddy Hair could have slipped past a hundred times without being noticed. What an idiot he was not to have thought of that before! He frowned, and marched up and down by the traffic lights, stamping his feet to keep them warm.

Then he saw it. A little, low sports car, zooming along the main road towards him. There was no mistaking it. Even if the number plate had not been EH1. Even if the car had not been painted in stripes of red, yellow and mustard colour. For there, at the wheel, was Eddy Hair himself, his huge bunch of purple curls almost filling the windscreen and a cheerful grin on his loony face.

Bounding with relief, Ian started to leap up and down beside the red traffic light, ready with his next set of false directions.

And for a moment it looked as though it was going to work. The sports car squealed to a stop and Eddy Hair leaned over and wound down the window.

'Please –' Ian started.

But Eddy Hair was obviously used to being stopped by waving children. He did not even give Ian a chance to finish his sentence. Instead, beaming all over his face, he shouted, 'Want an autograph, do you? Bless you, boy, you don't suppose I can *write*, do you?'

With a great screech of laughter, he banged the car into gear, roared the engine and was away as the lights changed, leaving only a cloud of exhaust fumes.

'Blast it,' Ian said softly. 'Blast, blast, blast!'

Then he began to run as fast as he could towards the school. He had to warn the others that the plan was not working perfectly. Luckily, he knew where he would find them all.

In the school boiler room, Harvey was shaking with fright, reading over and over again the instructions that Dinah had given him. 'It's quite safe if you do it in the right order,' she had said firmly. 'But if you don't, you might kill yourself.'

He looked at his watch. Why didn't the others come? It was after half past four. He could not leave it any longer. Oh well, he would have to do without their help. Pulling a torch out of his pocket, he looked nervously up at the big red handle on the wall which said MAINS SUPPLY.

'Here goes,' he murmured.

Gripping the handle tightly with his right hand, he pulled it hard down.

Instantly, the cellar was pitch black. Harvey switched on the torch and wrenched open the door of the fuse box. With his left hand he began to tug out the fuses, cramming them into his pockets.

There was a quick clatter of feet outside the door. Glancing nervously over his shoulder, he saw Mandy and Ingrid run in.

'Smashing!' Ingrid said enthusiastically. She leaped for the fuse box. 'We'll give you a hand.'

As her fingers reached for a fuse, Lloyd and Dinah came creeping in.

'OK, H?' Lloyd muttered. 'Everything else is going according to plan. Well – nearly. Ian's on his way. I saw him racing through the gate while we were on our way up here. Now let's get a move on with those fuses. Once we've chucked them away, they won't be able to do anything, even if they do get the lights and cameras here.'

They had just cleared the fuse box when Ian arrived. He pulled a face, gasping for breath. 'I couldn't stop Eddy Hair,' he panted. 'He really is as crazy as he seems on TV. But I've got the lorries locked up in the quarry OK, and – hey, Harvey!'

Harvey's hand, holding the torch, had begun to shake wildly, flashing light distractingly into everyone's eyes.

'Knock it off, Harvey!' Lloyd snapped. 'We've got to get out of here.'

'B – b – but –' stuttered Harvey, 'oh – look!'

He gestured despairingly towards the door, and the others spun round.

There, outlined in the doorway, was a tall figure in a gown. On either side of him stood Rose and Jeff, smirking.

'Well, well,' said the Headmaster. 'You've all been *very* busy today, haven't you?'

Chapter 14

The Headmaster
in Control

For a whole minute there was complete, horrified silence in the crowded boiler room. Then the Headmaster said, very quietly, 'Put the fuses back.'

'We won't!' Ingrid shouted. 'You're evil and wicked and we won't do anything to help you.'

The Headmaster smiled. 'I think you will.' He raised his voice slightly. 'Children – come along to the door.'

There was a tramping of feet in the corridor outside and suddenly the space behind the Headmaster was full of faces with blank, glazed eyes. Thirty or forty hypnotized children.

'We'd better do it,' Ian groaned. 'Otherwise they'll just make us. Come on, everyone.'

Despairingly, they began to push the fuses back into the box. Then Harvey switched on the mains supply again and they were all blinking in the sudden glare of light.

'That's better,' said the Headmaster, in a satisfied voice. 'Now we had better repair the rest of the damage you have done. Rose, where are all the teachers?'

'I saw Mandy and Ingrid lock them into the swimming pool.'

'And the prefects, Jeff?'

'Locked in their room,' Jeff said.

The Headmaster nodded and glanced back at the miserable

members of SPLAT. 'I have had you watched, you see. I am not entirely stupid. The only thing I did not know was what had happened to the camera crew. But from what I heard as we arrived, I would guess that they are shut up in the old quarry. If you are sensible, you will hand over all the keys to me. Now.'

Sullenly, Lloyd, Ian and Mandy tossed the keys on to the floor. At a signal from the Headmaster, Rose and Jeff scooped them off and ran away down the corridor. The Headmaster did not speak again until the sound of their feet had died away. Then he stepped further into the room and looked at Dinah.

'I think,' he said, 'that we had better discuss what is going to happen next.'

'I know what you want,' Dinah said stiffly. 'You want me to win the Great School Quiz for you. So that you can have a chance to hypnotize everyone in the country. Well, I won't do it. If it's the only way to stop you, I'll make sure I get all the questions wrong.'

The Headmaster raised his eyebrows. 'You have worked things out very cleverly. I can see that I have not over-estimated your intelligence. But you have underestimated my determination. You cannot refuse to do what I want.'

'Can't I?' Dinah stepped forward belligerently, but the Headmaster did not look in the least worried. Turning to the children massed in the doorway, he snapped at them in a brisk voice.

'Listen to my orders. In front of you are six straw dolls. They are no longer needed. You will advance on them and,' he drew a deep breath, 'you will tear them to pieces.'

Simultaneously, all the children swivelled their eyes to

look into the boiler room. They showed no signs of recognition. It was plain that they were seeing precisely what they had been told to see. As they started to advance, Dinah watched Lucy, who was in the middle of the front row. Her face was as calm and cheerful as if she had been going out to pick daisies.

Knowing it would be no use, Dinah began to yell at her as the children marched into the boiler room.

'Lucy! It's me, Dinah! And there's Lloyd and Harvey and the others. You can't hurt us!'

'She won't hear you,' the Headmaster said icily. 'She is programmed to listen only to me and the prefects.'

Dinah and the others cowered against the wall behind them as the children came steadily tramping towards them.

'Think, Dinah, think!' Lloyd yelled. 'There must be some way out of this. Otherwise they'll kill us.'

The foremost children had reached them now. Slowly they raised their arms, hands outstretched like claws.

'Oh, help!' Harvey yelled. 'Someone, help!'

The claw-like hands grabbed. Dinah found her blazer gripped firmly by Lucy and she heard Mandy's blouse rip. From beside her, Ingrid wailed, 'Oh, I'm frightened.'

More and more hands were pulling at them. Glancing across the room, Dinah saw the Headmaster smiling calmly, with no sign of wavering. Coldly, she realized that he would not relent. If he had to kill them, he would kill them. As someone started to tug at her hair, she shouted, 'All right, I'll do it! Whatever you say! Just stop them!'

At once, with a triumphant smile, the Headmaster said softly, 'Stop, children.'

Slowly, the arms dropped. Mandy gave a quick gasp of relief and Harvey drew a sobbing breath.

'You will be in the Quiz?' the Headmaster murmured.

Dinah nodded, hanging her head.

'And you will win?'

'If that's what I have to do.'

'Very well.' The Headmaster's mouth twisted in an unpleasant expression. 'But do not suppose that I shall be so foolish as to trust you. Your friends will be in the Hall, surrounded by these children. If you break your promise, all I have to do is to say, "Destroy the dolls!" and they will be dead. Is that clear?'

Dumb with despair, Dinah nodded again. Beside her, she heard Lloyd's familiar snort, comforting in its ordinariness.

'We may not be able to stop you,' Lloyd said scornfully, 'but we still think you're wicked. Wicked and pathetic. Fancy being prepared to *kill* us. Just for money.'

For the first time, the Headmaster looked startled. 'What do you mean?'

'That's what you're after, isn't it?' Lloyd said stoutly. 'You want to hypnotize everyone so that you can get their money and be the richest man in the world. Well, I think it's pathetic.'

To their amazement, the Headmaster suddenly flung back his head and laughed, soundlessly and horribly. When he stopped, he shook his head at them sadly.

'Money? Oh yes, I should be really pathetic if that was all I wanted. No wonder you have been my enemies. No wonder you think I am wicked.'

'Well you are, aren't you?' Ingrid said stoutly. He shook his head at her again.

'No, I am not wicked. My plans are for the good of every-one.' His voice rose, almost hysterically. 'My plans are glorious and splendid!'

'But you aren't going to tell us what they are?' said Dinah.

'You will see soon. Very soon now.' He looked round at them all. 'And when you do, you will understand how wrong you have been. Until then, I must remember that it is the fate of great men always to be misunderstood. Now – let us go to the Hall.'

They began to walk along the corridor, the Headmaster gripping Dinah's shoulder and the others marching in the middle of the crowd of hypnotized children. As she walked, Dinah was thinking busily. What was it that the Headmaster wanted? He, at least, must believe that it *was* good. But – *what was it?*

In the Hall, everything was in chaos. The television men had just arrived and they were leaping about at high speed, hanging lights, positioning microphones and connecting wires. In the centre of it all, a wiry figure with a crop of purple curls was dancing wildly from place to place.

'Come on, lads!' Eddy Hair was shouting. 'You can just do it. If you work hard.'

The Headmaster walked straight up the middle of the Hall, with all the children following. Dinah saw his face twitch with distaste as he stared round at the crazy scene. Then he forced a jovial smile and tapped Eddy Hair on the arm.

'Aaaagh!' With a scream, Eddy Hair fell to the ground as if he had been shot. 'You got me!' He lay on the floor, looking up at the Headmaster.

'I beg your pardon,' the Headmaster said gravely. 'I didn't mean to startle you.'

'Good for the soul, being startled,' chuckled Eddy Hair. 'Nothing like the unexpected for keeping people on their – TOES!' As he said the last word, he bounded to his feet. 'What can I do for you, O Master?'

'Do you want me to bring the school into the Hall yet?'

'Why not, why not?' Eddy Hair flapped a hand. 'Good for the lads here to have an audience. And I don't suppose they'll be finished until thirty seconds before the show starts. No time to set the audience up then. Yes, get the kids in now. And have your Quiz team ready at the side of the stage. But make sure they're all quiet. We don't want a racket.'

'Oh yes,' the Headmaster said, with an amused smile, 'I think I can assure you that all my pupils will be perfectly quiet.'

Dinah stood at the side of the stage, out of range of the

cameras, with the rest of the children taking part in the quiz. It had not occurred to her to wonder before who would be picked to make up the rest of the team. Now she discovered that it was to be Rose and Lucy. Rose was her usual unpleasant self, but Lucy, woken out of her hypnotized trance, was bubbling with excitement, hardly able to keep silent. She grinned merrily at Dinah. It was all that Dinah could do to grin back.

You nearly killed me an hour ago, she thought. But, looking at Lucy now, she found it almost impossible to believe. And if she could barely believe it, who else would?

The Manor Road Quiz team had just arrived and Lucy smiled at the boy with glasses. 'You're Alec Bates, aren't you?' she whispered. 'I saw you on television last week. You were very good.'

The boy grinned back at her, cockily. 'I've been practising since then. I'm even better now. You'll never beat us.'

One of the sound engineers frowned at them and wagged a finger. 'Ssh,' he said loudly. 'The show's just about to start.'

As the first notes of the opening music filled the Hall, Dinah craned her neck to see what was going on. In the front row of chairs were the other members of SPLAT, surrounded by wooden-faced children, all ready to attack them if the instruction was given. She shuddered and looked sideways at the Headmaster, who was next to her.

He was staring across at the stage. Out there, Eddy Hair had begun a fight with a giant plateful of spaghetti. And the spaghetti was fighting him back, huge white strands slapping slimily round his neck and spoonfuls of sauce splattering messily all over the stage. The Headmaster's face was white. His fingers twitched and he looked as though he were going to be sick.

He can't stand it, thought Dinah suddenly. *Mess actually makes him ill.* Somehow, that thought was rather comforting. At least he had weaknesses. The knowledge made her feel bold and, in a very soft voice, she asked the question that had been bothering her for days. 'If you hadn't got me in the school, how would you have arranged to win the Quiz?'

The Headmaster dragged his eyes away from the stage, and glanced at the other team. 'I should have hypnotized them and made them lose,' he murmured. 'But I shan't have to do that now. Shall I?'

'No. No, of course not,' Dinah said quickly, afraid. But she was not too afraid to risk another question. 'And what *will* you do after – after you've had your minute on television?'

But he just smiled at her and turned back to the stage, with a shudder. Eddy Hair had started to fling pepper at the spaghetti. He had three or four huge scarlet pepperpots with black stripes and he was shaking them frantically, spraying showers of pepper everywhere. And the spaghetti was sneezing. Its pale strands whirled everywhere like the arms of an octopus.

Dinah was left to wonder, desperately, what was going to happen. She was so deep in her own thoughts that she jerked with shock when the sound engineer prodded her.

'Quick!' he said. 'On to the stage.'

'What?'

'Didn't you hear? The Quiz is about to start.'

Chapter 15

The Great School Quiz

Lloyd, slumped in his chair at the front of the Hall, watched as the two teams filed out. The stage was a disgusting mess. Bits of spaghetti, broken eggs and torn paper lay all over the floor. On Dinah's chair lay one of the huge scarlet pepper-pots which Eddy Hair had used in his fight with the spaghetti. Lloyd saw Dinah pick it up and put it on the table in front of her while the Headmaster, with an expression of revulsion, kicked away a squashed banana from near his foot.

'Ghastly, isn't it?' Eddy Hair said cheerfully. 'The country must be in a mess when a show like this is so popular.'

He began to explain the rules of the Quiz. 'Ten questions for each team, with thirty seconds to answer. *If* you can.'

Dinah sat in her chair, with her hands clasped on the table in front of her. On her face was an expression of complete, total wretchedness. *It's worse for her than it is for us*, Lloyd thought suddenly. *We've only got to wait, but she's got to help him win*. He felt a sudden burst of pity for her and was surprised at himself. Was he getting soft?

'Right.' Eddy Hair reached for the question paper. 'Manor Road School first, and it's a real brain-buster. "King Bonk of Zoldovia has a hundred children. Ninety per cent of them have curly noses, eighty-five per cent of them are bald, eighty per cent of them have one leg and seventy-five per

cent of them lisp. How many bald, one-legged, lisping children with curly noses must he have?"'

Wow! thought Lloyd. But Alec Bates was already smiling confidently and scribbling on the paper in front of him. A moment later, he had answered.

'Thirty.'

'Right!' yelled Eddy Hair. 'And how pretty their holiday snaps must look. One point to Manor Road. Next question to the home team. And here it is. "Every room in my house has as many old women in it as there are rooms altogether. Every old woman knits as many knee-warmers as there are old women. I share the knee warmers out among seven of my worst enemies, giving each the same number and as many as possible, and I still have more than enough to cover my knees. How many have I got?"'

Dinah picked up the red pepperpot in front of her and

132

stared thoughtfully at its black stripes, but she did not bother to write anything down. 'Six,' she said in an unhappy voice.

The Headmaster gave a pleased smile as the scores drew level and Lloyd felt a cold shudder creep up his back. Only another nine questions each. And if they were no more trouble than that one, how could Dinah help winning?

But he had not counted on Alec Bates. Alec was the only one of the Manor Road team who seemed to have any brains at all, but he was crammed with them. Every time Eddy Hair asked him a question, he gave the same conceited grin and scribbled away furiously on his piece of paper. And, every time, his answers were right. When the score stood at 8–8, Lloyd suddenly realized that it could be a draw. What would happen then? The Headmaster had obviously realized it too. He was frowning and staring at Alec as the next question was asked, as if he were willing him to fail.

'Right, Smart Alec,' Eddy Hair said sarcastically, 'how about this one? "I have a certain number, made up entirely of sevens. One seven after another. And I can divide it by a hundred and ninety-nine. I want you to give me the last four figures of the answer. But – and here's the catch, folks – I'm not going to tell you how *many* sevens make up the number."'

Alec stared at him.

Eddy Hair did not say anything else. Just turned and looked at the big clock behind him where the second hand was ticking round from 30 to 0. 'Five seconds left,' he said at last. 'Come on, Genius. What's the answer?'

'I – I don't know,' Alec said, as the bell sounded. He did not sound embarrassed. Only furious.

'And the score is *still* 8–8!' Eddy Hair jumped off his barrel

133

and turned a quick cartwheel. 'Goodness me, the excitement's mounting here. What about our other genius? Will she be able to answer her question?'

Dinah looked at him, white-faced, and beside her the Headmaster smiled triumphantly. She gripped the pepperpot hard between her hands, until the knuckles showed white, and glanced across at Lloyd and Harvey, Mandy and Ingrid. When she answered the question, Lloyd could almost feel her reluctance. The score was 9–8 to them, now.

'My, my!' Eddy Hair looked out over the Hall and then raised his eyebrows at the Headmaster. 'What a quiet lot of children you have here. It's the first time your team has gone into the lead. Why aren't they cheering?'

The Headmaster shrugged. 'They can cheer if you want them to.' He raised a hand and instantly, obediently, all the children in the Hall started to cheer loudly and enthusiastically. Then he dropped his hand and they stopped. At once.

Eddy Hair gave him an odd look. 'That's remarkably well organized. I've never seen a school like it.' He grinned at the camera, baring his uneven yellow teeth. 'It's a good thing these bossy teachers don't run the country, isn't it, folks? They'd have us all doing just what they want. Like robots. And where would I be then?'

He chortled merrily. But the Headmaster's face gave a sudden, irritated twitch.

And all at once, Lloyd understood! That was it. That was what the Headmaster wanted. To run the whole country, so that it was as organized and joyless as the school. So that everything was neat and tidy and there was no freedom.

134

He looked frantically at Dinah, wishing there were some way he could tell her.

But, as his eyes met hers, he knew that there was no need to tell her. She had understood too. Her mouth had dropped open and her eyes were stretched wide, in complete horror. As the cameras turned towards the Manor Road team, waiting for their next question, she began to mouth furiously at Lloyd.

'That's what the prefects were talking about,' she said soundlessly. 'He's got them all set up to move people into work camps and –' Her mouthing became faster and more desperate, and Lloyd lost track of what she was saying. But he did not need to know any more. It was too terrible even to think about. It would be like having school everywhere, with no escape.

The Headmaster had seen her, too. He frowned and pointed down into the Hall, straight at the members of SPLAT. Then he looked at Dinah, his eyebrows raised in a question. Miserably, she shook her head. Lloyd could just imagine how trapped she was feeling. Now she knew what the plan was, she could still do nothing to stop it. Not without killing them all.

And there was not much time left. Alec had answered his last question and was grinning again.

'So the score is 9–9,' Eddy Hair said. He ran his fingers through his curls. 'The tension is killing me. Will it be a draw? Everything hangs on the last question.'

Lloyd looked anxiously at Dinah. She was gripping the pepperpot so hard that he wondered it didn't crack and she looked as though she were about to burst into tears.

'So,' Eddy Hair bellowed. 'Here we go. And it's a compli-cated one, so listen carefully. "I woke up and found I had lost my memory. I couldn't even remember what year it was. So I asked a man who was walking past. He told me: If you multiply my age now by twice my age next birthday, you will get the number of the year we are in. And I can tell you that I don't remember Queen Victoria, but I hope to live to the year two thousand." Got it?'

Dinah nodded. She was just about to open her mouth to give the answer. But before she spoke, she looked across at Lloyd.

And he knew that he could not let her do it. Even if it meant being killed. The idea of having the whole country run by the Headmaster, for ever, was too horrible. Frantic-ally, he shook his head, over and over again, until it felt as though it would fall off his neck.

Dinah shut her mouth again.

'Come on.' Eddy Hair looked at the clock. 'You can have a clue if you like. You only score half a point then, but that's enough to let you win. Do you want the clue?'

'Give it to her!' The Headmaster said sharply. He was looking incredulously at Dinah.

'The clue is this.' Eddy Hair looked down at his piece of paper. '"By the way," the man added, "I'm not quite as old as my cousin, Winston Smith." Got it?'

Dinah nodded sadly, as though that fitted in with what she thought, but she still did not say anything.

Glaring at her, the Headmaster looked down at the children in the Hall and cleared his throat, as if he were about to speak. Lloyd braced himself. Here it came. The end.

Sorry, H, he thought, *I couldn't protect you after all. This is more important.*

Then, from the other side of Dinah, came an excited yelp. Lucy, who had sat silently in her chair all through the Quiz, was bouncing up and down.

'I know the answer!' she yelled. 'I know it. Winston Smith's the name of the man in that funny book you told me about, Dinah! It's nineteen eighty-four!'

'That's the right answer,' Eddy Hair said gleefully. 'Well done, Tich. You've saved the day.'

As the giant panda appeared behind the chair of Manor Road's Headmaster, Lloyd began to shake uncontrollably.

Their own Headmaster had reached up and taken off his glasses. Ready for his turn to speak.

Chapter 16

'Look into my Eyes'

'That's dealt with the losers,' said Eddy Hair cheerfully, as the Headmaster of Manor Road tried to unwind the eels that the giant panda had tipped over his head. 'Now, how about the winners? A fantastic performance. Not a question missed. Come on, Headmaster. Tell us how you do it.'

With a feeling of sick defeat, Dinah saw the cameras swivel, pointing towards the Headmaster. He smiled into them, his large green eyes alight, and said softly, 'If you all look into my eyes, I will tell you. You must be feeling ready for some sense after all the crazy mess of this show. You must be longing to have everything sorted out tidily, everything settled for you.'

For ever, thought Dinah. *For ever and ever*. Oh, how could she stop what was going to happen? If she did not, life would never be worth living again. But if she tried, it would mean death for everyone else in SPLAT. She could see Lloyd leaning sideways now, whispering to them, explaining what was about to take place. And, as they understood, they all gasped.

'You are all feeling exhausted by the mess,' the Headmaster was saying into the camera. 'Tired and weary and ready to sleep . . .'

Through her misery, Dinah felt the familiar sleepiness start to creep over her. And all over the country, people sitting

138

in front of their televisions began to nod over their cups of tea, wondering why they were suddenly yawning.

'... you can hardly keep your eyes open. With every second that passes, your eyelids are growing heavier and heavier ...'

Millions of cups of tea, in homes everywhere, dropped to the ground unheeded as people slumped forwards in their chairs. In the Hall, the audience nodded and Dinah's eyes began to close. She struggled hard to keep them open, but the lids dropped irresistibly.

Then, just before they finally shut, she saw Harvey leap to his feet. He was pointing straight at her, pointing to the table in front of her. Muzzily, she looked at his lips, trying to see what it was that he was mouthing. If only she did not feel so tired ...

Harvey wagged his finger, pointing in a frenzy. And at last she managed to make out what it was he was saying.

'In your hand!'

Funny, she thought sleepily. Why was he interested in her hand? She looked down, forcing her eyes to stay open for a second longer. Oh yes, she thought vaguely. She was still clutching that silly red pepperpot with the black stripes.

'... so, so, *so*, sleepy ...'

She gave a huge, exhausted yawn. Pepper? she thought. Then – *pepper*!

That was it! Dragging together all the energy she could muster, she forced herself agonizingly to her feet, wrenched the bottom off the pepperpot and flung the contents, as hard as she could, straight into the Headmaster's face. Then she sank back on to her chair, knowing that she could not do anything more to resist that creeping, soothing voice.

But what had happened to the voice? It had stopped. For a moment there was silence, and she turned her head slowly sideways.

The Headmaster had gone purple in the face, his lips pressed tightly together, his green eyes bulging ludicrously. As she watched, his mouth was forced uncontrollably open in an enormous, a stupendous, sneeze.

'A – A – A – TCHOO!'

As though the strength of the sneeze had blown away her sleepiness, Dinah suddenly found herself wide awake. And, right across the country, people in easy chairs sat up and looked in bewilderment at the spilt tea on their carpets. In the Hall, everyone stirred and gazed in amazement at the sneezing Headmaster. His nose streamed, his mouth gaped ridiculously and his head jerked backwards and forwards.

'Atchoo! Atchoo! Atchoo!'

Then, from all over the Hall, unbelievably, came the sound of laughter. All the children were laughing at the Headmaster. Dinah could see the powerless rage in his eyes, but he could do nothing to stop them. From time to time he tried to speak. He managed to stutter out, 'Des – des – des —' in an effort to give his command to destroy the straw dolls, but every time he got as far as that, another huge sneeze overtook him, and he collapsed.

Eddy Hair was gazing at him ecstatically, as if a sneezing headmaster was what he had always wanted on his show. Raising his voice, he said, above the noise of the sneezes and the laughing, 'Well, folks, beat that if you can for a way to run a school! You know what I always say about this show – *you never know what's going to happen next!*'

As the final music began, he winked at the audience and cartwheeled away across the stage.

The Headmaster was just beginning to be able to control his sneezes. He pulled a spotless handkerchief out of his pocket, mopped his face and glared at Dinah with total hatred.

'Do you realize what you have done, you stupid girl?' he gasped. 'You have destroyed this country's chance of becoming the first properly organized, truly efficient country in the world.'

'No I haven't,' she said happily. 'I've saved it from being a miserable place full of scared robots, like this school. And I'm going to think of a way of saving the school from you, as well.'

'The school?' The Headmaster jumped to his feet and waved a scornful hand at the rows of giggling children. 'That rabble? Do you think – a – a – tchoo! – that I want to go on wasting my talents merely looking after *them*? When you've made a laughing-stock of me? A – a – tchoo! I shall resign at once, and let them all sink back into chaos.'

'What are you going to do, then?' Dinah said quietly.

He stood over her, glaring down. For a moment she was afraid that he was actually going to strangle her, in front of everyone. His large hands jerked, and his face was a mask of rage. Then he took a deep breath, and an unpleasant smile spread across his lips. 'Do you think I shall be so foolish as to tell you my plans? No, Miss Clever Glass. You must find them out for yourself. *If* you are clever *enough*. You have defeated me this time, but I know I was meant for greatness. I shall succeed in the end!'

With a loud, scornful laugh, he stalked off the stage and

began to stride down the Hall, between the chairs. As his black-clad figure went by, the children stopped laughing and glanced fearfully at him. He did not look either to the right or to the left, but passed them like a tall shadow.

Halfway down the Hall, he suddenly stopped, his body shaking.

'A – a – a – TCHOO!'

As if they had been released from a spell, the children began to giggle again, and Lloyd and Harvey grinned happily up at Dinah, while Ian, Mandy and Ingrid jumped up and danced a jig.

But Dinah did not grin back. She found that her hands were trembling, and she followed the Headmaster with her eyes, all the way, until the Hall door closed behind him.

'How did the show go?' Mrs Hunter said, opening the door. 'We were going to watch it, of course, but I'm afraid we had a – visitor.'

'It was fabulous! Marvellous!' Lloyd said jubilantly, bouncing into the house. 'We –'

'Can you save it?' his mother said, frowning slightly. 'We want you all to come into the sitting room. There's something we've got to talk to you about. Then you can tell us *all* about it.'

Lloyd winked at Dinah behind his mother's back. 'She'd get a shock if we did, wouldn't she?' he mouthed.

Dinah winked back happily, and walked into the sitting room. And stopped abruptly. There, on the settee, was Miss Wilberforce, looking solemn.

'Hallo, Dinah.'

'Hallo, Miss Wilberforce,' Dinah said, in a cold little voice.

Miss Wilberforce sighed, and looked at Mr and Mrs Hunter. 'I'm afraid you're right,' she said. 'It doesn't look as though she feels at home at all. And I was so *sure* she'd feel happy and relaxed here.'

'I don't think it's her fault,' Mr Hunter said sternly. 'I blame the boys.'

Lloyd stared round at them. 'What do you mean? What are you all talking about?'

'We're talking about Dinah.' Mr Hunter smiled apologetically at her. 'Mrs Hunter and I like having you here, dear. We've grown fond of you. But you don't seem to get on with the boys. You've been at each other's throats all the time, haven't you? So we've agreed with Miss Wilberforce that it would be better for everyone if you went back to the Children's Home.'

Dinah felt as though someone had hit her with a large lump of very cold ice. Her face stiffened. 'Yes, Mr Hunter,' she said, in a small voice.

'But you can't –' burst out Harvey. He stopped and looked helplessly at Lloyd.

Lloyd sat down deliberately in a chair and looked round at the grown-ups. 'I think you're all mad,' he said loudly. 'Why ever do you want to send Dinah away? Plum-coloured pumpkins! We want her here. For ever and ever. I think Mum and Dad ought to adopt her properly.'

Mr and Mrs Hunter goggled, their mouths dropping open. 'You like her?'

'Well, of course,' Lloyd said, as if it were a ridiculous question. 'I think she's fantastic. Except –' he grinned across at her '– except for being a bit thick, of course.'

Dinah had gone rather pink, and was staring at her feet.

143

She did not speak until Miss Wilberforce said gently, 'Well, Dinah? How do you feel about it?'

In a choking voice, as though she could hardly speak, Dinah said, 'Please. Oh please.'

'*That's* all right, then,' Lloyd said in a satisfied tone. 'Now *please* can we have something to eat? We're all absolutely starving.'

His mother looked at him in bewilderment. 'But you took a packed tea to school. You can't be hungry again. Whatever have you been up to?'

Lloyd, Harvey and Dinah looked at each other and grinned.

'Oh, nothing much,' they said. In perfect unison.

The Prime Minister's Brain

Gillian Cross

Illustrated by Sally Burgess

Contents

Chapter 1

The Octopus Game

'Dinah!'

Settling herself into the crook of the big, old pear tree, Dinah began to check the computer program she was writing.

```
2100 PRINT "IS SUN SHINING? (Y OR N):";
2110 INPUT A$
2120 IF A$ = "Y" THEN GOTO 2300
```

'Dinah!'

She was concentrating so hard that she did not hear the voices calling her from the other end of the garden.

```
2130 IF A$ < > "N" THEN GOTO 2100
```

But Lloyd was not the sort of person to put up with being ignored. He came stamping through the garden, with all the others following him, and stood beside the tree.

'DINAH!'

She looked down and blinked at him.

'Oh. Sorry. I was thinking.'

'Huh!' snorted Lloyd.

Harvey, Dinah's other adopted brother, raced up and interrupted, just as Lloyd was about to say something really rude.

'Di, aren't you ready? Look, everyone else is here. We want to get going.'

Dinah peered between the branches. Sure enough, there

were the other three members of S P L A T. Two tall figures –
Ian and Mandy – hauling along a smaller, chubbier one
that struggled crossly.

'Ingrid doesn't look very happy,' Dinah said.

'Ingrid *isn't* very happy!' shouted Ingrid, scowling fiercely.
'Ingrid's sick to death of the rotten Computer Club. We
went *yesterday*. Why do we have to go again today?'

'We voted to spend this week at the Computer Club.'
Lloyd gave her a stern look that was meant to shut her up.
'What's the point of having a secret society if we don't all
stick together?'

But it was not so easy to shut Ingrid up. 'What's the
point of having a secret society at all, if we don't do anything special? We were going to have a great time this
summer. A S P L A T picnic and a S P L A T camp in the
woods and a S P L A T visit to the Science Museum and –
oh, lots of things. But we've landed up trotting back to
school, like everyone else. To the *Computer Club*.' She
pulled a fierce, ugly face.

'It's only for another four days, Ing,' Mandy said gently.
'And if you'd only try to enjoy it, you'd see it's fun.'

'It's *boring*,' Ingrid said firmly. 'And anyway, who wants
to go back to school in the holidays?'

'We voted,' Lloyd said again. He folded his arms and
glared at Ingrid. 'Now stop moaning and behave properly.'

Up in her tree, Dinah started to get irritated. She didn't
want to listen to their squabbling. She wanted to get on
with her program.

'Look, Ing.' She waved the paper she was writing on. '*I*
haven't forgotten about the rest of the holiday. I'm writing
a program to help us plan it. Why don't you go on ahead
with the others and bag a computer? Then, when I get
there, you can help me run this program.'

'I'd rather run a ten-mile race!' Ingrid snapped. But she did not manage to sound quite as angry as before, and a moment later, she was letting Mandy lead her out of the side gate and away towards the school.

At the foot of the tree, Ian bowed low, in his usual teasing way. 'Well done, O Genius,' he drawled. 'How brilliant you are at handling people.'

'What do you mean *she's* good at handling people?' Lloyd looked furious. '*I* was the one who told Ingrid to behave.'

Ian grinned at him. 'Of course, of course, Great Leader. How stupid of me to forget. I grovel in the dust.'

'Be more sensible if we started going to the Computer

Club,' chipped in Harvey. 'If we're not there soon, I'll have to wait *ages* for a game of Diamond Dragon.'

He pushed them both and the three boys began to walk up the garden. Dinah watched them for a moment. Bossy Lloyd and tall, comical Ian. Having one of their friendly quarrels, while Harvey ran along behind trying to stop them. All quite normal and ordinary. She settled herself on her branch again and gave a private grin. Things were so pleasant and peaceful. Oh, it was going to be a good summer, with no excitements and lots of time to work. Now, where had she got to?

```
2130 IF A$ < > ''N'' THEN GOTO 2100
```

An hour later, she walked up the road towards the school gates, with the finished program tucked in her pocket. Her pale, thin face was as stiff as usual and she looked almost bored, because her feelings never showed on the outside, but inside her head she was singing.

Lovely, fantastic Computer Club! It meant that she could spend all day working out programs and trying new things, without the others nagging her for being dull and not joining in. And there were four more days of it left!

She was so busy planning what she would do on the other days, that she did not look where she was going. She ran up the school steps and nearly fell over two small, gloomy figures sitting at the top.

'Careful!' snapped Ingrid.

'Thought we were big enough to *see*,' muttered Harvey.

Dinah looked down at them in amazement. 'Whatever is the matter with you two? What are you doing out here?'

'Sulking!' Ingrid said. 'Because of the horrible Computer Club.'

Oh dear, thought Dinah. She sat down on the steps beside them, wishing she was Mandy, who was good at this sort of thing. 'You did promise to come, you know. And *you* liked it, anyway, Harvey. What's changed since yesterday?'

Harvey looked round woefully at her, and she remembered how cheerful he had been as he followed the others away an hour ago. What could have changed him?

'*That*,' said Harvey.

Twisting round, he stabbed a finger towards the glass door of the school. Stuck up there was a huge poster. Across the top, it said in large letters:

JUNIOR COMPUTER BRAIN OF THE YEAR

Underneath was a picture of a man in a white lab coat. He was very tall and very thin, with thick, pebbly glasses. Somehow, the blurred photograph made him look not quite human. More like an insect. Or a robot. Dinah actually found herself shivering and she gave a stiff little laugh to hide it.

'*He* can't be the Junior Computer Brain of the Year. He's much too old.'

'He's repulsive!' Ingrid pulled an extra-horrible cross-eyed face and stuck out her tongue at the poster. 'He's the Computer Director. The one who's running the competition to find the Junior Computer Brain. Mr Meredith brought the forms in this morning. And the game.'

'And that was it. Whang! Everything *ruined*,' said Harvey miserably. 'Yesterday was great. Like you said. We played all sorts of games and learnt some things as well. But today – well, no one will think about anything except the competition game.'

'They think they're going to win, do they?' Dinah said.

'*No.*' Ingrid looked impatient. 'It's not that. You don't understand. It's not the competition that's taken them over. It's the actual game.'

'But that's silly,' Dinah said. 'A game's just something for fun.'

'That's what we told them,' Harvey said. He sounded really unhappy. 'We told them it was only a game.'

'And what did they say?'

He looked even unhappier. 'They said, "Ssh!"'

'It's made them really *peculiar*.' Ingrid tapped her head and rolled her eyes. 'Remember what they were like when the Demon Headmaster was here?'

Dinah smiled her small smile and tossed her skinny plaits back over her shoulder. 'Oh, come *on*. They can't be that bad.'

Neither Ingrid nor Harvey answered her. They just stood up and hauled at her hands, one on each side, until she followed them into the school and along the corridor towards the Hall.

Dinah let them lead her, but she was still not taking them seriously. Because she could remember what the school had been like when the Demon Headmaster was there. The blank, bare walls. The quiet, hypnotized children moving round like robots. The cruel, bossy prefects. And the feeling of terror everywhere.

That had all changed since Mr Meredith became headmaster. Now it was an untidy, cheerful, noisy school, just like all the others Dinah had been into. How could it have changed back in a single morning?

And yet – it *was* rather quiet today. As they came to the Hall door, Dinah started to feel uneasy. And what she saw when she stepped inside was quite unexpected.

There were no crowds of children charging round everywhere or gathering in little huddles by the computers. There was no laughter or talking. Instead, all the children – about a hundred of them – were sitting crosslegged on the ground, in neat rows in front of one of the computers. They were watching the screen with a steady, blank stare. No one fidgeted. No one whispered. They almost seemed to be holding their breaths.

'You see?' Harvey hissed. 'They've all gone goo-goo eyed over this stupid octopus game. Even the SPLAT people. Look at them!'

Dinah could see that he was right. Lloyd and Mandy were sitting on the floor with the other children and Ian was actually at the computer keyboard. He was the one playing the game.

'They've been like that for ages,' muttered Ingrid, getting crosser and crosser. 'One person playing and the rest just staring. It's *stupid*.' Suddenly she lost her temper altogether. She pulled a face at the rows of motionless backs and yelled, '*You're all SILLY IDIOTS!*'

Ian jumped and looked round. Immediately, there was a loud BLUUURP! from the computer. And a wail from the watching children.

'Ing, you're mean,' Mandy said. 'You distracted him.'

'Oh, sor*ry*,' Ingrid jeered. 'What's the matter? Was he going to be Junior Computer Brain of the Year?'

'Me?' murmured Ian. 'Of course not. I'm just an ordinary moron having fun. I can tell you, it needs a *genius* to win this game. No one stands a chance except –' Then he caught sight of Dinah. 'Oh, there you are!'

'We've been waiting for you,' Lloyd said. He jumped up and began to organize things as usual, catching at Dinah's arm and trying to pull her forwards. 'You've got to have a go at this game. It's brilliant.'

All the others had turned round now. They were staring at Dinah, nudging each other and whispering. Dinah wriggled uncomfortably. She hated people to fuss over her and she wasn't interested in computer games. She wanted to go and work on her own program.

'Come on!' called Mandy. 'I bet you can do it.'

Dinah looked pink and stubborn. 'I don't think I'll bother, thank you.'

'Oh, come *on*, Di.' Everyone was shouting it now. 'You've *got* to have a go. You could win the whole competition.'

Dinah felt like a snail dragged right out of its shell. All the children were staring at her and telling her what to do. And it was no good saying she didn't want to. They would never leave her alone until she had a go at their wretched game. Slowly she walked through the crowd towards the computer.

'Traitor!' hissed Ingrid.

'Oh *Di*!' Harvey looked at her sadly and turned away.

'Shut up you two,' said Lloyd. 'Just because *you* don't like the game, it doesn't mean that no one else can play.' He pulled Dinah closer to the front. 'You'd better watch first, so you know how to do it. Mandy can show you. She's the best one so far.'

Mandy shook her red hair out of her eyes and smiled across at Dinah. 'I'm not really good. I mean – I can't *do* it or anything. You'll be loads better than I am.'

'Oh, get on.' Lloyd pushed her down into the chair in front of the computer. 'Come on. Start.'

Obediently, Mandy pressed the first key and the name of the game flashed on to the screen.

Octopus Dare.

158

'It's a treasure hunt,' muttered Ian helpfully. 'You have to steer your way through invisible shoals and then dive down and try and get past the –'

'Ssh!' hissed everyone else.

They had already turned back to the screen, staring with glazed dull eyes. Ian shrugged.

'Sorry I spoke. I just thought Dinah might like to know –'

'Shut *up*!' snapped Lloyd. 'Mandy's concentrating.'

She was. She was frowning and biting her lip as she pressed the keys to move a tiny ship around the screen. Shoals and sandbanks kept appearing and disappearing and her ship zigzagged backwards and forwards frantically trying to avoid them. As each one appeared, the watching children held their breath. And when Mandy managed to steer the ship past, a sigh of relief went round the Hall.

Dinah managed not to look impatient. She was used to having to wait while people struggled with things that were simple and obvious to her. But – couldn't Mandy *see*? There was a definite pattern to the shoals. Once you'd worked that out, you could go straight through and not round the long way. The thing was a puzzle that had to be worked out, not a test of quick reflexes. But Mandy obviously *couldn't* see. She went on frowning and steering at desperate speed.

Dinah passed the time by looking round at the faces of the others. They were all staring at the screen with the same eager attention, even though the game seemed quite ordinary. Was it the shoals that they found fascinating? Dinah did not think so. They seemed to be waiting for something else. Something that came later. But why on earth were they so excited about it?

Suddenly the ship and the shoals all vanished and a message flashed on to the screen.

YOU HAVE REACHED THE SPOT.
YOU MAY NOW DIVE BY PRESSING 'D'.

Mandy sat back and mopped her forehead. 'Phew! I thought I wasn't going to manage it this time. Just let me get my breath.'

'Hurry up,' said Lloyd. 'We want the octopus!'

'Yes! Yes!' everyone else shouted. 'The *octopus*!'

Dinah looked round at them, puzzled by their eager faces. So that was what they'd all been waiting for. That was what the ship had to get past in the next bit of the game. That was what had made them sit so still and watch the screen so anxiously. But – why?

Mandy leaned forward again and pressed 'D'. At once, the screen was filled with a pattern of long, waving tentacles. They moved and twisted, twining in a complicated pattern of curves and loops, constantly altering and yet always keeping a balance, swelling and shrinking and dancing . . .

Dinah could not look away. As the curves shifted and changed, her eyes followed them. Backwards and forwards. Up and down. Crossing and uncrossing. It was a strange sensation. Watching them made her feel dreamy and excited, both at once.

Octopus – s – s – s – s! murmured her mind.

It was a second or two before she realized that there was a small blob up in the top right-hand corner of the screen. Mandy's submarine, that she was trying to steer past the octopus to reach the sunken treasure. But there was not much time to watch it. In less than a minute, Mandy faltered and the tentacles reached out and engulfed the submarine.

BLUUURP!

Mandy turned round, laughing. 'You see? I'm hopeless. You have a go, Di.'

160

'Dinah doesn't want a go at your stupid octopus game,' Ingrid said from the back of the crowd.

'She thinks it's boring,' called Harvey.

Dinah stared at the screen. Trying to remember *exactly* what the octopus had been like. Trying to work out how to get past the tentacles. Because she was *sure* it could be done logically, like avoiding the shoals. Only she could not see how, and the problem nagged and teased at her.

'Dinah!' shouted Ingrid. 'Tell them you don't want to do it.'

But her words seemed to come from the other side of a wall of glass. On this side, there was nothing except the octopus. All Dinah could think of was that she knew she could work out the puzzle. If only she could see the octopus again . . .

Almost in a daze, she sat down in front of the computer.

Chapter 2

Dinah Plays Octopus Dare

'Lloyd!' whispered Harvey.

'Ssh!' Lloyd hissed, flapping a hand to make him go away. 'You'll disturb Dinah.'

Harvey prodded him. 'Ingrid and I are *bored*. Can't we go off to the swimming pool?'

'What? No!' Lloyd pulled a face and glanced quickly sideways. 'Be quiet. Wait until Dinah stops if you want to talk.'

'But she's been playing that wretched game for FOUR WHOLE DAYS!' Harvey said crossly. 'She never stops. And the rest of you just sit and stare at the screen. What's so great about a rotten octopus?'

Lloyd sighed impatiently and forced himself to turn round. 'Look,' he said, 'it's an important competition. Dinah kept the octopus on the screen for ten minutes last time, and she nearly got past it. She could *win*.'

Ingrid came up behind Harvey and her stubborn face peered over his shoulder. 'That's not why you're watching. You're just hooked on the octopus. You *can't* look away.'

Lloyd exploded. 'You don't know what you're talking about!'

'Ssh!' said all the others.

He lowered his voice. 'Why don't you two push off? Go and play Space Invaders or something on one of the other computers. I'm sick of your moaning.'

'You haven't had a chance to be sick of it,' Harvey said bitterly. 'You've hardly spoken to us for four days.'

He and Ingrid wandered off and Lloyd turned back to look at the screen, just as Dinah brought her ship safely through the shoals. The watching children leaned forward eagerly, their eyes on her finger as it reached out to press the 'D' key. The key that would bring the octopus to the screen.

Lloyd found himself leaning forward like the others, with his eyes fixed and his mouth open. Out of the corner of his eyes, he saw Harvey nudge Ingrid and point to him. Well, let him. They were both wrong. He could look away from the screen whenever he chose. And he would. In a minute. In a minute . . .

Octopus – s – s – s – s!

Quickly and deftly, Dinah began to flick the keys, her thin plaits hanging down on either side of her face, her eyes narrowed. The submarine moved backwards and forwards and sideways in a complicated dance, just out of reach of the weaving tentacles.

Lloyd felt his fingernails digging into the palms of his hands. He had forgotten all about looking away. All about Harvey and Ingrid. He could not think of anything except the octopus.

The tentacles were flying faster now and it seemed impossible for the submarine to escape. But each time, just before the octopus snatched it, it darted away in complicated loops. More and more complicated each time.

With a shock, Lloyd realized that he did not want Dinah to win. And he did not want her to lose. He just wanted her to keep on and on playing, whirling her submarine free so that the octopus stayed on the screen, waving and wheeling and winding . . .

163

But Dinah was too good. In a final, nerve-racking rush, she began to press keys like a fury and her four days of practice triumphed at last. The submarine soared up in a great arc, over the top of the curling tentacles and down the side to reach the sunken treasure. It was there!

At once, the computer seemed to go mad. It began to play a loud marching tune and big letters flashed across the screen.

WINNER!

WINNER!

WINNER!

For a moment there was a total, awed silence. Then Lloyd yelled, 'She's done it! Di's done it! Someone go and fetch Mr Meredith!'

Ian raced off and everyone else crowded round, slapping Dinah on the back, cheering her and telling her how clever she was.

And Dinah burst into tears.

Lloyd was astounded. Dinah was crying? *Dinah*, who kept all her feelings locked away like the Crown Jewels? He couldn't understand it at all. It was Mandy who took control of the situation. Waving everyone back, she put her arm round Dinah's shoulders.

'It's all right, Di, don't worry. It's just a reaction, because you've been concentrating so hard.'

Dinah sniffed. 'No, it's not that.' She shook her head from side to side and wiped her eyes fiercely. 'It's just – well, I know it sounds silly, but this has been the most *fantastic* problem to solve. I haven't thought about anything else since I started. And now it's finished. What am I going to do without the *octopus?*'

'You see?' said Ingrid, loudly and rudely from somewhere

164

near the back. But no one took any notice of her, because, at that moment, Mr Meredith, the headmaster, came bustling across the Hall, chattering to Ian.

He was a short, fat man, so enthusiastic that the sight of him set everyone grinning. The children had found it very hard to get used to him, after the Demon Headmaster. Mr Meredith was popular, but it was hard to believe that he was really in charge of the school.

Now he was chuckling with delight as he pushed his way through the crowd and bent to examine the computer, which was still playing its triumphant march and flashing its message.

WINNER!

WINNER!

WINNER!

'Well, well, well,' he said, rubbing his hands together. 'My goodness me. Fancy you being so clever. Well done, Dinah.'

Dinah was her usual controlled self again. 'Thank you, sir,' she said calmly.

'Well, well, well,' Mr Meredith shook his head from side to side as though he could hardly believe what he saw. 'I suppose you'll be wanting me to find the forms now, eh? To send off to the Computer Director to say that you've qualified for the final of the competition? Mmm?'

Dinah hesitated.

Lloyd knew what she was thinking. She hated people to make a fuss about how clever she was. He couldn't understand it. If he were as clever as that – well, of course he *was* in his own way, but if he were clever in *her* way – he'd be standing on top of the town Clock Tower, shouting about it. It really annoyed him when she kept quiet and pretended to be ordinary.

165

'Yes, she does want to go into the final,' he said loudly. 'Find her a form, sir.'

Mr Meredith looked at him and then at Dinah, with unexpected shrewdness, but all he said was, 'Well, well, a modest girl. Nice to see.'

Then he began to rummage in his pockets, taking out pens and rubber bands and handkerchiefs, while children scrabbled round on the floor, picking up things he dropped. Finally, with a flourish, he produced a sheaf of papers from an inside pocket. Half of them slipped through his fingers and fluttered to the ground, but he only laughed when people bent down to pick them up.

'Doesn't matter. Unless lots of you were thinking of going on to the final.'

'Us? Win *Octopus Dare*?' Ian pulled a comic, horrified face.

'If it took Dinah four days, none of us will ever do it.'

Mr Meredith grinned and started to fill in one of the forms with Dinah's name, age and address. He signed it with his big, untidy signature. Then he patted Dinah on the head. 'Better get it posted then. Before I lose it. Eh? Eh?'

He shambled off, followed by most of the children, and Ian gave his slow grin.

'Time to celebrate, I should think. What d'you want, Di? Champagne? Fish and chips and a glass of dandelion and burdock?'

'Sackcloth and ashes and a plate of cold porridge!' said a hollow voice from the back of the Hall. Ingrid came stalking towards them. Harvey followed her.

'That's a bit mean, Ing,' he said reproachfully. 'After all, it was clever of Dinah to win the game. We ought to congratulate her on that, even if we *are* sick of the octopus.'

'*Congratulate* her? On having her name sent off to that Computer Director?' Ingrid gave a slow, dramatic shudder.

As usual, it was Mandy who moved to soothe everyone. She put one hand on Ingrid's shoulder and the other on Harvey's.

'Cheer up, you two. Just think – it's *over*. We can talk about the rest of the holidays now. We've finished with the Computer Club. And the octopus.'

'That's what *you* think,' Ingrid murmured darkly.

Chapter 3

The Letter

A week later, the doorbell rang while the Hunters were having breakfast. Harvey jumped up to answer it. He loved answering things – telephones, doors, people stopping to ask for directions in the street. Harvey met them all with a cheerful grin on his round face.

This time it was the postman. He handed Harvey a fat bundle of letters and nodded at him. 'Having a piece of toast, were you?'

Harvey grinned wider, brushing the toast crumbs off his tee-shirt as he shut the door. Then he wandered back into the kitchen, sorting through the letters.

'You've got one Mum and Dad's got five. And – hey, there's one for you, Di!'

'Me?' Dinah sat up, with a small flicker of excitement. She hardly ever got any letters. Only a postcard, every now and then, from the house-mother at the Children's Home where she had lived before the Hunters adopted her. 'A real *letter*?'

Harvey held it out to her. It was in a long, stiff white envelope, with her name and address typed on the front. She took it carefully and began to slide her finger under the flap, running it from side to side.

'Thundering hamburgers!' Lloyd exploded. 'You're not *natural*! How can you bear to be so slow? I'd have ripped the envelope off.'

'*And* dropped it on the floor,' murmured Mrs Hunter.

'*Mum!* How can you say that? You know I'm the tidiest person in this family. Except for Di, of course, and she's inhuman. Oh, and you and Dad –'

Dinah grinned to herself at Lloyd's typical blustering and lifted the flap of the envelope, sliding out what was inside. It was not a letter. It was a stiff card, like a birthday card. She glanced down at it and her eyes opened wider as she saw the patterns snaking across the front. Twisting, twining tentacles. Curling and rolling across the card so that they almost seemed to be moving. Spiralling and twirling and . . .

Octopus – s – s – s – s!

'Dinah?' said Mr Hunter. It seemed like weeks later. 'Aren't you going to *open* the card? See what it says?'

'I – what? Oh yes.' Blinking and shaking her head from side to side to clear it, Dinah flicked the front of the card back. 'Oh! It's from the Computer Director. The one who organized that competition.'

'Eugh!' Harvey pulled a face and made sick noises into his plate.

Dinah could see Mrs Hunter getting ready to send him out of the room. Quickly, to save him, she started to read her card out loud.

'Dear Miss Hunter,

Congratulations on solving *Octopus Dare*. This makes you one of the contestants to qualify for the final round of the Junior Computer Brain of the Year Competition.

The final round will take place in London from August 28th to September 2nd at the Saracen Tower, Turk's Island –'

'What a weird address,' muttered Lloyd. 'An island? In the middle of London?'

But Dinah had been skimming on, ahead of what she was reading, and all at once she saw something terrible. Her voice died away, and she lowered the card, her hands shaking.

'What's the matter?' Mrs Hunter said anxiously.

Dinah breathed hard and stared down at the shiny, twining front of the card. 'I can't go to the final. Not unless I've got a Saladin microcomputer. And I've never even *heard* of a Saladin.'

She stopped sharply and clenched her fists. Because she was beginning to panic inside her head. She was going to miss the final. And there would be beautiful octopus patterns there to solve. She was *sure* of it. She had to go. She *had* to. If she couldn't go she would scream and scream and scream –

She made herself breathe very slowly, to get back her self-control. She *never* screamed. What was she thinking of? Why had she suddenly started to feel so desperate? It frightened her, but she could not stop herself. The very sight of the octopus patterns on the front of the card made her feel that she had to go to the final. She *had* to go, she *had* to go . . .

'*I've* heard of Saladins,' Lloyd said airily. 'They're brand new. Just come on the market. Ginger Frost says his uncle in Edinburgh has got one. Cost about five hundred pounds.'

'Oh Dinah!' Mrs Hunter looked upset. 'I *am* sorry.'

Dinah screwed up her fists. She wouldn't cry. She *wouldn't.* And she didn't. But instead she heard her voice say, very high and loud, 'Well, you'll just have to buy me one, that's all.'

'What?' Mr Hunter stared at her. 'I'm sorry, Di, but we haven't got five hundred pounds. Not to spare.'

'Well, sell the car.' Dinah was panting. Gasping for breath. 'Mortgage the house. Get a bank loan. I don't care what you do, but you've got to find the money. *I must go to that final!*'

They were all staring at her. All four of them. And she knew why. She was the person who never asked for things. Never made a fuss. Good, quiet little Dinah, who never wanted anything for herself. Only she *did* want this. It was senseless. It was selfish. But the more she gazed and gazed at the octopus patterns on the card, the more she knew she could not bear to turn down the invitation. Whatever it cost.

'Please, *please*!' she shouted. 'You said you'd buy me a bike. Well, I don't want a bike. That's some of the money, anyway. And you must be able to find the rest somehow.'

'It's not that simple,' Mr Hunter said gently.

Dinah was past listening to him. All she could think of was the octopus, the octopus, the *octopus*. And all she could feel was panic. Terrible panic that she might be going to miss bigger and better and more complicated octopus patterns, lacing and weaving and curving . . .

'A Saladin!' she yelled. 'You've got to buy me a Saladin! I must have one!'

'Dinah!' Mrs Hunter stood up, looking very solemn. 'Please go up to your room until you've calmed down.'

'*I must have a Saladin!*'

'Your room!' Mr Hunter gripped her shoulders and turned her round towards the door. 'You'll hate yourself if you go on shouting at us like that.'

'I'll come and see you in a bit,' Mrs Hunter said.

Still sobbing and gasping for breath, Dinah gave a last scream, flung the card at them and ran out of the room. As she went, she heard Lloyd give a low, astounded whistle.

'Wow!' he said.

'Ssh!' muttered Mr Hunter quickly.

Dinah pounded up the stairs, flew into her bedroom and flung herself face down on the bed.

And was quite calm. Instantly.

It was so peculiar that she sat up and blinked, testing out her feelings just as she might have prodded her arms and legs to see if she had any broken bones. There was no doubt about it. She was perfectly cool and controlled.

At once, an embarrassed, miserable shiver ran up her back, when she remembered how she had just been behaving downstairs. But she squashed it. No point in wallowing in guilt and self-pity. Of *course* she had behaved terribly. She had behaved quite unlike her usual self. But why? And how had she managed to get back to normal so quickly?

She slid off the bed and went to look in the mirror. Her face was still red and blotchy, but the awful screams and sobs seemed a million miles away. Oh, it was annoying that she was going to miss the final, but she quite understood. Of course they couldn't afford to buy her a Saladin. And it didn't *matter*. Not enough to shout and scream at Mum and Dad who'd been so lovely to her. Who'd taken her into their home and adopted her.

'How *could* I have done it?' she whispered to her reflection in the mirror.

Think, the reflection seemed to say back. *Think hard. What started you off?*

Dinah stared into the depths of the glass, puzzling.

'It was when I saw the card. From the Computer Director. I was all right before then, and I'm all right now. But as soon as I started to look at the card I felt – weird.'

But what about *the card?* said her reflection.

Dinah thought back over what had happened. She had opened the envelope perfectly calmly, listening to Lloyd bickering with Mum. She had slid out the card. And – yes – she had still been all right when she did that. Then she had looked down and seen – and seen –

She was nearly there, on the verge of understanding it all, when there was a knock on the door. 'Can I come in?' said Mrs Hunter's voice.

Dinah jumped up and opened the door. 'I'm sorry,' she said awkwardly. 'I'm sorry I made such a fuss.'

Mrs Hunter put an arm round her shoulders and led her across to the bed. 'Sit down beside me, Dinah. I want to talk to you.'

Meekly Dinah sat down. She supposed she was going to be told off. It wouldn't be nice, but she had deserved it, after all. She folded her hands and waited.

'When people start living together,' Mrs Hunter began slowly,'– the way you've started living with us – they have to try hard to get used to each other. Now, you've put a lot of effort into getting used to *us*, Dinah, but I'm not sure we've understood properly about *you*. You're not an easy person to find out about, you know.'

Dinah stared at her, utterly bewildered. 'But you've been lovely to me.'

Mrs Hunter smiled, a little sadly. 'Well, of course we've tried. You're our daughter now, and we want *all* our children to have what they need to grow up properly. But –' she laughed suddenly '– we're not *used* to having a child as clever as you. Perhaps you need more things than Lloyd and Harvey do. Or different things, anyway. Because of the kind of brain you've got.'

Dinah had a terrible feeling that she knew what was coming. 'Mum –'

But Mrs Hunter went straight on talking. 'After you'd gone, Lloyd explained all about this Junior Computer Brain Competition. We think it could be a really important chance for you. You *ought* to be in the final. And if you have to have a Saladin to do that – well, we'll just have to buy you a Saladin.'

Dinah gasped. 'But you can't afford it! You know you can't.'

'Ah.' Mrs Hunter suddenly looked very pleased with

herself. 'You didn't know about this, did you?' She put a hand into one pocket of her big, untidy cardigan and pulled out a long, heavy gold chain set with turquoises. 'This is my nest-egg. It belonged to my grandmother. I've never worn it, but I knew I'd need it one day. And if I sell it, I should get enough to buy your Saladin.'

Dinah's eyes prickled with tears. She didn't deserve anyone to be so good to her. And she didn't even *want* it any more. Not in the wild, desperate way she had wanted it downstairs. She couldn't let Mum sell her chain for nothing.

'Look –' she began.

Mrs Hunter put a hand over her mouth. 'Not another word. We're going to buy your Saladin. We really want to. You just take care of this, in case you need it.'

Reaching into the other pocket of her cardigan, she pulled out the card that Dinah had flung at them. The card from the Computer Director, with the octopus tentacles curling across it. Dinah looked down and saw the swirling patterns.

Octopus – s – s – s – s!

It was no good! She *had* to have the computer, because she *had* to go to the final in the Saracen Tower. She had to, she had to, she had to . . .

'Oh Mum,' she whispered, as she felt the panic starting again, 'I'm scared.'

'You funny girl.' Mrs Hunter laughed. 'What is there to be scared of?'

She did not get an answer. Instead Dinah, who never showed her feelings, hugged her hard and buried her face in the big, untidy cardigan.

Chapter 4

Turk's Island

Dinah looked round at the SPLAT meeting and took a deep breath. 'I need help,' she said quietly.

'Help? You?' Lloyd stared at her. He could never remember her asking for anything like that before.

She wriggled awkwardly on her chair. 'I'm sorry, but I do. It's this competition. I feel –'

'Not the *competition*!' Ingrid gave a loud disgusted snort and rolled over on the floor, burying her head under a cushion. 'I don't want to hear *anything* about the creepy Computer Director and his smelly competition.'

'Nor do I.' Harvey put his fingers in his ears. 'They've ruined enough of the holiday already.'

Lloyd sighed. No one would think this was supposed to be a serious meeting! Ingrid and Harvey were behaving like three year olds, Mandy, who hated quarrelling, looked ready to burst into tears, and Dinah had turned very pale and stiff.

'It doesn't matter,' she said in a small voice. 'Forget it. I'm sorry I spoke.'

'Of course it matters!' spluttered Lloyd. 'This is supposed to be a secret society, not a playgroup.' He nodded to Ian. 'Help me sort these two out.'

There was a short scuffle, with grunts from Harvey and loud, dramatic shrieks from Ingrid. Two minutes later everyone was sitting very still and solemn, staring at Dinah.

'*Right,*' said Lloyd. 'Now, what is it?'

Dinah looked even stiffer and more embarrassed. 'It's this final. I can't explain why – I don't *know* why – but I'm scared of it. There's something wrong, something I can't understand. And the nearer it gets, the more nervous I feel.'

'What a stupid problem!' Ingrid said loudly, before anyone else had a chance to speak. 'It's obvious what you've got to do. Just don't go if you don't want to. No one can force you to.'

Dinah shook her head, looking miserable. 'It's not that simple. Mum and Dad have bought me this Saladin computer just so that I can go to the final. It was really expensive. I can't suddenly turn round and tell them I've changed my mind. And anyway, I haven't changed my mind. I still want to go to the final. Every time I look at that invitation card, I feel as though I'll *die* if I don't go. But – I'm scared.'

'I want you all to come with me.'

For a moment there was complete silence. Then three voices burst out at once.

'No one would let us –' said Lloyd.

'Why should we want to –?' shrieked Harvey.

'*I'm not going near the Computer Director –*' yelled Ingrid.

Dinah looked even more miserable, and Mandy got up and put an arm round her shoulders. 'I think we should try and go,' she said stoutly. 'Dinah wouldn't have asked us unless she felt *really* upset. And I bet you could make a plan if you tried, Lloyd. You could say *we* all want a trip to London too. If Dinah's getting one. We could go and stay with your Auntie Alice and visit the Science Museum.'

Lloyd was tempted. He loved organizing things. Especially huge, complicated plans. A SPLAT trip to London! That would really be something. Only – Ingrid and Harvey were still looking rebellious.

Then, unexpectedly, Ian spoke. Until then, he had been lounging back in his chair, looking slightly superior. But now he jumped to his feet, taking them all by surprise. '*I* think we should try and go, as well. We're being pathetic. Not like S P L A T at all. It's supposed to be a fighting organization. Remember? The Society for the Protection of our Lives Against Them. When we started it, we were strong – the Demon Headmaster couldn't hypnotize any of us except Dinah, and we defeated his plans. But look at us now! We've wasted all this morning, just bickering!'

He glared round in disgust, and the others looked sheepish. Even Ingrid stopped pulling a sulky face and hung her head. Ian snorted.

'We need something to do. We've got *feeble*! If the Demon Headmaster came back now, he'd have us all in his power in a couple of seconds.'

He snatched the heavy, plush cloth off the table and draped it round his shoulders, so that it hung in long folds, like a teacher's gown. Then his fair, lazy face set into stern lines, like the face of the Demon Headmaster.

'Funny that you should all be so sleepy,' he crooned. 'Look into my eyes. Look deep, deep into my eyes.'

Ingrid giggled. 'Don't be thick. You don't look like him at all. Even *you* aren't ugly enough.'

'Quiet!' snapped Ian. 'Do not disturb the others. They want to go to sleep.' His voice slowed, soothingly. 'They're so, so sleepy. They can't lift their arms or their legs.'

They all began to play up to him. Mandy let her head slump forward. Lloyd and Harvey flopped sideways and Ingrid gave a snore. Even Dinah relaxed.

'That's better,' crooned Ian. 'Much more orderly. Now, close your eyes, all of you. Sleep, sleep, sleep . . .'

Obediently, they shut their eyes. Ingrid opened one again and peeped at him, but he glared so fiercely at her that she shut it quickly.

'Now,' he said, in quite a different voice, sharp and precise, 'I will give you your instructions. Tomorrow we will plan to take over the world and run it efficiently, but today we have more important things to do. We have to solve Dinah's problem. Everyone repeat after me – we will do our best to go to London with Dinah.'

'We will do our best to go to London with Dinah,' chorused the others.

'And we will succeed,' Ian said firmly.

'*And we will succeed.*'

It was not as difficult as they had expected. On the morning of 28 August, all six members of SPLAT climbed off a train in the middle of London. Feeling tired and thirsty in the dry, summer heat, they dragged their cases up the platform. Dinah had the most to carry, because she had brought her Saladin as well, but it was Ingrid who complained the loudest.

'I still don't see *why* we've got to do this. I don't want anything to do with the Computer Director. Why can't we *really* go to your Auntie Alice's, Lloyd? And visit the Science Museum?'

'We've *told* you,' Lloyd said impatiently. 'Six million times already. We're SPLAT, and we're going with Dinah.' He gripped the back of Ingrid's neck and pushed her up the platform and through the ticket barrier.

'I still think it's mean to trick Auntie Alice,' muttered Harvey. But he followed the others to the telephones. They all crowded round while Lloyd made the phone call. They could not hear everything he said, but snatches of talk drifted out.

'... terribly sorry, Auntie Alice ... *enormous* bright red spots ... this morning ... yes, all of us ... yes, all over ...'

When he came away from the phone, he did not look very happy. 'Well, that's done,' he said. 'But it was horrid. She was ever so nice and sympathetic.'

'Ah, but you *had* to do it, didn't you?' Ingrid said nastily. 'So that we can be S P L A T and go with Dinah.'

She was still in a really bad temper. When they went down the steps into the Underground station, she trailed behind, making loud, rude remarks to Harvey. And when they got to the Underground train, she persuaded him to sit up at the far end of the carriage with her, pretending not to know the others.

'Oh *dear*.' Mandy frowned. 'Do you think I ought to go and talk to them?'

'Whatever for?' Ian looked amazed. 'They're having a *lovely* time. You know how Ingrid likes sulking.'

Mandy did not seem convinced, but she settled back in her seat anyway. 'Oh well, they'll probably be all right when we reach Turk's Island. That's what the place is called, isn't it, Dinah? It sounds wonderful. This horrible, dusty heat is making us all crotchety. Just think how lovely it'll be to see a beautiful river, full of water.'

Dinah frowned. Until then she had not joined in the conversation at all. She had sat, very still and upright, on the edge of her seat, looking wooden because she was so nervous. But now she said, 'I've been wondering about that. Yes, the place *is* called Turk's Island. I've got to go to the Saracen Tower on Turk's Island. So there must be a river. But I can't work out which one. We won't be anywhere near the Thames.'

Lloyd waved a hand. 'Don't worry. I bet there are millions of rivers in London.'

'Perhaps this is a nice little one,' said Mandy. 'With reeds at the edges, and waterfalls.'

'Oh sure,' Ian said sarcastically. 'And herons and salmon and otters. All in the middle of London.'

Lloyd licked his lips. 'I'll settle for just the water. It's so *hot* in this carriage.'

They sat back, dreaming of cool, clear running water and trying to ignore the rude snorts that came from Ingrid and Harvey at the other end of the carriage.

All at once, Dinah sat up. 'Get ready,' she said. 'It's the next stop.'

'Oi!' Ian yelled down the carriage. 'You two ugly mugs! Get off at the next stop.'

'Huh!' Ingrid tossed her head and she and Harvey turned their backs, but at the next station they did get off, even though it was by a different door. They charged up the steps and through the ticket barrier, ahead of the others, and Lloyd could hear them muttering as they climbed the second staircase, towards the open air.

'. . . beastly computers . . . putrid Computer Director . . .'

'. . . spoilt the whole summer . . . and . . .'

'*OH!*'

They both said it together, as they reached the top of the steps. Stopping dead, they looked from side to side, staring. Quickly the other four raced up behind. Their heads were full of beautiful, refreshing pictures of grass and water and ducks.

'*OH!*' they all said, as they reached the top.

Because there was no grass. Not a single duck. In fact, there was not a river in sight.

Instead, they were standing in the middle of an enormous

motorway intersection. The station looked tiny, completely surrounded by bridges and tunnels and cars. Roads looped up above them, high in the air, supported by concrete arches. Roads plunged down, vanishing into the darkness of underpasses. More roads ran round them at ground level, on every side. And the traffic sent up a steady, unbroken roar.

For a moment, they were utterly bewildered. Then Ingrid said triumphantly, 'You see? It's all a load of rubbish. Well, *we're* not standing about here, are we Harvey? We'll go and sit on that bench over there, until they all decide to be sensible and go to Auntie Alice's after all.'

The two of them marched off and Mandy looked distressed. 'We've got to do something, or they'll get unbearable. Haven't you got any idea where to go, Dinah? What about the instructions in your invitation?'

'Well –' Dinah hesitated. 'They're a bit peculiar. They just say, *Turn to the north and you will see the Saracen Tower on Turk's Island.* That doesn't seem much help.'

'Ah.' Ian shook his head wisely. 'This isn't a holiday camp you're going to, remember. It's a special session for Brains. I bet the rest of them could work out how to get there. They're probably all knocking on the door now. Horrible little wizened fellows, with great bulging egg-heads. And tiny little pebbly glasses. And backs all bent from stooping over their books. And –'

In spite of her nervousness, Dinah grinned and sloshed him. 'Yes, but what are *we* going to do?'

'We could try the instructions,' Mandy said mildly. 'It's easy enough to work out where north is, after all. The sun's more or less in the south at this time of day, and there's no missing that. Not in this heat.'

'Right,' Lloyd said bossily. 'Everyone face north.'

They turned their backs on the sun and stared. But what they saw was just baffling. In front of them were more and more loops of motorway, arching up towards the sky and down under the ground. And apart from those, there was only one other thing to be seen. In the exact centre of the intersection rose a tall, modern tower block, high and narrow.

It stuck up into the sky like a finger of light, reflecting the sunshine back blindingly into their eyes. Its whole surface seemed to be composed of large squares of mirror, with no sign of any windows or balconies. And it was completely isolated in the middle of the roaring traffic. Nothing else was visible. Only roads, roads, roads – and that single, dazzling pillar.

Then, suddenly, Dinah said, 'Oh! I'm stupid!'

'She's realized at last!' Ian applauded. 'Well, when you've finished cheering, perhaps you'll explain things to us sub-zero morons.'

'Look!' Dinah pointed straight at the gleaming tower. 'Don't you see? Turk's Island isn't an island in a river. It's an island in the *traffic*. And that's the Saracen Tower!'

Lloyd and Ian and Mandy looked amazed, but, from the bench round the corner, Ingrid laughed scornfully.

'Call yourself clever, Dinah Hunter? We worked that out ages ago, didn't we, Harvey?'

'What a naughty taradiddle,' murmured Ian. 'Didn't your mother ever tell you not to boast?'

'But we *did*,' insisted Harvey. 'Look.'

He pointed away to his right. Walking closer to the bench, the others found that they could see a flight of steps plunging down into a small pedestrian subway. At the top of the steps was a notice.

Mandy shook her head, gently. 'Why didn't you *say*?'

'Why should we?' Ingrid shrugged. '*We* don't want to go near the Computer Director. He's bound to turn out to be a robot or a vampire or something.'

'Well, tough luck,' said Lloyd. 'Because the rest of us are going there now. And I've got all the money. So if you don't come with us, you'll have to sit here and stare at the traffic. There's nothing else to do round here.'

He led the way down into the subway. And five pairs of feet followed him.

Chapter 5

Into the Saracen Tower

It was very dusty in the subway. Dusty and dirty and dry. And the narrow passage was lit by bright white fluorescent tubes which showed up every cobweb.

It was cold, too, and slightly musty. For the first few seconds the cold was a relief, but by the time they had gone a yard or two it made their skin feel clammy, as though they had walked out of the sun into a deep dungeon. And their footsteps echoed eerily ahead of them, the noise re-bounding off the hard surfaces of the walls.

'Do you think it's far?' whispered Mandy. Somehow it seemed right to whisper.

Lloyd forced himself to answer in a normal voice. 'It looked about two hundred yards. Going straight across from the station. But the subway isn't quite straight, of course.'

It curved gently, first to the left and then to the right, so that they could not see anything ahead of them except the passage. Ingrid and Harvey shuddered and walked closer to the others.

The end came quite suddenly. The subway bent round, a little more sharply than before, and they were facing a steep flight of steps leading upwards to the open air. At the top, they could see the blinding brightness of the sun, reflected from the walls of the tower block.

Lloyd took a deep breath and then marched up the stairs,

slightly ahead of the others. They needed to be given a lead. He could feel them hesitating. He would go first.

As he emerged from the subway, he found himself staring into his own eyes.

For a moment it startled him so much that he could not understand the reason. Then he realized. The walls of the huge tower were not just *like* mirrors. They *were* mirrors. The whole surface, right to the top, was made of mirror panels, and he was looking into the eyes of his reflection.

'Wow!' muttered Ian, behind him. 'What a sight.'

'I think it's stupid,' snapped Ingrid. She pulled her cross-eyed face at the reflections and stuck out her tongue.

Lloyd took another deep breath, ready to give orders, and immediately found himself spluttering. Here in the very centre of the intersection, the air was foul with exhaust fumes. Before he could recover, Ian had turned to Dinah.

'Right, what do we do now? What do your instructions say?'

Dinah glanced down to check. 'It says *Present yourself at the door and request admittance.*'

'Hey!' Mandy grinned. 'That sounds very grand. Do you think there's a butler or something?'

'More likely to be a bouncer,' drawled Ian gloomily. 'A huge, hairy thug hired to keep out unwanted visitors like us.'

Ingrid tossed her head. '*We're* not unwanted visitors, are we, Harvey? We're unwant*ing* visitors.'

'Shut up, all of you.' Lloyd rubbed his eyes, which were starting to smart. He had never known SPLAT be so diffi-cult to keep in order. 'Now listen. We don't know what's going to happen, so we'll just have to take our chance. We'll all go with Di when she requests admittance and if there's any opportunity for the rest of us to get in, be ready to seize it. If not, we'll have to use our wits.'

'But you *will* get in?' Dinah asked anxiously. 'I don't want to be stuck in there by myself.'

'Of course we will,' promised Mandy. 'Now where do you think we go? It just says *the door* in your instructions, doesn't it? Do you think it could possibly mean that one?'

She pointed. The door facing them was a very strange shape. It was about ten feet high, but only about two feet wide, and it was made of metal. Engraved across the middle were the words *The Saracen Tower*. And that was all. No opening. No handle. No nothing. Only, beside the door, was a small metal panel set into the mirror wall, and, above that, a knob like a bellpush.

For a moment everyone hesitated. Then Lloyd marched over and pressed the bellpush.

'Let's just see what happens,' he said stoutly. 'They can't eat us, after all.'

But what did happen took him by surprise. From somewhere above his head came a voice. A queer, mechanical voice.

'If You Desire Admittance, Please Punch Out
Your Name.'

At the same moment, the metal panel in the wall slid aside, revealing a row of buttons lettered with the letters of the alphabet. Lloyd stared for a moment and then began to press them.

L-L-O-Y-D-H-U-N-T-E-R.

As he finished, there was a short pause. Then the mechanical voice sounded again.

'I Am Not Programmed To Admit You. Please Go
Away.'

188

Lloyd stepped back.
'You try, Di. But the rest
of us will be ready. When
the door opens, we may
all be able to rush in.'

Dinah gulped and then
pressed the bellpush.

'If You Desire Admit-
tance, Please Punch
Out Your Name.'

Again, the metal panel
slid aside. With a quick
glance over her shoulder
at the others, Dinah began
to punch.

D-I-N-A-H-H-U-N-T-E-R.

A pause. Then –

'Please Step Into The
Half Circle In Front
Of The Door.'

For the first time, they
noticed that the concrete
ground in front of the door
was marked by a metal
groove. It ran in a perfect
half circle, exactly the
width of the door and a foot
from front to back.

Carefully, Dinah stepped
over the groove, standing
with her feet neatly together
and her arms in front of

THE
SARACEN
TOWER

her, clutching the handles of her suitcase and the Saladin computer. The others crowded close, but there was not room for anyone except Dinah in the circle. Still, they were all prepared, holding their breath, ready to charge forward as soon as the door started to swing open.

But it did not swing open. Instead, with bewildering speed, it turned, like a revolving stage, taking the half circle of ground with it.

Without moving a step on her own, Dinah was spun away from them, into the building. There was a brief glimpse of a narrow corridor and then the turn was complete. Dinah had vanished and they were staring at the opposite side of the metal door, which looked exactly the same as the first side. Ten feet tall and two feet wide, with *The Saracen Tower* engraved across the middle. And there was nothing else to be seen except their own startled faces, reflected in the mirror walls.

'Well,' said Ian, after a moment of stunned silence, 'what now, O Leader?'

'We – we –' Lloyd racked his brains frantically. If you want to be in charge of people, there are moments when you must produce a plan. It doesn't matter what, but there must *be* a plan. And Lloyd knew that this was one of those moments. 'We'll try to get in just like Dinah did,' he said.

He stepped forward again and pressed the bellpush once more. But this time, when the mechanical voice asked him to punch out his name, he winked at the others over his shoulder and punched out.

D-I-N-A-H-H-U-N-T-E-R.

A pause. Then –

'This Person Has Already Been Admitted. Please Leave Otherwise The Police Will Be Summoned.'

'Oh dear,' Mandy said softly, 'it's going to be ever so hard to get in. What can we do?'

'I think we should just go back to the station and get a train to Lloyd's Auntie Alice's,' said Ingrid.

Harvey nodded. 'We can say we've been miraculously cured.'

'But we couldn't do *that*.' Mandy was shocked. 'We promised we'd get into the building and make sure Dinah was all right. SPLAT-swear. We can't let her down now.'

'Well, I'll really enjoy seeing you get inside,' said Ingrid. 'Go on. Show me how you're going to do it without getting us all arrested.'

And she and Harvey sat down cross-legged on the pavement and folded their arms, looking up at the others with irritating smugness.

Lloyd tried to ignore them. There *had* to be a way of getting into the building. There just *had* to be . . .

Chapter 6
The Brains

When the ground began to turn under her feet, Dinah was too surprised to do anything. She did not have time to shout to the others or jump backwards to safety. All she could do was concentrate on not toppling over. Clutching the handle of her suitcase with one hand and gripping the Saladin's case with the other, she was whirled round, away from the sunshine, away from the open air, away from the other members of SPLAT into – total darkness.

It snapped round her as though the lid of a box had slammed shut. She was standing in a completely strange place and she could not even see her clenched hands in front of her or her feet on the floor below.

Automatically, she put her suitcase down and felt behind her, trying to push at the door she had come through. But the wall on this side was lined with metal and the door fitted so perfectly that she could not even find the cracks at its edges.

Keep calm she kept muttering to herself. *Don't panic.* She couldn't have been brought all this way just to be shut up in the dark. There must be a reason for it. Something must be going to happen. Mustn't it?

But she knew that she could not stay in control of herself for ever. She could not have been there for more than a minute, but already the darkness was straining her eyes and she was beginning to breathe faster. Something must happen soon. It must, it must . . .

And then it did. Suddenly, in front of her, a tiny green light appeared, floating in the blackness. She could not tell whether it was near to her or far away. It was out of the reach of her hand when she stretched towards it, but beyond that she had no way of telling, nothing to measure it against in the blackness. It just hovered, staying in the same place but vibrating constantly as though it changed shape all the time. But it was either too small or too far away for Dinah to make out the shapes properly.

Then she heard the mechanical voice that had spoken to her when she was outside.

'You May Advance Towards The Light.'

She shuddered. The sensible part of her mind knew very well that the voice was made by a machine. In fact she knew she could do the same thing with her Saladin if she loaded the right instructions. But – it was hard not to think of that jerky, inhuman voice as the voice of the Computer Director himself. She imagined his mouth opening and shutting like the mouth of a robot, while his pebbly glasses gleamed above.

'Please Advance Towards The Light,' the voice said.

It was hard not to be terrified at the thought of stepping forward into – nothing. But there were no other choices. Dinah bent down to pick up her suitcase and then began to shuffle forward, very slowly, step by step, feeling the ground in front of her with her feet before each move.

Both her hands were full, so that she could not reach out to feel whether there were walls on either side. The floor was covered with something soft, like carpet, so that her footsteps made no noise. Cautiously, she coughed once or twice to see if she could tell by the sound what sort of place she was in. She had an impression of walls close to her on both sides, as though she were in a long, straight corridor, but she could not be certain. The only thing she could be certain of was the green light hanging in the air in front of her. With her eyes fixed on it, she shuffled closer, inch by inch.

And slowly, very slowly, it grew larger as she got closer, until she could see that it was made up of tiny, shifting, snaking green lines of light. Like the lines on a computer screen. Something about those lines made her move faster, trying to get near enough to see them plainly. Her quick walk changed to a trot and then a stumbling, awkward run as the lines came clearer and clearer and larger and larger and she *recognized* them.

She really was looking through the darkness at a computer screen. And there, dancing across it, winding and shifting and writhing, were the familiar patterns of not one octopus, but *two*. Two beautiful, complicated octopuses of green light, hovering in the darkness of the Saracen Tower. Dinah was panting by the time she got close to the screen.

'Stop Now,' the mechanical voice said suddenly.

Dinah put down the box and the suitcase, reached out with one hand to touch the glass of the screen in front of her and then ran her fingers down it to see if there was a keyboard below.

That was the last thing she remembered properly. After that, the beautiful, shifting lines of light held her fast, so that she was not aware of anything else around her. She could only see their twirling and twisting and turning and . . .

Octopus – s – s – s – s!

*

194

It could have been a minute later that she came back to herself or it could have been five hours. She had no way of telling. But suddenly the octopus patterns vanished and she realized that she could see.

She was standing in a lift, in a glare of light, with a blank, dead screen in front of her where the octopuses had been. At her feet were her suitcase and the Saladin. Behind her, the lift doors were open and from the room beyond came a faint hum of voices.

I'm here, Dinah thought. Wherever *here* was. The air was cool and damp and when she glanced over her shoulder she had a quick picture of a hard, bright room. The windowless walls were covered in white plastic and lined with shiny metal cabinets all the way round. And the whole large room was full of people. Full of strangers. Dinah picked up her belongings, swallowed hard and turned round to face them.

They were sitting with their backs to her, in rows of separate desks, and for a moment she had an impression of inhuman neatness and order. All the desks were identical – white-topped, with shiny metal legs. They were ranged in perfectly straight lines, with the gaps between them as regular as though they had been measured in millimetres. On each desk stood a Saladin computer and in front of each desk was a gleaming white-and-metal chair. Sitting in the chairs were dozens and dozens of children dressed in identical spotless white lab coats, their backs hunched as they leaned over the desks. The Brains.

For a second Dinah stood nervously in the lift, re-membering Ian's jokey description of them. Perhaps, if she moved or spoke, they would turn and look at her with identical faces, white teeth and metal glasses gleaming under high, curved foreheads. She stared at their backs, gathering her courage, and then stepped out of the lift. The soles of her shoes clacked on the hard, bright floor outside and at once every head in the room moved as the Brains turned to look at her.

The bright, mechanical tidiness was completely shattered. Black faces and white faces, brown ones and yellow ones all gazed at her, some smiling and some just inquisitive. Boys and girls from sixteen or seventeen right down to eight or nine. Some of them had dark hair, some of them had fair hair, some were ginger and some were mousy. There were plaits and curls and spikes and crew-cuts and fringes. And the clothes which showed at the necks of the lab coats were just as varied – a hotchpotch of colours and shapes. Red and mauve frills, green shirt collars, pink and blue and khaki tee-shirts, yellow-striped, purple-spotted or gold-streaked jumpers. The mere sight of them made Dinah begin to smile.

Before she could move any further or say anything, one of the girls stood up and launched towards her with her hands held out.

'Oh how lovely to see you I'm Camilla Jefferies and I wondered who was going to come and sit in this desk next to me because it's the only empty one and I thought perhaps there was no one else –'

She was the most beautiful girl Dinah had ever seen. One of the oldest there, tall and willowy with smooth pink and white skin. A great cascade of curling chestnut hair fell down over her shoulders, almost to her waist, and a flood of words tumbled from her lips as though she never needed to breathe.

'– look here's your desk next to mine and this is my

brother Robert behind you and Bess on the other side of you –'

Meekly Dinah let herself be ushered across to the empty desk and helped into the white lab coat that was hanging over the back of the chair. Then she sat down and nodded at Robert and Bess.

Bess seemed to be the youngest person there. She was shy and nervous, and she was clutching a teddy bear on her lap. 'Hallo,' she whispered, smiling up at Dinah.

'Hallo,' Robert said quietly from behind. He looked very much like Camilla only younger. About the same age as Dinah. But he was as silent as his sister was talkative and he did not say anything else, just looked shrewdly at Dinah before he bent over his desk again.

'– have you brought your Saladin oh good well you plug it in here let me show you –'

With a stream of instructions, Camilla got Dinah settled into her desk and then leaned back with a happy sigh.

'Oh isn't this *nice* we're really here and settled and everyone's friendly and it's going to be really fun isn't it –'

'Hrmph!' came from Robert.

Bess gave a pale, polite smile and clutched harder at her teddy bear. 'It seems all right so far,' she murmured.

Dinah knew what they meant. Nothing bad had happened yet, but still, at the back of her mind, was the niggle that had been troubling her for weeks. The feeling that there was something *wrong* about the final – about the whole competition. But she could not think of any way to start explaining it. So she just smiled back at Bess and waited to see what would happen now.

She did not have to wait long. Almost as soon as she was settled the mechanical voice rang out over the room.

'The Computer Director is Approaching.
Please Stand And Be Silent.'

Even Camilla stopped talking, and everyone stood very quietly, facing the front. There was a faint hissing sound from behind them. Dinah decided that the lift was coming back. Then, sharply, making them all jump, the sound of feet in hard shoes stepping out of the lift and walking across the floor.

A double line of men in white coats marched briskly up the room keeping perfectly in step with each other, not looking to the right or to the left. When they reached the front of the room, they spread out in an exact straight line, facing the desks, four of them on one side and four on the other.

In the centre, dominating the whole room, they left a space.

I won't look behind, Dinah thought sternly. *I won't.* Glancing from one side to the other, out of the corners of her eyes, she saw that Camilla and Bess were staring ahead in the same stubborn way. They were too well-behaved to gawp over their shoulders, but they were full of curiosity. They were waiting, the men at the front were waiting, the whole room was waiting for the Computer Director to appear.

Then, from the entrance of the lift, a voice spoke. Very sharp and precise.

'Good morning.'

Dinah stiffened. That voice! She could not believe that she had heard right, but now she did not *dare* look round.

'Now that you have all arrived,' the voice said crisply, 'we shall start work without wasting any further time.'

Footsteps sounded as the owner of the voice began to walk up between the desks. Dinah hung her head so that her plaits fell on either side of her face, hiding it from anyone walking by.

No, she was thinking frantically, *no, no, no, it can't be true.* She was nervous and anxious and excited and because of that she must have made a mistake about the Computer Director's voice. She *must* have made a mistake.

But, all the same, she could have sworn that the voice she had just heard was the same as a voice she knew only too well. One that she had good reason to fear.

The voice of the Demon Headmaster.

Chapter 7

Another Way In

'Are we going to stand here for *ever*?' moaned Ingrid. 'All you've done, ever since Dinah went in, is talk, talk, talk. And now you've even stopped talking. I'm bored.'

'Be quiet,' muttered Lloyd. 'I'm trying to think.'

'No you're not,' Harvey said. 'You're just hoping an answer will float into your head. We can't wait for that. We've got to *do* something.'

'Well, you tell me what, then!' snapped Lloyd, losing his temper. 'If you're so clever.' Why did people never understand how hard it was to have ideas?

'Boys, *boys*,' murmured Ian soothingly, 'I know you're enjoying your little quarrel, but why don't you stop it and help the rest of us decide what to do? Are we going to try and get into the Saracen Tower?'

'We *must*,' said Lloyd. 'We promised we would. And Dinah's not an idiot. If she thinks there's something peculiar about all this, I bet she's right.'

'OK then.' Ian glanced round at the other four. 'So – what are we going to do? We've tried everything we can think of to get through this door and it's hopeless.'

'Why not look for another way in?' That was Ingrid. She was sitting sulkily on the ground, with her back against the metal door. 'I know you're all older than me and cleverer than me, but you're being really *thick*. It's no good trying to fool our way in through this door, but there might be another one. Why don't we go and look?'

That's what I was going to say, thought Lloyd crossly. He took charge at once, before things could get out of hand. 'Well done, Ing. That's what we'll do. I'll go this way round the building, with Ian. Mandy, you take Ingrid and Harvey and go the other way. Got your S P L A T notebook?'

'Of course.' Mandy took it out of her pocket and waved it.

'Good.' Lloyd nodded. 'Well, write down everything you see that could be a way in. Even locked doors and tiny windows. *Everything*. I'll do the same and then, when we meet at the back, we'll make a plan. Come on, Ian.'

It did not take very long. Because there was nothing to write down. Lloyd and Ian walked off to the left and down the side of the building without seeing anything that broke the sweep of the huge mirror panes. Not a single window or door. Not even an air vent.

As they came round the corner to the back of the building, they saw the others appear from the far side. Lloyd waved his empty notebook at Mandy and turned his thumb down to show how useless it was. Mandy did the same. Nothing on her side either.

At that very moment they saw it. All together. Not a door, but a wide opening. It led on to a ramp sloping down under the building. They charged towards it and met in the middle, peering down into darkness.

'Of *course*!' breathed Mandy. 'It's the car park. Do you think there's a door into the building from down there?'

'Could be,' Ian said. 'Shall we risk the terrible darkness and the shadows that lurk in the corners?' He pulled a horror-comic face. 'I've brought the S P L A T torch.'

He produced a little plastic flashlight from his pocket and pressed the switch. Nothing happened.

'Should have brought the SPLAT batteries as well,' murmured Ingrid nastily.

'Oh, give it to *me*. I bet I can work it.' Harvey snatched the torch from Ian and began to fiddle with it. After a few seconds, it gave out a pale, feeble light. 'Told you so.'

'Right then,' Lloyd said briskly. 'Here we go. Try not to make too much noise, everyone. I should think there's a terrible echo in there.'

It was like walking down into a giant cave. As they walked down the ramp, light faded round them and the car park stretched away into the darkness, a vast, empty expanse with a few cars dotted round it.

'We'll go all the way round the edge,' Lloyd decided. 'Then if there's a lift door or something we'll be sure to find it.'

They began a long, slow trek round the dark car park. Their feet echoed loudly on the chilly concrete floor and their whispering voices floated eerily through the shadows, as Harvey swept the torch beam up and down the walls. But there was no sign of any door.

Then, when they were about three-quarters of the way round, they saw a dark hump in front of them, huddled in the next corner. Harvey shone the light towards it and picked out a rounded glass body set on spindly legs with wheels at the bottom. The rotors at the very top sent strange elongated shadows up the wall and the torchlight glinted back off the glass.

'*A helicopter!*' said Harvey. He was so surprised that he spoke in a loud squeak that made everyone jump. 'Look. What a weird thing to find down here.'

Without waiting for the others, he darted forward at a run. Ingrid followed him and before Lloyd could gather his wits the two of them were pulling themselves up into the helicopter's cockpit. There was no door to keep them out and they squashed together into the single pilot's seat, chattering in excited whispers.

'Lloyd!' Mandy hissed, sounding shocked, 'you can't let them do that. Suppose they *break* something? You've got to get them out.'

'Of course I'm going to get them out,' Lloyd said irritably. Why was everyone so busy telling him how to organize things? Even Mandy was getting bossy now. He marched across to the helicopter, feeling his way along the wall with his fingertips. 'Harvey! Ingrid! Get out of there!'

'But it's really interesting –' began Harvey.

'Come *down*!'

'You could just have a look –' Ingrid sounded quite excited, even good-tempered, but Lloyd did not listen.

'Come down at once! How can I organize things if you two just go off and do whatever you want to?'

'But it's not like that,' protested Harvey. 'We thought this might be important and –'

'– and we've found something ever so odd –' Ingrid said.

'– and it wouldn't take a second if you just –'

'– scrambled up here and had a *peep* and –'

'*Down!*' Angrily, Lloyd reached up, grabbed Harvey round the leg and tugged. 'We're not here to play games.'

Harvey squealed, caught off balance, and lurched wildly. For a second the light in his hand swept out towards the centre of the car park, into the darkness. Then he dropped the torch. It hit the concrete floor with a crunch and the light went out.

At the same time, Mandy gave a tiny scream and clutched at Lloyd's arm.

'What's the matter?' Ingrid said sourly. 'Afraid of the dark?'

'No,' whispered Mandy. 'But I saw *people*. Tall figures. In the middle there, between the pillars.'

For a moment there was a horrible, cold silence. Harvey and Ingrid slid out of the helicopter and stood with the others, shivering. Then Lloyd squared his shoulders. After all, he *was* the leader. 'Stay here. I'm going to investigate.'

Slowly he padded across the floor in the direction Mandy had pointed out. As his eyes grew used to the dark, he started to make out the shapes that she had seen. Three of them, very tall and straight and still.

Very still. Surely people would not be as still as that? And people would be thinner. These shapes were very solid.

Then, as he came up to them, he saw what they were – not people, but tall metal cylinders. They were about six feet high, on little wheels, and they stood under a sort of overhang like a hood sticking out from the side of the pillar. Lloyd did not need to wonder what they were for. His nose told him.

'It's all right,' he called out, trying not to laugh. 'They're not people. They're *dustbins*. Big ones, like the ones at school.'

He was just turning to go back to the others when suddenly, from above his head, came a loud WHOOSH! There was a sound of rushing and sliding. Then, from the overhanging hood, a great mass of peelings and empty packets dropped into one of the dustbins.

And an idea dropped into Lloyd's head. A disgusting, repulsive, sick-making, *brilliant* idea.

'Hey, you lot,' he shouted. 'Come over here and have a look.'

'Why should we?' Ingrid called sulkily. 'We're not here to play games, you know. *You* wouldn't come up and look at our helicopter, so why should we –'

But Lloyd was feeling so pleased with himself that he did not bother to get angry with her. 'Oh, shut up, Ingrid and stop being silly. You've all got to come over here. *I know how we're going to get into the building!*'

Ian guessed first. When he reached the dustbins he saw Lloyd standing close beside them, peering up under the hood, and he pulled a face.

'Yuck! You're joking, of course?'

'Of course *not*!' Lloyd said. 'Here, give me a leg-up. If I climb on top of this bin, I'll be able to see better.'

Clambering on to Ian's shoulders, he gripped the rim of the nearest dustbin and hauled himself up. For a moment he was balancing on his stomach over the edge. He caught a horrible whiff of rotting vegetables, potato peelings and old tea-leaves and for one ghastly second he thought he was going to overbalance and plunge head first into the middle of it all.

Then he had pulled himself up and was sitting on the edge of the bin with his legs dangling and his head up underneath the hood.

'It's all right,' he called down softly. 'There's a chute about eighteen inches wide. I can't see any light at the top, but it seems to go on a long way. And there must be an opening *somewhere*, so that people can put the rubbish in. It should be quite easy to climb if I put my back against one side and walk my legs up the other.'

Ian coughed politely. 'Were you – er – thinking of

making this trip alone? Or is it going to be a jolly outing for all of us?'

'Of course you've all got to come,' Lloyd said. 'We're SPLAT, aren't we? We've got to stick together.'

'You didn't stick with *us* when we were investigating the helicopter,' argued Ingrid. 'You wouldn't even listen when we tried to tell you about —'

'Ingrid,' Lloyd said dangerously, 'if you don't shut up about that helicopter, I'll drag you up here and throw you into the middle of the rubbish!' The smell from the dustbin was beginning to make him feel peculiar and he wanted to start climbing. 'Come on, everyone, follow me.'

He turned his back on them all and stood precariously on the rim of the dustbin. Balancing carefully, he leaned back against the inside of the chute. Then he lifted one leg and planted his foot firmly against the opposite side. Right. Now for the tricky bit.

'Of course,' murmured Ingrid innocently, 'if the walls of the chute are too greasy you'll fall straight into the bin.'

Lloyd ground his teeth. 'Of course,' he hissed, 'from up here I could spit straight on your head. Be *quiet*. I'm concentrating.'

Pressing hard against the sides of the chute, he lifted his second leg and planted that foot beside the first. And there he was, wedged across the opening.

Carefully he walked his feet up the wall until they were almost level with his body. Pressing his hands backwards on either side of his bottom, he levered his body up another six inches. Then his feet started to walk again.

It was not exactly difficult, but it was very tiring and he had to concentrate hard. As he got higher, he could hear the others below him, clambering up on the dustbins and then working out how to follow him up the chute. But he could not let himself listen to them. He had to think about levering his body and walking his legs, levering his body and walking his legs, levering his body . . .

He had fallen into a rhythm when suddenly he levered his body up, leaned his head back and found the wall giving way behind him. He was so startled that he nearly fell down on top of the others, but just in time he realized what had happened. He had reached one of the openings in the side of the chute. It was covered by a flap, hinged at the top, and it could be pushed open from either side.

Finding the edges of the opening with his hands, Lloyd gripped them and hauled himself up until he was sitting in the gap, with his legs dangling down. By leaning slightly backwards, he managed to push the flap open a little way with his body, so that he could peer through the opening, over his shoulder, and see what was on the other side of the flap.

It was the most amazing room he had ever seen.

For a moment he could not do anything except stare. Then he remembered the others, on their way up. 'You can come,' he called softly. 'It's quite safe.' Then he pushed the flap open wider, so that he could study the room properly.

It was obviously a kitchen. The walls and the floor were very clean and white and shining. From one side to the other stretched row after row of worktops, covered with food in various stages of preparation. There were pots of potatoes, casseroles full of stew, huge dishes of milk pudding.

But there were no cooks. Instead, long thick rods ran from side to side of the room, just above head height. Attached to the rods were all kinds of mechanical arms.

Some of them were stirring, some of them were slicing and some of them were scooping rubbish together. But nowhere was there any sign of a person controlling them.

Robot arms, thought Lloyd. *Like those machines they have in car factories*. They must all be run by some sort of computer.

It was so fascinating that he just gazed and gazed while the others clambered up the chute below him. Enormous saucepans and casseroles were being lifted out of microwave ovens and lined up on the worktops. Then mechanical arms were loading them on to little heated trolleys which ran along rails set in the floor. When the trucks were full, the doors in their sides shut automatically and they ran silently along their rails into a lift on the far side of the room.

Lloyd was just about to crawl right out of the chute into

the kitchen, so that he could investigate the lift more closely, when his eye caught something large moving quickly towards him from half-way across the room.

A thick, strong metal arm, much longer than the others, was rearing up over the tables. On the end of it was a giant scoop. While Lloyd watched, the scoop skimmed the worktops, collecting all the little heaps of wet, smelly rubbish. Closer and closer it moved – and suddenly Lloyd realized what it was doing.

'Watch out, you lot!' he shouted downwards. 'Rubbish!'

'*You're* rubbish!' shrieked Ingrid.

'Get out of the way!' shouted Harvey.

'Please,' Mandy added.

And, from the very bottom of the rubbish chute, Ian bellowed, 'Hurry *up*! I can't bear sitting on this pongy dustbin much longer.'

There they all were, with their faces turned up and their mouths open as they shouted.

And when Lloyd looked back at the kitchen, there was the huge scoop, full of tins and packets and peelings and scrapings, poised over the rubbish chute. Slowly tilting . . .

Chapter 8

The Brains are Programmed

Dinah sat very, very still at her desk, hardly daring to breathe. Up at the front of the room, in the middle of the men in white coats, stood the Computer Director. Only now she did not think of him as the Computer Director. Ever since he had reached the front of the room and she had been able to see him, she had known who he really was.

He was dressed in a spotless white lab coat, without a single crease, and his eyes were covered by thick, pebbly glasses. He looked exactly like his photograph on the posters that Mr Meredith had stuck up at school. But his voice and the way he walked and the way he held his head were all unmistakable. And Dinah knew that if he took off the thick glasses she would find herself gazing into a pair of strange sea-green eyes. Huge eyes, that had the power to hypnotize her, so that she felt she was drowning in their depths. So that she forgot what happened and did everything he told her. The eyes of the Demon Headmaster.

That was what she had expected, as soon as she guessed who he was. She thought he would start by hypnotizing all the Brains. But she was wrong. Instead, without any introduction or any polite speech of welcome, he had begun to dictate notes in a fast, clipped voice.

Dinah was so paralysed with fear that she had to make a great effort to pick up her pen and start writing. She was terrified that any noise from her, or any tiny movement, might attract his attention. Then he would recognize her, and – and – she did not know what would happen after that, but she knew it would be horrible. Keeping her head lowered, she scribbled down the notes, trying to concentrate on what the Headmaster was saying.

'You will all have noticed the rows of cabinets round the walls,' said the cold voice. 'These are parts of the Super-Saladin, the world's most advanced computer. There are other parts, throughout this building, but this room is the centre. The main control room. It was the Super-Saladin's voice that you heard when you first entered the Saracen Tower. Among other things, it runs the building.'

The Brains gasped, awed by the enormous size and power of the Super-Saladin. Several of them turned round to gaze at the rows of cabinets, but Dinah stayed hunched in the same position, desperate not to attract attention. And the Headmaster's voice went on.

'You have, I presume, all brought your little Saladins with you, according to instructions. And I imagine that you are not too stupid to work out how to connect them up where you are sitting. As well as being microprocessors on their own, these little Saladins are now acting as terminals to the Super-Saladin. Each one of you is in contact with the most powerful computer in the world.'

The most powerful computer in the world. It ought to have been incredibly exciting, Dinah thought miserably. She should have been sitting on the edge of her chair, longing for a chance to use her terminal. But the only thought in her head was *SPLAT. I do want SPLAT.* Where could they all have got to?

It was no use thinking like that! She gave herself a mental

prod. She had to keep track of what the Headmaster was saying. He had started to give details of how to operate the Super-Saladin. If she didn't learn *those*, he would be sure to notice her. Bending over her notebook, she began to scribble at top speed, like all the other Brains.

And scribble and scribble and scribble. The Headmaster kept pouring out information without waiting for them to understand or ask questions. It took all Dinah's energy to keep pace with him. Out of the corner of her eye, she could see that Camilla and Bess were just as breathless, scrambling to make a note of everything. And it seemed that the voice would never stop. On and on it went, with every sentence giving another important fact. On and on and on . . .

Until at last, suddenly, the stream of words stopped dead and the Headmaster nodded.

'Right. That covers everything you need to know. In a moment, you will be sent to have your lunch. While you are eating, you should learn these notes. After the meal, you will be starting work on the final stage of the competition and I shall expect you to *know* everything I have told you. Otherwise, you will be sent home.'

Giving another brisk nod, he walked quickly down the room towards the lift. Dinah shuddered as he passed her, but he did not look at any of the Brains. He just strode into the lift and slid away.

'Christmas *pudding*!' said Camilla breathlessly, 'you don't mean he really expects us to learn everything he's told us do you realize he's been speaking for *two hours* and –'

'Silence!' barked one of the men at the front of the room. 'No talking until you are sent down to the canteen!' His voice was dead and expressionless and at the sound of it Dinah shuddered again.

213

Then she glanced sideways at Bess, to make sure she was all right. But Bess already had her head bent over her notebook, her lips moving slightly as she began to memorize what she had written.

Nursing her wrist, which ached from holding a pen for so long, Dinah flipped back through her own notes. Pages and *pages*! How could she ever learn them? She was already exhausted. She had worked harder in the last two hours than she had ever worked in her life, and it looked as though that was only a start. Help!

The white-coated men were walking down between the desks now, sending the Brains into the lift, two rows at a time. The Brains went solemnly and silently, their eyes on their notebooks and their faces concentrating hard.

When it was Dinah's turn, she went with Camilla and Bess and Robert. The men packed the lift so tightly that none of them could move and then pressed a couple of switches.

Immediately, the door closed and for a second there was total darkness. Bess caught her breath, but before she could say anything a green light came on. The octopus patterns began to writhe their way across the computer screen on the wall of the lift.

For an instant, Dinah felt the uneasy, worrying niggle that had been at the back of her mind ever since she entered the Saracen Tower. Octopus patterns *again*?

Then as the beautiful familiar curves filled the screen, she slid into a daze, watching them loop and arch and intertwine and . . .

Octopus – s – s – s – s!

The next thing she was aware of was the lift doors opening.

The Brains blinked as the octopus patterns disappeared and light filled the lift. Then they started to push their way out, looking like any other crowd of hungry children.

They were in a vast, windowless canteen, with long tables set out in line from end to end. Very neat, regular lines. Perfectly straight and evenly spaced. Strip lights glared down from above, filling the room with a harsh brightness, and everything was so clean and hard and shining that it was almost painful to look at.

As Dinah stepped out of the lift, she heard the mechanical voice of the Super-Saladin.

'Collect Your Cutlery From The Clean Cutlery Dispenser And Then Sit At A Table.'

The message was repeated every ten seconds or so as they all lined up in a neat queue in front of a slot in the wall labelled *Clean Cutlery Dispenser.* As soon as someone stood in front of it, a bundle appeared in the slot. A knife, a fork and a spoon, wrapped in a paper napkin. The waiting person took the bundle, but the next bundle did not appear until the next person stepped forward.

Very hygienic, thought Dinah. *No chance for the things to get dirty.* But the efficiency of it made her even more miserable. It was just the sort of thing the Headmaster *would* think of.

She took her cutlery and sat down at a table with Robert, Camilla and Bess. As she settled herself, she looked sideways at Bess. The little girl was pale and quiet and she had brought her teddy bear with her.

'OK?' Dinah said.

'I think so.' Bess gave her a small, shy smile. 'It was marvellous hearing all about the Super-Saladin. I just hope I can learn everything in time.'

215

'*You* hope you can learn it. Goodness, what about me,' said Camilla, 'I'm the world's worst learner it takes me ages doesn't it Robert and –'

'Hrmph!' said Robert.

Dinah looked curiously at him. The two girls were nervous and excited, but they seemed quite pleased with their morning. Robert was different. His face was sharp and solemn and Dinah wondered what he was thinking. But before she could ask him anything the voice of the Super-Saladin sounded again.

'Please Remain Seated. Your Food Will Be
Served To You.'

All the Brains were sitting down now, most of them busy trying to learn their notes. At the sound of the voice, they looked up, wondering who was coming to serve them. Would it be the men in white coats or would it be other people? More friendly people?

But no people appeared at all. Instead, the lift doors swished open and a line of little trucks ran out of the lift and along the floor beside the tables.

'Oh look!' Bess beamed all over her face. 'Aren't they *sweet*!'

It was a comic sight. The trucks were running alongside the tables, stopping at each occupied place. When they stopped, doors opened in their sides. Mechanical arms unfolded, lifted out plates and served hot food from inside the trucks. It was like being served by a procession of fat, square gnomes.

But, after a moment or two, some of the other Brains began to wail from the other end of the room.

'But I don't *like* carrots!'

'I can't eat milk pudding. It brings me out in a rash!'

'I'm a vegetarian!'

The trucks, of course, took no notice. They simply went on serving out the same portions to everyone. Carrots, potatoes and stew for the first course. Milk pudding and prunes for the second course. Each meal looked exactly the same and each meal was exactly the same size.

'I'll never eat all *that*,' muttered Bess, as she was served. 'It's enough to last me for a week.'

'I'll have what you don't want please,' Camilla said hastily. 'I'd be glad to because otherwise I'll starve to death and it's not that I'm greedy only –'

All over the canteen, similar swaps were going on as

people tried to make sure they got meals they could eat. Robert looked grimmer and more solemn.

'You see what's happened?' he murmured.

Dinah nodded. 'The computer's been programmed so that the robots feed us all the same meal. All average portions. And we're not all average.'

'That's right.' Robert pulled a face. 'Worse than school dinners. At least the dinner ladies *listen* when you tell them you can't eat something.'

'But it's quite fun watching all the things work, isn't it?' Bess said timidly. 'Now we know how they all fit into the main computer system. Fancy the Director having programmed in everything we're going to do while we're here!'

'No!' Robert said violently. 'I *don't* fancy it!'

Bess looked hurt, as though he had kicked her. 'What do you mean?'

'Don't we get any *choice* about what we do?' Robert murmured. 'Or are we just another set of things for the computer to control? Like the rest of the robots?' He waved an arm at the figures all round the room. The Brains had sorted out the food and now they were silent except for the sound of rustling paper as they turned the pages of their notebooks. 'Look how we're being forced to work with our meal!' Robert sounded disgusted. 'It's *bad* for us. We're not machines. We're people. We need time to rest.'

'But Robert don't forget this is special,' protested Camilla, 'and if we don't work as hard as we can we'll be wasting it so you'll be sorry if you're lazy and you don't do what the Director said –'

'I'm not lazy,' Robert said quietly. 'I'm worried. It's all too – too efficient. Clean and precise and mechanical. And *controlled*. We're so controlled that we don't even know how we got to this canteen.'

'Oh Robert don't be so stupid of course we know we came up in the lift and –'

Camilla's voice died away suddenly as she realized what Robert meant, and Bess finished the sentence for her.

'– or *down* in the lift. But we don't know which, do we? Because we were all too busy watching the octopuses wriggling.'

'Exactly.' Robert nodded. 'Don't you think there's something *peculiar* about the way the Director uses the octopuses to distract our attention? It's as though he can switch off our minds with them whenever he wants to. And that's creepy.'

At the back of Dinah's head, an uncomfortable memory stirred. A miserable, strange memory of herself screaming at Mum and Dad to buy her a Saladin so that she could see more octopus patterns. 'It's like an addiction, isn't it?' she said slowly. 'Like when people get stuck on drink or drugs. We're all stuck on the octopuses. That's *terrible*.'

'It might not be the most terrible thing,' said Robert. He was looking even gloomier. 'The important question is – if we *are* addicted to the octopuses, why is the Director using them to control us? Why does he *need* to control us? *What does he want us to do?*'

Chapter 9
Harvey Walks into Trouble

'Shut your mouths! Close your eyes! *Hold on tight!*' yelled Lloyd.

He just had time to screw up his own face before the great

scoop full of rubbish tipped right over. A mountain of wet carrot-scrapings showered down on to his hair. Slimy potato peelings slithered over his neck and something that smelt like sour milk dripped down his nose and his chin. On and on went the stream of rubbish. He spat out tea-leaves, brushed flour away from his eyelashes and peeled burnt rice pudding skin off his cheek. And all the time he was frantically pressing his back and his feet against the sides of the chute so that he did not get knocked down on top of the others.

Their shouts didn't help, either.

'Eugh!'

'Yuck, *yuck*, YUCK!'

'Lloyd, what are you *doing?* Have you forgotten we're down here?'

'*Stop* it, Lloyd!'

As if he was responsible for all the rubbish, instead of catching the worst of it himself. But he couldn't answer or explain, because if he opened his mouth it would fill with muddy water and bits of fat and gristle and eggshells and buttery paper and . . .

As soon as the flood of rubbish stopped, Lloyd gripped the edge of the opening behind him and flung himself backwards through it.

'Come on quickly!' he called down the shaft. 'Before it happens again.'

One by one, the others appeared through the flap. They were soggy and bedraggled and very, very angry. But as they crawled out of the chute and into the kitchen, their faces changed. Their eyes opened wide and they gaped.

'Exploding eggshells!' said Harvey. 'What sort of place is this?'

'It's wonderful,' breathed Mandy. 'I've never seen any-thing like it.'

Even Ian, who was always so cool, gave a low whistle when he saw the robot arms swinging and bending around as they cleaned up the kitchen. Only Ingrid was not im-pressed.

'More horrible, loopy arms!' She pulled a sick face. 'Just like the beastly octopuses. I knew how it would be, from the moment we looked inside the helicopter and saw –'

'Ingrid, will you shut *up* about the helicopter!' Lloyd said fiercely. 'We don't want to listen to you moaning on and on. We've got to get out of this place.' He glanced across the room. 'There's a lift over there. I saw a whole lot of trucks of food going into it a little while ago. Perhaps we could –'

'Not *yet*!' wailed Mandy. 'We can't go anywhere looking like this. We're – we're disgusting!'

Lloyd looked. At any other time it would have been funny. Harvey had bits of potato peel in his hair and the front of Ian's white tee-shirt was spattered with tea-leaves. Ingrid's face was streaked with flour and gravy. Even Mandy, who was always so neat, had carrot-scrapings nestling among her red curls.

'You do look a bit – strange,' Lloyd said.

'*We* look strange!' Harvey nearly exploded. 'You should just see yourself. You look like a compost heap.'

'Like the inside of a dustbin lorry,' said Ingrid.

Lloyd ignored them and let Mandy brush him down and comb his hair for him until most of the rubbish was out of it. But he was impatient to get on with finding Dinah. As soon as Mandy let him go and started on Harvey, he ran across the room, dodging the robot arms. He wanted to examine the lift.

It did not take long to examine. There was nothing to see,

except two smooth, strong doors, tightly shut. Lloyd hunted all round, peering up at the ceiling and crouching down to look along the floor, but he could not find any buttons to press. No handles, no knobs, no levers. The lift might come, but as far as he could see there was no way of calling it.

And it was impossible to open the doors of the lift shaft. Even when Ian and Harvey came to help him, they did not succeed in moving them so much as a crack apart.

'Charming!' said Harvey. He kicked crossly at the doors. 'I suppose we'll have to use the stairs. That'll take for ever. Don't you remember how tall this building is?'

'I don't want to bring tears to your dear little eyes,' murmured Ian, 'but it's *worse* than that.' He had been staring round him in every direction. Now he turned back to face Lloyd and Harvey. 'You haven't realized, have you? There *aren't* any stairs. Look for yourselves. The lift is the only way up.'

Harvey suddenly looked very pale. 'You mean – we're trapped in here?'

For a moment, Lloyd made the same mistake. *I was the one who brought us all here*, he thought. *And now we may never get out.*

Then Ingrid spoke scornfully. 'Don't be a dumbo, Harvey. Of course we can get out. The same way we got in. And the sooner the better, if you ask me.'

Wriggling away from Mandy, who was trying to comb her hair, she darted back towards the rubbish chute.

Of course! Lloyd thought. *What an idiot I am!* He raced back across the room, chasing Ingrid.

'Stop a minute, Ing! You've got it wrong!'

Ingrid looked round. She had already opened the flap of the rubbish chute and hooked one leg over the edge. 'What d'you mean I've got it wrong? I'm the only person with any sense round here. *I* was the one who remembered the chute.'

'Of course you did,' Lloyd said soothingly. 'And you're right. We are going to use it again. But we're not going down – we're going on *up.*'

'*UP?*' Ingrid looked ready to bite him. 'You mean you haven't had enough of this place? You want *more?*'

'We've got to find Dinah,' said Mandy. 'We promised.' She turned to face the rubbish chute. 'It's not very nice in there, but if it's the only way we'll have to use it.'

'It *is* the only way,' Lloyd said firmly. Pushing Ingrid aside, he lifted the flap and clambered through the hole. 'I'll go first. And I'll come out through the next flap. Wherever that is. Right?'

It was harder to start off this time, with nothing solid under his feet, but at last he got himself safely wedged and began to wriggle, walking his legs and levering his body and walking his legs . . .

He had climbed about five feet when it suddenly struck him that he had a long way to drop if he fell now. It was probably twenty feet or more down into the bin in the car park. One slither, one second's loss of concentration and he would be falling, falling, falling . . .

But it was stupid to think like that. It was no use thinking about what was below. He should be worrying about what was coming. Tilting his head back, he tried to see an opening somewhere in the darkness above him. But there did not seem to be even a crack of light. Nothing but a great pillar of shadowy black, stretching up as far as he could see or imagine.

The opening, when it came, took him completely by surprise, like the first one. Suddenly, as he levered his back up the wall, there was nothing behind him. The flap gave way and he was tumbling backwards and out of the darkness, pushing at the edges of the hole to make sure that he got through and praying that there was no one waiting for him on the other side.

But no angry voices shouted at him. No one squealed with shock at his sudden appearance. Instead, he hit hard floor and uncoiled himself with his back to the room.

When he turned round, for a second, he could not make any sense of what he saw. He seemed to be looking down a long, narrow corridor, lined from floor to ceiling with baked bean tins. It was immensely tall – about twice as tall as a normal room – but so narrow that he could have stood in the middle with his arms outstretched and touched the tins on both sides. And why would anyone want to decorate a corridor with *baked bean tins*?

Then, as he picked himself up off the floor and stepped sideways to hold the flap open for the others, the mystery was explained. Because as he moved a few feet to the left he found himself looking down another corridor, identical to the first one except that it was lined with packets of sugar and tea.

Of course! They weren't corridors but the alleys between stacks of shelves. He had come out into a long, high storeroom with rows of tall shelves running from one end to the other. He moved a bit more and saw shelves filled with bags of flour, sacks of rice, tins of tomatoes.

The whole place was cool and airy and spotlessly clean. The floors were polished so perfectly that they reflected the packets and tins above them. And every packet and tin and sack and box was set neatly in its place, next to others of the same kind, with no waste of space and no squashing together.

225

'What's up here, then?' Harvey asked, as he came tumbling out of the chute. He picked himself up and peered round. 'What a fantastic place!' Then his expression changed. 'What's that?' he said sharply.

Something large and fast ran across their field of vision, travelling along an alley that ran crosswise, cutting the long, straight rows at right angles. Lloyd stiffened. People? Friends or enemies? He leaned even further sideways, trying to catch another glimpse of whatever it was.

When it reached the alley full of sugar packets, it turned towards Lloyd and Harvey and began to move in their direction. For a second they were both terrified. The thing was a tall, open truck, with sides made of wire netting. It was about six foot high and crammed with tins and packets, and it was hurtling straight towards them.

'Lloyd!' whispered Harvey in horror. 'How does it know we're here? It's automatic. There's no one in there to drive it.'

'Perhaps it picked up the noise you made,' snapped Lloyd. He was just about to call down the chute, to warn the others, when the truck stopped. Robot arms unfolded from the side and began to lift out more packets of sugar. As they picked up each one, they held it for a second and then stacked it neatly in the empty space next to the other sugar packets.

Lloyd let out his breath. 'Phew! It's not after us at all. It's just putting the packets on the shelves.'

Harvey frowned. 'But how does it know *where* to put the packets? There's all sorts of other things in it, besides sugar. How did it know it had to put the sugar packets in *that* place?'

As he spoke, the robot arms picked out a packet of tea. They held it for a moment, turning it round and round, and

226

then the whole truck swivelled and moved a little further along the alley, to reach the space on the tea shelves.

'You see?' Harvey said triumphantly. 'It *knew*. It knew it had a packet of tea this time instead of a packet of sugar. But how could it? It's creepy.'

'No it's not,' Lloyd said firmly. He didn't want to cope with Harvey getting scared. 'It's just a machine. Machines can't be creepy.'

'But how does it *do* it?' persisted Harvey.

For a moment, Lloyd was baffled. Then, as he saw the robot arms turning the next packet of tea over and over, scanning the surface he suddenly realized. 'Bar codes!'

'Bar *what*?' said Harvey.

'Bar codes. You've seen them a million times. Those funny patterns of thick and thin black lines that you see on packets and tins and things. Computers can scan them with light pens and read them. We did it at school.'

'So?' Harvey said.

'So this truck's *computerized*, thicko.' Lloyd felt very pleased with himself for working it out. 'It can scan the bar codes and read what it's picked up. And then it's programmed to take the things to the right part of the store-room.'

Slowly, light dawned on Harvey's face. 'Brilliant!' he said softly. 'Oh, *brilliant*. I must watch it doing it.' He moved away, towards the truck.

'Not yet,' called Lloyd. 'We've got to wait for the others.'

But just at that moment his attention was distracted by Mandy, who appeared through the flap. When he had helped her to scramble clear, she looked round.

'Where's Harvey?'

Lloyd looked over his shoulder, but there was no sign of

227

Harvey or of the truck. Somewhere out of sight beyond the next lines of shelves feet were pattering up and down. 'You all right?' he called.

'Course I'm all right,' Harvey's voice came back. 'It's sensational.'

Lloyd shrugged and raised his eyebrows as he turned towards Mandy again. 'He just couldn't wait until the rest of you got here. We'll have to go after him, but shall we wait until the others have arrived?'

Mandy nodded and put out a hand to help him keep the flap open. While Ian was climbing the last few feet, they could hear Harvey, still moving to and fro.

It was when the three of them were hauling Ingrid through the flap that the shout came.

'Help!' Harvey's voice. Shrill and terrified.

'Where are you?' Lloyd shouted. 'What's the matter?'

'Help! Help! It's got me!'

'Come on!' Lloyd yelled to the others.

They dashed along the baked bean alley, following the sound of Harvey's shouting, turned left and then right and then left again. Then they skidded to a stop, between shelves of dried peas and shelves of spaghetti.

'HELP!' wailed Harvey.

He had been caught by the truck's robot arms. One grab was round his body and one round his left leg. As the others watched, the arms began to lift him high in the air, towards the top of the truck.

'Help! Get me down!'

Chapter 10

A Task for the Brains

'You Will Now Return To The Computer Room.'

As the voice of the Super-Saladin grated across the canteen, the men in white coats marched out of the lift and down the room.

'Goodness I haven't finished Bess's dinner yet,' moaned Camilla, 'and I'm sure I don't know those notes well enough to –'

'Silence!' One of the men stopped beside her table. 'You will not talk any more until you are told to.'

'But can't I just ask –?' Camilla fluttered her beautiful eyelashes at him.

'No, you may not. Stand up and prepare to enter the lift,' the man said coldly.

'How *horrible*,' Bess whispered to Dinah, as soon as he had gone past. 'He didn't even look at her.'

'Silence!' snapped the man again. He glared over his shoulder, trying to see who had whispered, but Bess was looking very small and angelic, clutching her teddy bear, and he did not suspect her. 'Go to the lift!' he said at last.

All over the canteen, the same thing was happening. Men were giving orders and children were standing up, forming silent queues and moving towards the lift. They walked slowly, with their heads bent and their eyes fixed on their notebooks.

'See?' murmured Robert in disgust. 'We're all turning into robots.'

Suddenly, over on the far side of the room, there was a disturbance.

'No, I *won't*!' shouted a boy's voice. 'I'm sick of being pushed around. I don't like the food and I don't like being shut in. I'm going home.'

Immediately, two men in white coats appeared, one on either side of him. Smoothly they took hold of his arms.

'It is not possible to go home,' said the first man.

'You are to stay here until September the second,' said the other.

Both of them spoke in level voices, with no expression. Exactly the same voices they had used all the time. Dinah found herself shuddering. That was how the prefects at her school used to talk. When the Headmaster was in charge. Coldly. Almost like machines. It was never any use appealing to them or trying to get them to have pity or see sense, because they were not free to soften. They were hypnotized by the Demon Headmaster and under his control. And now these men were the same. She was sure of it. However much the Brains argued with them, they would just go on carrying out their orders.

But the boy who was shouting did not know any of that of course. He shrieked at the men.

'I want to go home!'

The Brains who were near him clustered round, worried and excited. Some of them tried to soothe him and others tried to persuade the men to let him go. There were dozens of voices talking at once and above them all rose the yells of the boy, who was almost hysterical by now.

'I WANT TO GO HOME!'

For about a minute, there was total chaos in that corner of the canteen.

But only for a minute. Then, quite calmly, more of the men walked over. Four of them picked the boy up, ignoring his struggles and screams, and carried him towards the lift. A fifth man marched ahead, going into the lift first.

All at once, the whole canteen was quiet. The Brains stopped talking. They stopped moving. They almost stopped breathing as they waited tensely to see what would happen. Bess slid a shaking hand into Dinah's and held on tightly.

The screen inside the lift flashed suddenly bright with flickering, shifting green lines as the octopus patterns were switched on. The kicking, screaming boy was carried in and his feet were lowered so that he was held in a standing position, facing the screen.

Within five seconds, he had stopped struggling. His eyes swivelled towards the screen and stayed fixed there and he stood perfectly straight and still, with a man on either side of him.

'*Oh!*' said Bess softly.

Robert nodded, and his face was dark and frowning. 'Total control,' he muttered out of the side of the mouth. 'That's what they want. And they're using the octopus pictures – and our addiction to them – to make sure of it.'

The doors slid shut and they heard the hiss as the lift carried the boy off. But even after he had gone, the Brains were quiet, looking pale and solemn, as though they had received a shock.

'What do you think they'll do to him,' whispered Camilla and even she was subdued, 'do you think they've just taken him back to the Computer Room ahead of us –?'

'No I don't,' Robert whispered back. 'I think something peculiar's going on. And *I'm* going to find out what.'

Dinah felt the back of her neck prickle, sensing danger. '*How* are you going to find out?'

'I'm going to speak to the Computer Director, of course,' said Robert firmly. 'I can't believe he knows how these men are treating us. I'm going to tell him he's got to alter it – or give us a satisfactory explanation.'

'But that won't be any use!' Suddenly Dinah realized how stupid she had been not to tell them all about the Headmaster in the beginning. 'He won't listen to you. I *know* what he's like. He used to be our Headmaster, you see, and –'

But before she could begin on her explanation, a man in a white coat was at her side.

'Silence!' he said, in his blank, hypnotized voice. Putting a hand on her elbow, he hustled her off towards the lift.

I must explain to Robert and Camilla and Bess, Dinah thought frantically. *I must tell them about the Headmaster.*

She was so busy clinging on to that thought that she forgot about everything else. As the man pushed her into the lift, squashing the others in behind her, the words thudded in her head. *I must tell them. I must tell them. I must.*

The doors slid shut. As the lift was engulfed in darkness, Dinah looked up at the others ready to start her explanation again. But she had forgotten the lighted screen. At the very second she looked up, it flashed on, catching her eye, with its fascinating, flickering patterns. *I must tell* – for an instant longer she managed to cling on to what she was thinking. Then everything slipped out of her head as the patterns started to swirl and swoop and sweep and . . .

Octopus – s – s – s – s!

When the lift doors opened again, it was too late. She was swept out as the Brains hurried to their desks. And, even

232

before she sat down, she had seen the tall figure standing at the far end of the room, dominating everything.

The Computer Director was already there, standing very still and straight, with the bright lights flashing off his glasses, so that it was impossible to tell which way he was looking.

Quickly Dinah scuttled into her seat, keeping her head bent and hoping that he would not notice her. If only he did not discover that she was there, she would at least be free to try and work out what was going on and why he had bothered to gather the Brains together like this, from all over the country.

'Good afternoon.' He spoke suddenly, breaking into her thoughts. 'You all had an easy time this morning. Now you must be prepared to work hard.'

'Easy time this morning,' whispered Camilla, 'goodness, he must be joking –'

Mercifully, the Headmaster did not hear her. 'This afternoon,' he continued in his precise voice, 'you will be beginning on the task for which you were summoned here. I will start by explaining –'

'Not for a minute, please!' Robert's interruption astonished everyone. He jumped to his feet and spoke politely but loudly. 'Before we start on anything, I think there are some things we would like to get clear –'

'Sit down,' said the Headmaster coldly.

'But I want to ask a question.'

The Headmaster frowned. 'Questions are an unnecessary waste of time. I shall tell you everything that you *need* to know. I am not here to settle your idle curiosity about other matters. Now sit down. If you speak again, you will be dealt with in a suitable manner.'

233

Please, Robert, thought Dinah, still keeping her head bent. Terrified that the Headmaster would look down from Robert's face and see her, sitting immediately in front. *There's no point in arguing with him. He's not like that.* But she did not dare to say the words aloud, and Robert had obviously decided that he was not going to give in.

'I'm sorry, sir,' he said, still polite, but stubborn, 'but I don't think this *is* just idle curiosity. I want to know –'

The Headmaster's lips went very thin, pressed tightly together, but he did not speak. Instead, he made a small, sharp movement with his hand.

'Look out Robert!' shrieked Camilla. 'Oh why did you have to be so stupid you should have guessed what would happen –'

But her warning was no use. From the back of the room, the men in white coats advanced on Robert, picked him up bodily and carried him towards the lift. All the way, he went on shouting loudly, making a speech to the Brains.

'You see? He won't tell us what's going on! And now he thinks he's going to shut me up by showing me those octopus pictures! He thinks we're all so hooked on them that he can use them to control us! Don't let him! Fight back! *Shut your eyes!*'

Even when the octopus pictures began to flicker greenly in the lift, his shouts went on. He stood there with his eyes screwed shut, yelling warnings to everyone. But it made no difference. The lift doors still snapped shut and the lift still carried him off.

Its hiss sounded very loud in the sick, shocked quietness of the Computer Room. No one spoke until, after a second or two, the Headmaster broke the silence.

'Perhaps now you all understand. You are not here to amuse yourselves. You are here to do something difficult

234

and complicated. Something that requires discipline, obedience and silence. Anyone who disturbs other people will be treated in the way that you have just seen.'

No one spoke. Not even Camilla. They were all too stunned. *It's worse than being hypnotized*, thought Dinah, *because we know what's happening to us. When the octopuses fail, he's using fear to keep us under control.*

'Is there anyone else who wants to make trouble?' said the Headmaster, in a voice of ice. 'Are there any more – *protesters?*' He made the word sound like the name of some loathsome disease. 'If so, let them speak up at once, so that they can be dealt with.'

No one made a sound. Dinah could almost feel the trembling that had come over them all. They might be Brains, but they were only children and they were afraid and confused by what was happening.

'No one?' The Headmaster gave a satisfied nod. 'Then perhaps we can go on without any more stupid interruptions.'

Dinah saw Camilla stir unhappily in her seat and knew that she was worrying about Robert. But there did not seem any point in saying anything. They both picked up their pens, ready to write down what the Headmaster was saying.

'You have all got through the first round of this competition,' he began, 'because you have quick reflexes, you understand computers and you are good at doing puzzles. Now we are going to go a step further. This puzzle will test your powers of lateral thinking.'

So that's why he hasn't hypnotized everyone! For the first time in the whole day, something made a tiny fragment of sense to Dinah. *It's no use hypnotizing us and making us act like robots if he wants us to think.* She sat up straighter, alert now. Because the crucial question was – what were they going to have to think *about?*

The Headmaster walked across to the Super-Saladin's central keyboard, at the front of the room, and began to tap at the keys. For a second or two, there was no sound except the patter of his moving fingers. The Brains watched expectantly and Dinah knew what they were thinking, because she could not help thinking it herself, in spite of everything that had happened.

Would there be more octopuses?

Bigger, better, more complicated octopuses?

The Headmaster straightened at last and the light flashed from his glasses as he moved his head to scan the rows of children.

'The Super-Saladin is now connected to another computer,' he said. 'Through the Super-Saladin, your little Saladins, too, are connected to that computer. You could have access to it – except,' he paused in the middle of the sentence and waited to make sure that they were all listening eagerly before he finished, '– except that it is protected by a code or a password. I want you to crack the code or discover the password.'

It's impossible, thought Dinah. *We could be here for a hundred years trying to do that.*

'To help you concentrate,' the Headmaster said silkily, 'I should tell you that the boys who have been taken away will not be brought back until you have completed your task. If you want to see them again, you had better begin to work at it.'

Camilla went very white and her eyes widened with disbelief. 'Does he really mean –?' she whispered.

The Headmaster repeated what he had said in even plainer language, so that there should be no mistake.

'I want you to break into the computer.'

Chapter 11

On the Shelf

'Lloyd! Help! Ian, Mandy, Ingrid! Help, help!'

Harvey's voice shrilled out over the huge store-room, echoing from the rows of tins and the high ceiling. His hands and feet flapped uselessly as the robot arms held him up in the air, six feet above ground. He twisted and wriggled with all his might, but he could not struggle free.

'Help!'

'Be quiet!' Lloyd hissed up at him. 'If you go on yelling, someone will come and find us here. Then we'll be worse off than ever.'

'I *can't* be worse off!' wailed Harvey. 'Ouch! Yerk! Ee-ow!'

Slowly the mechanical arms began to turn him this way and that. One held him steady, firmly gripped, while the other moved methodically over his body.

'What's it doing?' Ingrid said curiously. 'Why is it stroking him?'

'It's not str – spfflt!' Harvey spluttered, as the end of the moving arm tickled his nose. 'It's not stroking me, you stupid lunk-head. It's searching for my bar code.'

Ian looked up. 'I never knew you had one of those.'

'Of course I haven't got one!' snapped Harvey. 'I'm not a tin of baked beans, am I? Not a – aarrgh! yeeow! – not a packet of rice. Why don't you stop making jokes and *get me out of here?*'

'Oh *dear*,' said Mandy. 'Don't get so upset. We'll think of something. You don't suppose it'll put you down, do you? When it's checked all over and not found a bar code?'

'More likely to sound an alarm,' Lloyd said grimly. 'That's what machines do when they come across something they can't sort out. They call a *person*. We've got to get Harvey down before that happens. Can't *you* do something, H?'

'Oh sure,' Harvey said bitterly. The arms had turned him right upside down now. His legs jerked madly, high up in the air, and his face was slowly turning purple. 'What do you want me to do? Turn myself into a packet of lard or a tin of soup?'

'Don't be silly!' Lloyd found it hard to be sympathetic. 'Of course we don't want *that*.'

But Ian's eyes suddenly brightened. 'Yes we *do*,' he said. 'Or something like it. How d'you fancy being a packet of spaghetti, Harvey?'

'Ian!' Mandy shook her head at him. 'Can't you tell that Harvey's really upset? Stop joking.'

'I'm not joking,' drawled Ian. 'I seem to be the only person doing any proper thinking round here. The rest of you are just running round in circles, twittering like a load of starlings. And the answer's obvious. We should have seen it straight away.'

He turned round to the shelf behind him and took a packet of spaghetti off the nearest one.

'Here!' he called up to Harvey. 'Catch this. If the machine wants a bar code, then *give* it a bar code.'

Taking aim carefully, he threw the long packet of spaghetti high into the air. Reaching out a hand, Harvey grabbed at it, just as the arms began to turn him the right way up again. Quickly, understanding what Ian meant, he found the white square with the pattern of thick and thin black lines which was the spaghetti's bar code. Then he held it out towards the end of the moving arm.

Very delicately, the tip of the arm moved backwards and forwards over the bar code, scanning it. Then, having found what it was looking for, at long last, it stopped its restless searching. The two arms held Harvey still and steady, six feet above ground.

'Phew!' breathed Lloyd. 'That was a narrow squeak. I reckon it was just about to sound the alarm.'

'Thanks, Ian.' Harvey rubbed a hand across his eyes. 'I'm glad *one* of you had some sense. I'll be glad to be down on the ground again.'

'On the ground?' Ian raised an eyebrow, looking amused. 'I'm not sure you've quite understood, Harvey. You see –'

But before he could explain, the robot arms began to move again. Instead of putting Harvey down, they began to lift him *up.* Up and up, higher and higher, until he was fifteen feet up in the air, nearly at the ceiling.

'What?' he shrieked. 'Hey! What's going on?'

'I'm afraid,' Ian said mildly, 'that you've just told the machine that you're a packet of spaghetti. And it believes you. So it's going to put you with all the other packets of spaghetti.'

'Oh, of *course*,' murmured Mandy.

'Yes,' said Lloyd. 'That figures.'

Even Ingrid nodded wisely, as though she understood. But Harvey was not comforted. 'What do you *mean*?' His voice floated down to them. 'What's going to happen to me? I want to come *down*!'

'All in good time, my little packet of pasta,' crooned Ian

soothingly. 'Let's get you safely *up* before we worry about getting you *down* again.'

The arms stretched out, carefully moving towards the topmost shelf. All the shelves below were crammed full, but on the top shelf there was a space about three feet wide, next to all the other packets of spaghetti.

'Don't wriggle, Harvey,' Mandy said anxiously, 'or you'll make all the packets tumble down.'

'Never mind the packets,' moaned Harvey. 'What about

me? I feel seasick up here. I feel like a tightrope walker. I feel –'

'Keep *still*!' Lloyd called up. Really, Harvey was making a stupid fuss about nothing.

Carefully, the robot arms pushed and tweaked, until Harvey was placed neatly in the gap on the shelf. When he was settled there, they finally unclamped themselves and reached down for the next thing in the truck. It was a large packet of paper. As soon as its bar code was scanned, the truck set off, trundling at top speed towards the far side of the store-room.

Mandy let out a long sigh of relief. '*Phew!* You were a real genius to think of that, Ian.'

Ian bowed solemnly. 'Don't mention it. Thank you, fans. Just because I look like a brainless hatstand, it doesn't mean I don't have any ideas.'

'Well, how about another one?' came a small miserable voice from high above his head. Ian turned, with Lloyd and Mandy and Ingrid, and peered up towards the ceiling. Harvey's pale, frightened face looked out from between the packets of spaghetti. 'How am I going to get down from here?'

'Can't you climb down the shelves?' Ian said. 'As if they were rungs of a ladder?'

Harvey looked even more frightened. 'They're terribly far apart. Suppose I fell?'

'You'll have to try,' Lloyd said firmly. He was just about to order Harvey to start when he had a better idea. 'Hang on a minute, though. While you're up there, you might as well be useful. Have a look round. What can you see?'

'Much too much!' wailed Harvey. 'I want to come *down*!'

'Come on. It could be useful. Tell us what you can see.'

242

Harvey took a deep breath. 'Right.' He sounded annoyed now. 'I can see baked beans and peas and spaghetti and tins of rice pudding and rolls of paper and stacks of string and light bulbs and floor polish and –'

'Don't be thick!' shouted Lloyd, wishing he could reach Harvey and shake him. 'I don't want a shopping list.'

'But that's what it's like,' said Harvey, in an injured, innocent voice. 'All the way across to the other side. It's a huge store-room. Not just for food, but for all sorts of things. And there are three or four computerized trucks – like the one that caught me – all busy unloading *more* stuff.'

Lloyd wished he were up there himself. It was so frustrating having to explain. 'Can't you see anything *else?*'

Harvey grinned cheekily. 'I can see shelves and the ceiling and the floor and the doors of the lift and –' Then he stopped dead. And suddenly crouched down among the packets of spaghetti. In quite a different voice, he whispered, 'Hide!'

'What?' Lloyd said irritably. 'What are you playing at?'

'I'm not playing.' Harvey's voice was so faint that they could hardly hear it. 'The lift doors are opening. *Hide!*'

Before any of them had a chance to move, they heard a boy's voice, shrill and desperate, coming from the far side of the room.

'Help! Help! Is there anyone there?'

Chapter 12
Only Joking?

This is ridiculous, thought Dinah. *Don't they understand? Don't any of them understand?*

She looked round at all the Brains, searching for one of them, just *one* of them who looked worried. Who might be wondering *why* the Headmaster had given them this peculiar, impossible task. She was certain that what they were trying to do was wrong. The Headmaster did not do things like this for fun.

But no one else seemed troubled at all. All the Brains were crouched over their keyboards, wrestling with the problem. Some of them were juggling with long strings of numbers, working out ingenious codes. Others were inventing complicated patterns of letters, trying to trick the strange computer into giving away some crumb of information about its password. They were all completely absorbed in what they were doing.

They don't think it's real. Suddenly, Dinah understood. They were all so used to playing games with computers, and solving puzzles set for fun, that they did not for one moment think they were trying to break into a *real* computer. They just thought it was another game, that the Headmaster had set up as the final round of the competition. All they were thinking about was winning.

But no one seemed anywhere near doing that. Even from

where she sat, Dinah could see the same word flashing up on screen after screen as the strange computer answered all the attempts to communicate with it.

ERROR

ERROR

ERROR

Camilla looked worse than anyone else, more frustrated and more desperate to solve the puzzle. She was bent forward over her Saladin, thinking so hard that a deep frown ran up between her lovely eyebrows. As she worked, she was twisting the ends of her hair and chewing her fingernails.

Poor Camilla, thought Dinah. *She's not thinking about winning the competition. She's thinking about getting Robert set free.* But she was not having any more success than the other Brains. The computer answered all her efforts with the same one-word snub.

ERROR.

Dinah sighed. She had been looking at the problem herself. Testing out one useless idea after another. But she could not concentrate on it in the same way as everyone else. Because, all the time, the same uncomfortable thoughts niggled away at the back of her mind.

What computer was she trying to get into?

Why did the Headmaster *want* to get into it?

What was he up to?

As she shifted unhappily in her chair, she glanced up at the Headmaster. He was just turning towards her part of the room. Help! It was dangerous to sit here doing nothing. At any moment his eyes would reach her. If she was not working, he would notice her and – and – Dinah switched her Saladin on again and began to tap the keys. Letters flashed up as the strange computer answered her attempt to get in contact.

WHAT DO YOU WANT?

In the last hour, she had used up a lot of energy staring at that question, thinking up clever, complicated answers. Useless answers. Every one of them had got the same reply. Now she did not even try. She just typed in the first thing that came into her head, so that she would look as if she were working.

PLEASE LET ME IN.

No surprises there. She got exactly the response that she expected.

ERROR.

But, out of the corner of her eye, she could see that the Headmaster was still looking in her direction. Head bent, she typed again, industriously.

DON'T BE A MEAN OLD COMPUTER.

That was one good thing about machines. They never got insulted or annoyed. The reply was just as calm as before.

ERROR.

Oh well, Dinah thought. *I can keep this up all day.* The Headmaster would never notice, and she would be able to stop worrying about his plans, because *she* was not going to be helping them. She would just amuse herself.

The idea of tricking him, even a little bit, made her feel a lot more cheerful. She went on looking as solemn as before, her pale face just as earnest as everyone else's, but to match her mood she typed in something silly, as a joke.

KNOCK KNOCK

Then she froze. For a second she could not do anything except stare at the Saladin's screen. At the words which had lettered themselves across it. It was almost impossible to believe, but there it was. This time the computer had given a different reply.

246

The right reply.

WHO'S THERE?

The next line of the joke.

Dinah felt as though an invisible hand had dropped an ice-cream down her neck. There was a slow, cold slither, the length of her spine. Putting out a trembling finger, she typed another word.

DINAH

Instantly, the answer was there.

DINAH WHO?

Was it possible? Was she really going to do it? Half of her mind was screaming, *Stop now, before it's too late!* But the other half would not let her stop. She had to know if she had really solved it.

DYNAMITE – BOOM!

she typed in.

HA HA – THAT WAS FUNNY. TELL US
ANOTHER.

The words flashed across the screen as soon as she had finished.

What had happened? For a moment she hesitated, not quite sure whether she had managed to break into the computer or not. Then she decided that all she could do was carry on, as she had been told to. Obediently, she started another joke.

KNOCK KNOCK
WHO'S THERE?
OWEN
OWEN WHO?
OWEN ARE YOU GOING TO LET ME IN?
HA HA THAT WAS FUNNY. TELL US
ANOTHER.

247

Oh well. Dinah shrugged and began again.

KNOCK KNOCK . . .

After the third joke, she realized what had happened. She had got herself on to a loop. The computer would go on and on, tirelessly giving the same answers however many jokes she told. Unless she managed to hit on the right joke. The one that would get her off the loop.

In spite of where she was, and the fact that she was mixed up in one of the Headmaster's plans, Dinah began to feel excited. She was sure that she was well on the way to solving the problem. The password was a 'knock knock' joke. The only question was – which one? There must be hundreds and hundreds, and she could not think of any way of choosing. She tried

HARRY UP AND LET ME IN

and

POLICE MAY I COME IN

and

MARY CHRISTMAS I'M A CAROLSINGER

and dozens more, but it was no use. The computer replied to each one, very politely, in the same way.

HA HA THAT WAS FUNNY. TELL US ANOTHER.

This is silly, thought Dinah. *I could spend weeks doing it like this.* What she ought to be doing was thinking, trying to work out how she had hit on the right idea in the first place, and seeing if that would help her. Twiddling the end of one skinny plait absent-mindedly, she sat and brooded, forgetting all about the people round her and the nagging voice at the back of her head that had kept telling her not to go on. All her attention was fixed on one question.

What joke would have been chosen by the person who

invented the password? The first stage was deceptively simple, after all. If you wanted to get in, you said 'Knock knock'. It even made a crazy sort of sense. So what else made the same sort of sense? What did you say when you felt as though you would go *mad* if you didn't get off the loop?

Then it came to her. Like magic.

She was absolutely sure that she was right. It had the right feel, somehow. But she could not resist trying it out, just to make certain.

KNOCK KNOCK
WHO'S THERE?

answered the computer.

OLGA
OLGA WHO?

Right. Dinah breathed hard and then typed the answer in, very slowly and carefully.

OLGA MAD IF I DON'T GET OFF THIS LOOP

The effect was so sudden and so startling that she gasped aloud, unable to stop herself. As soon as she had finished, the screen wiped clean and her joke was replaced by a heading and a catalogue of sections. The sight of them filled her with total, paralysing horror.

PRIME MINISTER
PERSONAL INFORMATION
ACCESS TO PM
SECURITY AND PASSWORDS.

She had broken into the Prime Minister's computer. If she wanted to, she could look at all the security arrangements and learn the passwords which would get her in to see the Prime Minister face to face.

And that meant that the *Headmaster* would be able to get in and see the Prime Minister face to face. If he got his hands on the information. The Headmaster would be able to stare directly at the Prime Minister, with his huge, mesmerizing sea-green eyes. And then . . . He must *not* find out that she had solved the puzzle!

But before Dinah could do anything, Camilla, who had heard her gasp, leaned over towards her.

'Goodness Dinah you did sound funny are you sure you're all right you seem very pale and –'

Then she caught sight of the screen of Dinah's Saladin and, before Dinah could stop her or say anything to warn her, she let out a great shriek of delight.

'Oh you're so clever you've *done* it you've *done* it and now we can get Robert back and –'

At the front of the room, the Headmaster turned when he heard her voice. Slowly, he began to walk between the rows, towards Dinah's desk.

Chapter 13

The Prisoner

Lloyd crouched uncomfortably, with his chin jammed against his knees, trying to look like a tin of tomato soup. He had dived for that space, next to all the other tins of tomato soup, because it was the nearest one he could see.

When the strange boy had shouted 'Help!' Lloyd had hesitated for a second, like Ian and Mandy and Ingrid, not quite sure what to do. But before they could dash to the rescue, the shout was choked off with a queer kind of gasp, as though a hand had been jammed against the shouter's mouth. From the top shelf, Harvey had pulled a wide-eyed frightened face, frantically flapping a hand to tell them all to get out of sight. So now Lloyd was squashed in with the tins of soup. It was not a very good hiding place, because someone walking past would have seen him instantly, but it was the best there was. At least the alleys between the shelves would *look* clear if anyone glanced down them.

Across the way, facing Lloyd, was Ian, among a lot of packets of dried peas. Mandy was further down, surrounded by staples and paper clips and rubber bands. And Ingrid had vanished round the corner, to squeeze herself between huge boxes of apples.

They were all breathlessly silent, listening to the voices coming from the far side of the store-room.

'I can hold the boy while you request a rope,' said one man's voice.

It was a curious, dull, lifeless voice. Lloyd frowned, trying to remember where he had heard something like it before, but he could not track the memory down. It was the tone he recognized, not the actual voice.

When the second man spoke, it was in exactly the same tone. 'Is it correct to use the rope? Our information said that the children could be restrained by use of the octopuses.'

'Where the octopuses do not work,' said the first man, 'it is correct to use rope. We are also ordered to leave everything secure when we go off duty this evening. To leave *this* boy secure, we must tie him up.'

'Very well then,' the second man replied. 'I will order a rope.'

In among his tins of tomato soup, Lloyd shuddered. There was something frighteningly cold and unfeeling about the men's voices. And yet – the boy had sounded scared all right. What *was* going on? And how were the men going to *order* a rope?

He should have known the answer to that last question, because he had seen the computerized trolley at work, but he did not remember until a mechanical voice sounded over the store-room.

'Please Remain Beside The Computer Terminal
And What You Have Ordered Will Be Brought
To You.'

Of course! That must be the computer's voice, the same voice they had all heard outside the tower. And the trolleys were used to fetch things out of store as well as to stack them away.

Anxiously, Lloyd looked round to see if the rope was anywhere near them. He did not like the idea of seeing another trolley bearing down on him. But he could not see any rope and, after a moment or two, there was a faint hiss of wheels on the far side of the room.

'I have the rope,' said the second man. (What *was* it about their voices?)

'Very good,' the first man answered. 'Help me get the boy back into the lift and then we will take him upstairs to the Restraint Room.'

Whatever the Restraint Room was, it was obvious that the boy did not like the sound of it. Lloyd heard scuffling noises, and the boy must have got free for a second, because there was a clatter of running feet and shouts echoed down the aisles of shelves.

'The Computer Director is dangerous! He is evil! No one is free and – aargh!'

Heavier feet rattled after him and his words were interrupted by an anguished scream. Then the scream, in its turn, was cut short. Cautiously, Lloyd peered out from his shelf, up the alley, driven nearly mad by not being able to see anything.

At the far end of the alley, three figures were struggling. Two men in white coats were trying to get a grip on a boy of about Lloyd's age. A boy with curly chestnut hair, who was fighting wildly to escape.

But before Lloyd could call the others, or decide whether they should attempt a rescue, the men got the upper hand. Wrenching the boy's arms unmercifully behind his back, they dragged him off up the aisle. A moment later, Lloyd distinctly heard the smooth, sliding sound of the lift doors closing and the hiss of the lift moving away. He gave them a second to get clear and then called softly to Harvey.

'OK?'

'I think so.' Harvey looked almost green as he peeped

253

over the edge of the top shelf. 'It was terrible. They *hurt* him. They pulled his arms and jerked his head back and –'

'And did you hear what they *said*? came Ingrid's triumphant voice. She strolled round the corner, eating an apple and looking pleased with herself. 'Did you hear them talking about the octopuses? It's just like I said. The whole place is riddled with those beastly octopuses. All the way up from the helicopter and –'

'Ingrid,' Lloyd only just managed to stop himself from shouting. 'Will you please *shut up about that wretched helicopter*! We've got enough problems, without you driving us all mad.'

'Please yourself,' sniffed Ingrid. She turned her back on the others and crunched loudly at her apple.

Harvey did not even seem to have heard her. He was still talking about the men, babbling on and on in a nervous, shocked voice. 'And the worst part about it was that they weren't angry. They just hurt him mechanically, like robots. That's what this whole building is, you know. A giant robot, all controlled by a computer. And the computer's controlled by the Computer Director. And you heard what that boy said about the Computer Director –'

His voice rose higher and higher as he spoke, and Ian nudged Lloyd. 'What are we going to *do?*' he murmured anxiously. 'We've got to get him down fast. And he's not in any state to climb.'

Lloyd thought for a moment. 'Ropes,' he said briskly. 'If those men could get ropes out of the store, so can we.

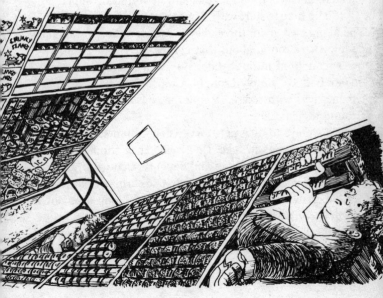

255

They'll help Harvey get down safely. *If* we can find them. I don't think we ought to risk trying to use the computer.'

'I don't think we *need* to use the computer,' said Mandy. She took a step backwards, so that she could see the top shelf better, and called gently upwards. 'Harvey! Did you see where the trolley went, to get the rope for the men?'

Harvey nodded nervously. 'It was a great long rope and they're going to tie him up with it and –'

'And we're going to help him,' Mandy said soothingly. 'We'll get him free, don't you worry. But we've got to get you down first. If Ian and I go off to look for ropes, do you think you can watch us and tell us which way to go?'

The unhurried steadiness of her voice seemed to have an effect on Harvey. He knelt up on the top shelf, ready to watch, and when he spoke again, he sounded calmer.

'Go up here to start with. That's right . . . now turn left . . . go along past about three alleys . . . turn right . . . should be somewhere round about that corner.'

A couple of minutes later, Ian and Mandy were back. They had not simply brought a rope. They had garlanded themselves with ropes, looping the coils on both arms and round their necks.

'This one's to help get Harvey down,' Ian said, 'and the others are for us to take. One each. They should come in useful if we have to go up and down that chute any more.'

'I know it's like stealing,' Mandy said earnestly, 'but we're only borrowing them. And – it's an awful long drop down to that car park.'

'I think we should take everything we can!' Ingrid said fiercely, turning round at last. 'It all belongs to the Computer Director, doesn't it? And he's just as bad as I said he was. I warned you –'

Lloyd gritted his teeth. 'Ingrid, will you *shut up!*' He wished he could gag her. 'Stop wasting time and let's start by getting Harvey down.'

Reaching for the neat coil of nylon rope that Ian was holding out to him, he stepped back, ready to throw it up to the top shelf. 'Watch out, Harvey! It's coming!'

It was the sort of thing that always looked very easy on television. When people threw ropes in plays, they landed exactly in the right place, in reach of the person who was waiting. But it took Lloyd seven attempts. Twice Harvey nearly fell off the shelf and once the rope sailed right over the top and landed in the next alley.

But at last it was done. Harvey held the coil of rope in his hand. For a moment he stared stupidly at it, as though he could not guess what he should be doing with it. Then he got the idea. Wriggling his way along the shelf until he reached one of the upright supports, he began to knot one end of the rope round it.

'Mind you tie it tightly,' called Mandy in an anxious voice.

Harvey nodded and tested his knot carefully by tugging at the rope before he started to climb down. It did not take long. In a few seconds, he was standing on the ground beside the others.

'Petrified pancakes!' he whistled. 'That was really awful. I feel like a jelly in a jungle.'

'Don't be so *feeble*,' Ingrid said scornfully. 'You ought to be pleased. Now we've got the ropes, we'll soon be out of this place and –'

'What did you say?' Lloyd stared at her.

'Well – we must get out of here, mustn't we?' Ingrid gave a defiant toss of her head. 'You heard what sort of thing was going on. With those men around, we're in *danger*.'

'Oh *Ing*!' Mandy said. 'What about Dinah?'

Ian walked slowly round Ingrid looking her up and down. 'You really are a prize specimen, aren't you? You ought to be in a museum. Labelled *Selfish Little Creep*.'

Ingrid tossed her head again. 'I'm not a creep. And I *do* care about Dinah. But what's the use of staying in this horrible, dangerous building, climbing up and down the rubbish chute? We haven't found Dinah yet. We haven't done anything useful at all. I think we should get out and call the police.'

'But what would we tell the police?' Mandy said gently. 'We saw that boy being taken off, but we don't know why. And that's all we've seen. If we start telling the police, they'll probably arrest *us*. For illegal entry and trespassing and stealing ropes and –'

'I think it's *stupid* to go on,' said Ingrid, pulling a stubborn face. 'Ask Harvey. *He* knows. He watched the men knocking that boy around.'

They all turned to look at Harvey. He was still very white and shaken. Mandy put a hand on his arm.

'What do you think? *Could* you bear to go on?'

'It was *foul*,' Harvey said softly. 'It scared me silly watching the way that boy was treated. There's something really *bad* going on in here.'

'You see?' Ingrid put her hands on her hips and looked triumphantly round at them all. 'Harvey agrees with me.'

But Harvey shook his head. 'No, you've got it wrong, Ing. What I said is not a reason for going back. It's a reason for going *on*. We've got to save Dinah, and we've got to *rescue that boy*. Come on, let's get started.'

Picking up one of the coils of rope, he looped it over his shoulder and began to walk towards the rubbish chute.

Chapter 14

'The Prime Minister's Brain'

The Headmaster strode down the room towards Dinah. He seemed to tower taller and taller, like a nightmare. She could not move an inch. As if she *were* in a dream, she was paralysed by the thought of what would happen next.

But none of her terror could have shown on her face, because Camilla went on congratulating her in the same happy, relieved voice.

'– you're *brilliant*, Dinah, you really deserve to be the Junior Computer Brain and I know it's silly to be worrying about Robert, because he's sure to be all right but I'm so pleased you've done it and he can come back and –'

And the Headmaster can get on with his plans, whatever they are, thought Dinah. Fear was making her stupid. She could see the tall figure getting nearer and nearer and she could see the precious, secret information on the screen of her Saladin, but it was not until the Headmaster was almost at her desk that she realized what she ought to be doing. A very simple, obvious thing.

Jerking forward in her seat, she tapped quickly at her Saladin's keyboard, ordering it to disconnect and to wipe everything she had just done off its screen and out of its memory. Just in time, as the Headmaster stopped beside her, the screen went blank.

'Dinah?' Camilla said, sounding puzzled.

Dinah sat back calmly, folding her hands together, and waited to see what the Headmaster would do. For a second he did not speak. He stood very very still and stared down at her through his pebbly glasses, without any expression. She kept just as still, not watching him but gazing down at her fingers.

'Well, well,' he murmured at last. 'Clever Little Dinah Glass. How did you get in here? The computer was programmed to keep out anyone called Glass.'

Dinah did not look up. 'I'm called Dinah Hunter now,' she said, in a level, matter-of-fact voice. 'The Hunters adopted me.'

'Extraordinary.' The Headmaster raised his eyebrows. 'People waste so much energy on totally pointless actions. Well, Miss Dinah *Hunter*, what was all the noise about? Am I to understand that you have solved my little problem?' He glanced at her blank screen. 'Apparently not.'

'Oh but she has she has,' Camilla said eagerly, 'I saw the heading on her screen it said Prime Minister Personal Information and that's right isn't it that's what we were supposed to be doing –'

The Headmaster's eyes were suddenly alert. 'So you *have* found the password. I must congratulate you. When I ran a projected feasibility study on the Super-Saladin I worked out that the odds were that *one* of you would discover the password. But not for three days. You have been very quick.' His voice sharpened. 'So – why is your screen blank?'

'Because I'm not going to let *you* get at the Prime Minister's personal information.' Dinah jumped to her feet and looked round the room. All the Brains had stopped working. They were staring in her direction, wondering what the disturbance was about. Raising her voice, Dinah shouted so that they could all hear. 'Listen, everyone, I know what's been going on. We've been trying to break into the Prime Minister's computer. And it's not a game. It's *real*!'

There was an awed gasp and then total silence as they all waited to hear what she would say next. Quickly, she gathered her thoughts. It was no use beginning on a long tale about what the Headmaster had done before. She needed to get the Brains on her side. Quickly.

261

'I have just discovered the password that the Computer Director wants,' she shouted. 'But that password means *power*. I don't think we should give anyone power like that without knowing why he wants it. I think we should ask the Director to explain what he's up to!'

A rumble of agreement came from all over the room. All the Brains sat back and folded their arms. The message was clear. They were stopping work until they discovered what was going on.

An irritated frown crossed the Headmaster's face, but he did not get angry. Instead, he glanced round the room and then began to make a speech, in a calm, reasonable tone.

'All of you must often have thought how badly this country is run. Money not shared equally among people. Parents bringing up their children on junk food and letting them roam the streets. Inefficiency, strikes, waste. Doesn't it all worry you?'

Heads nodded in every part of the room.

'And haven't you ever thought,' the Headmaster went on, 'that everything could be much better run by one man – one man who cared more about efficiency and order than about his own wealth or comfort?'

Some heads nodded again. Not as many, but still quite a few.

'*I* am that man.' The Headmaster said it quite simply. 'Ask this girl who knows me.' He turned to Dinah. 'Do you deny that I am extraordinarily efficient?'

'No, of course not,' said Dinah, 'but –'

He swept on, not letting her add anything. 'And am I concerned with making money for myself?'

'No,' Dinah said reluctantly, 'I don't think you are, but –'

Interrupting her again before she had finished, he turned

back to face the rest of the room. 'You have heard what sort of man I am. Now I am glad to tell you that I have prepared a vast, efficient scheme for running this country properly. It is stored on discs in this very building occupying several floors, and it will be run by the Super-Saladin. Once it is in operation, this will be the most disciplined, orderly country in the world.'

'But even supposing all that's true,' Dinah finally managed to say, '*what's it got to do with the Prime Minister's computer?*'

There was a tiny, tense pause. All the Brains were alert. This was the question they all wanted answered.

'It is difficult to make people be sensible,' the Headmaster said at last. 'They waste time being stubborn and arguing. Claiming they have a right to choose what happens. My plan will cut out all that wasteful choice. Once I have spent an hour or so with the Prime Minister, my scheme will be the *only* choice that people have.'

Bess rubbed her forehead. 'It all sounds rather miserable,' she said timidly. 'I *like* to choose. I like to choose my clothes and my books and presents for my family and –'

'All completely wasteful,' the Headmaster interrupted sharply. 'Once my scheme is in operation, you will wear the clothes you are issued and read the textbooks which will teach you what you need to learn. Presents and other books are simply a distraction from work.'

There was a horrified gasp as people started to understand just what kind of country he was planning. Then Camilla spoke, sounding puzzled.

'But what I don't see is how you're going to persuade the Prime Minister because however good your arguments are and however much time you have to explain, Prime

Ministers always have their own ideas don't they and they can't just swap over –'

'He won't be trying to persuade anyone,' Dinah said. Suddenly she felt very tired and afraid. 'He doesn't need to *persuade*. He can hypnotize people – almost everyone – and make them do exactly what he wants. I don't suppose the Prime Minister's any different.' She could see from the doubtful faces round the room that the Brains did not believe her. Banging the desk with her fist, she spoke more fiercely. 'Don't you understand what we've been doing? We haven't just been finding him a way into the Prime Minister's computer. We haven't just been finding him a way into Number Ten Downing Street, even. *We've been finding him a way into the Prime Minister's brain!*'

'You seem to have grown very excitable,' the Headmaster said. 'But now you have finished ranting, perhaps you will give me the password you have discovered. I'm sure you can remember it, even though you may have wiped it off your computer.'

Dinah gaped. 'You're mad! Do you really think I'm going to tell you? Do you think I'm going to have anything to do with your plans for turning people into robots?'

The Headmaster's lips pinched together impatiently. His face was stern and motionless. But when he spoke again he sounded surprisingly smooth. Almost kind.

'Wouldn't you like to think again?' he said softly. 'It's always a mistake to take important decisions in a hurry, and you have had a very exhausting day.'

Dinah had expected him to start shouting at her. For a moment she did not understand why he was so gentle.

'I've tired you all out, I'm afraid,' crooned the Headmaster. 'You must be feeling very weary, very sleepy . . .'

Dinah was nearly taken in. She nearly relaxed, thinking that the worst of the danger was past. Then, just in time, she noticed the Headmaster's hand, which was moving slowly up towards his face as he spoke. Ready to take off his glasses. Ready to uncover his eyes.

His eyes! In the split second before they gazed into hers, Dinah understood what the Headmaster was up to. Once he was staring straight at her, with those huge, extraordinary sea-green eyes, he would be able to hypnotize her. He had done it often enough before for her to know that she had no chance of resisting. Once she looked into his eyes she would be lost, and he would be able to get her to do anything. Even tell him the password.

Just in time, she screwed up her eyes, shutting them so tightly that she could not see anything except the lights that danced in the blackness behind her eyelids.

The Headmaster's voice stopped for a moment. Then he said, 'Open your eyes, Dinah.'

'I *won't*!' Dinah said defiantly, clenching her fists and flinging her head up. 'I know you want to hypnotize me, but I won't open my eyes, and then you can't.'

He drew his breath in sharply, irritated. 'What a tiresome girl you are.'

'You can't make me open my eyes,' Dinah said more quietly. 'Can you?'

There was no answer.

That was more unnerving than any bullying. It was torture not to be able to see what the Headmaster was doing. But she was not going to let herself get caught by something as simple as that. *It's only a trick*, she told herself severely. *Don't be fooled.*

Even so, it was very dark and lonely standing there with

her eyes shut. What could she do next? Could she trust Camilla to tell her when the Headmaster had gone – or was Camilla too concerned about Robert? Would Bess –?'

And then Bess screamed. A high, shrill shriek of pain and terror. The sort of noise that cannot be faked. Automatically, Dinah's eyelids flew up. There was no way that she could have stopped them.

'Bess, are you all right –?'

But the second her eyes opened, she found herself staring into the Headmaster's wide green ones. He gave a satisfied smile, dropped Bess's arm, which he had been twisting cruelly behind her back, and began to murmur at Dinah.

'Interesting that you should be so concerned about your friend – when you're so tired. So tired and sleepy that you can hardly hold up your head. Look into my eyes and feel the sleepiness washing over you . . .'

Dinah felt that she was sinking into the depths of the green eyes. Deeper and deeper and deeper. Until, gradually, her eyes clouded over and her mind blanked out.

Chapter 15

The Restraint Room

'Dear Mum, I am having a really lovely time in London.'

Ingrid's sarcastic voice floated up through the darkness of the rubbish chute. Wedged uncomfortably between the narrow walls, Lloyd looked down and frowned. 'Ssh!'

But she did not take any notice of him. Just went on muttering in the same cross voice, still making up her imaginary letter.

'You will want to know what we have been doing. Well, we have spent most of our time so far climbing up a dustbin and wriggling up a rubbish chute. Now we are so high that Lloyd has made us rope ourselves together for safety. *Just like a holiday in the Alps.*'

'*Ingrid!*' Lloyd hissed. 'Be quiet! Someone's bound to hear.'

'Huh!' snorted Ingrid. 'Fat chance of that. I don't think there's anyone left in the building except us.'

Somewhere even further below, there was a mutter of agreement from Harvey. They had climbed and squirmed their way so far up the chute that they had lost count of how many floors they had passed but all they had found was one empty room after another. Strange, cold rooms, lined with metal cabinets or filled with shelves of discs.

'This can't *all* be to do with the computer, can it?' Mandy had muttered after the fourth or fifth floor like that. 'It must be *massive* if it needs all this space and all these discs.'

But there had been no one to answer her. The others just grunted and went on climbing, feeling more and more as though they had got tangled up in the workings of a machine. A spotless, gleaming, huge machine, perfect in every way – and completely inhuman.

They were all getting very tired. Wriggling their way up and down the chute made them use all kinds of strange muscles and they ached in unexpected places.

It's dangerous, Lloyd kept thinking. He had made them rope themselves together, but even so he could not forget the drop beneath them. If they went on like this, sooner or later someone was bound to slip, simply from exhaustion. Already Harvey and Ingrid were getting irritable, and that meant they would be getting careless.

Then, immediately behind him, Mandy sighed. Lloyd was sure that she had not meant him to hear. Mandy never complained about being uncomfortable. But it was a very weary sigh and at the sound of it, Lloyd made up his mind.

'We'll climb out of here at the next floor,' he called softly downwards. 'Whatever there is there, we'll stop for a bit, because we all need a rest. But please *shut up* until then.'

He knew he had made the right decision, because no one attempted to argue. They all whispered 'OK' and went on silently following him up the chute.

It was only another few feet to the next opening. Lloyd squirmed towards it until his head was level with the flap and then pushed it open a crack, so that he could see what was on the other side.

He was so surprised that he nearly lost his grip and slithered all the way down into the dustbin. Because there, on the other side of the flap, not ten feet away, was the boy who had shouted and struggled in the store-room.

He could not shout or struggle now. He was sitting in a chair, tied round and round with rope so that he could not possibly move. A tight, painful gag was strained across his mouth and Lloyd could see a red mark where it had rubbed his cheek sore.

But the really strange thing was his eyes. They were tightly closed, screwed up until they almost disappeared in a tangle of creases. And his head was twisted sideways, awkwardly and uncomfortably. Instead of facing forwards – away to Lloyd's right – he was forcing his neck round so that his face was towards the opening of the rubbish chute. It was as though he was trying not to look at something.

Lloyd hissed, very very softly, to attract his attention. Slowly and cautiously, the boy opened his eyes. And opened them even wider when he saw Lloyd's face, peering round the edge of the flap.

Lloyd pointed at himself and then out at the room, raising his eyebrows to signal *Can I come in?* Instantly, the boy pulled a sharp warning face and shook his head very slightly. The message was clear. It was not safe to come through the flap.

So – what could they all do? While Lloyd was wondering, hesitating where he was, he heard voices coming from the room. Even though the speakers were out of sight, he recognized the dull, lifeless sound of the men in white coats.

'Are both the boys secure?' said one.

'They are,' said another. 'We can leave them like this.'

'Very good,' said the first speaker. 'Then our instructions are to go off duty, as usual. The Director does not require any of us here after half past five.'

'And we report tomorrow, as always, at eight o'clock?'

'That is correct.'

Feet walked across the room, still out of sight, and then Lloyd heard the sound of the lift doors closing and the hiss of the lift going down. This time he did not need to signal to the boy who was tied up. Once the lift was gone, the boy nodded and grunted at him, clearly meaning, *You can come in now.*

Gripping the edge of the opening hard with both hands, Lloyd kicked with his feet against the opposite wall of the chute and pushed himself backwards through the flap. He

landed with a bump on the floor, picked himself up and began to hurry over to the strange boy, ready to untie him.

He had only taken a couple of steps when he realized that there was another person in the room. Another boy, of about the same age. But he was not tied up. He was simply sitting in a chair, staring with a blank face straight in front of him. In the very direction that the other boy seemed to be trying to avoid.

Curiously, Lloyd glanced round, to see what there was in that direction. He was vaguely aware that the first boy was shaking his head and grunting frantically, but he did not take any notice. After all, he had already been told that the room was safe. What could be the harm in looking at something?

On the far wall was a big screen, about five foot square. When he saw it, Lloyd gave a smile of pleasure and re-cognition. Because the green designs that swirled across it were very familiar. Only they were even better than the ones he had seen before. This time there were *two* octopuses curling and weaving and twining. That was worth a second look! In a moment, he would untie the prisoner, but first he must watch the curves and arcs and twists and . . .

Octopus – s – s – s – s!

By the time Ingrid and Harvey reached the opening, it was almost impossible to get out of the chute. Lloyd and Mandy and Ian were all standing just by the flap, perfectly still and silent, staring towards the right-hand wall.

Ingrid came first. She did not waste time arguing. She simply shoved hard at their legs.

'Why don't you shift, you great ugly lumps? Have you gone blind and deaf as well as thick?'

They didn't answer her back, which was peculiar. They simply moved sideways, where she pushed them, and went

271

on staring. Ingrid scrambled out of the chute, glanced round to see what they were gazing at, and gave a loud sniff.

'Harvey, you're never going to believe this,' she called. 'Come and see. It's *pathetic*.'

Harvey had kept close behind her, because he did not fancy being the only one left in the dark. As he climbed out and looked where Ingrid was pointing, he shuddered.

'*More* octopuses! I don't like it, Ing.'

'*I* think it's stupid,' Ingrid said firmly. 'Fancy gawping at them like that, instead of untying that poor boy. Here, Mandy, what do you think you're doing?'

'Mmm?' Mandy turned towards her with a sweet, vague smile and then turned back to stare at the octopuses before she had time to answer.

'You see why I don't like it,' Harvey said miserably. 'Those octopuses really make them go peculiar.'

'Well, *I'm* not putting up with it,' Ingrid said stoutly. Marching over to the screen, she bent and switched off the plug underneath it. The octopus pictures vanished immediately and Lloyd and Ian and Mandy blinked, looking around as though they had just woken from a deep sleep.

'Wha – at? Where am I? How did I get here?' The boy who had been sitting staring at the screen shook his head from side to side and then stood up, gazing at the others with a dazed expression. 'What's going on?'

'There's only one person who looks as if he's got any sense round here,' Ingrid said. 'Why don't we get him untied and ask *him*?'

'Oh, of *course*! Oh, you poor *thing*!' With a horrified gasp, Mandy ran across the room towards the boy who was tied up. 'How *can* we have been so awful? Fancy stopping to watch octopuses while you were still roped up.'

'Not your fault,' croaked the boy hoarsely, as soon as she had loosened the gag. 'It's those octopuses. All I could do not to look at them myself. It seems we're all addicted to them. I think they must echo our brain patterns in some way. And the Computer Director is using them to keep people under control.'

'You *see?*' Ingrid burst out triumphantly. 'It's just what I've been telling you all the time. Ever since we saw –'

'Ingrid,' Lloyd said dangerously, 'if you *mention* that helicopter again, I'll lynch you.' He glared at her until she stopped. It was bad enough having to be rescued by her, without having her going on about how brilliant she was. When she was quite quiet, he turned back to the boy. Mandy had untied him completely now and she was rubbing at his sore wrists. 'Are you one of the Brains?'

'One of the *what?*' The boy grinned. 'Oh, you mean am I in the competition. Yes. My name's Robert Jefferies.'

'I'm Doug Grant,' muttered the other boy, still looking dopey and confused.

Lloyd decided that Robert was the only one likely to answer his questions. 'What's going on in this building?' he said urgently. 'There's something wrong, isn't there? And have you seen our sister, Dinah Hunter?'

'Oh, you're *Dinah's* brother.' Robert looked surprised. And then very pleased. 'Well, if you're *her* brother, *you* should be able to tell *me* what's going on. You probably know more about it than I do.'

'We don't know anything about anything,' murmured Ian. 'Except the inside of the rubbish chute. We're experts on *that*.'

Robert frowned. 'Well, Dinah seemed to. She said that she knew the Computer Director before she came here.'

'*Knew* him?' Lloyd looked puzzled. 'She never told us that.'

'I'm sure that's what she said. Something about how he used to be your headmaster.'

For a moment there was a frozen, appalled silence. Then Mandy said, in a shaky voice, 'The Headmaster?'

'Well, well, well.' Ian gave a low whistle. 'No wonder he's so good at mesmerizing people with octopuses. That's just his sort of thing.'

Harvey shuddered and sidled up to his brother and even Ingrid looked taken aback. They were all staring at Lloyd, waiting for him to make a plan, to tell them how to deal with this new shock.

But all Lloyd could feel was a terrible rage, so great that his brain would not function. The *Headmaster*! The Headmaster had set up this whole competition and used the octopuses to keep people quiet. And *he* had been caught by them. Him! Lloyd Hunter, who was immune to being hypnotized. Who had set up SPLAT as a resistance group and used it to defeat the Headmaster once before. He had been fooled and drugged with octopus patterns just like any – any stupid *Brain*. It was almost too humiliating to think about.

But there they were, still looking at him and waiting. Even Robert, who hardly knew him, was listening for what he would say. Unless he *did* organize them, they would never get down to anything – and the Headmaster would triumph. Squashing down his black, blinding fury, Lloyd took a deep breath and began to give orders.

'Right then. Now we know who we're facing – and we know how he's been keeping everyone quiet with octopus patterns. Whatever the Headmaster's plotting, it *can't* be good. It's our duty to defeat him and rescue the Brains. So we'll have to be double careful. *And not look at any octopuses!* He turned to look at Robert and Doug. 'Are you two coming with us?'

'Of course.' Robert nodded vigorously and, after a second's hesitation, Doug copied him, as though he were more afraid of being left on his own than of following.

It took some time to rope everyone up and to explain to Robert and Doug exactly how to climb up the chute, but in the end they set off again on the upward journey that seemed endless. This time, with seven of them, progress was even slower than ever, but Lloyd did not have to remind anyone to be quiet. All the SPLAT members were shaken by what they had just found out and Robert and Doug knew, only too well, what the Computer Director was like. So they were all silent, making no sound except the slow shuffle of feet against the wall and the occasional soft grunt as people heaved their backs upward in the dark.

And that was why Lloyd was able to hear Dinah's voice so clearly. It came floating down from above them, sounding flat and strange.

'Knock knock.'

Harvey gave a small squeak and Lloyd sshhed him as loudly as he dared. The next moment he nearly squeaked himself, when he heard the voice that answered Dinah.

'Who's there?'

The Headmaster's voice. But – was it possible? Dinah seemed to be telling him a joke. A *joke?* Lloyd felt as though he had gone mad. He tugged gently at the rope, signalling to the others to stop climbing. He wanted to think before he did anything else. To try and make some sense out of what he was hearing.

Dinah's voice came again. 'Olga.' Still in the same expressionless, mechanical tone. Like the voices of the two men in the store-room and the men in the Restraint Room. Like – Lloyd was still groping in his memory for what those voices meant.

'Olga who?' said the Headmaster.

Then Lloyd got it. Hypnotism! The Headmaster had hypnotized Dinah, to make her do what he wanted. And he had hypnotized the men in white coats. Just as he had hypnotized almost everyone in the school when he was there. That was why Dinah was speaking in such a dull, level voice. She was in a trance.

But why should the Headmaster hypnotize her and then make her tell *jokes*?

Everything seemed even crazier than before.

Chapter 16

The Computer Director's Triumph

'You can wake up now.' The Headmaster's voice broke into Dinah's sleep and she woke instantly.

As soon as her eyelids opened, she knew what had happened, even though she could not remember anything. It was obvious from the triumph on the Headmaster's face and from the bewildered stares of the Brains. One moment they had been listening to Dinah defying the Headmaster and shouting about the wickedness of his plans. The next moment, they must have heard her helping him. Telling him the password to the Prime Minister's computer. No wonder they were puzzled.

She had opened the way for him to go ahead with his plans.

Dinah felt as though she wanted to stand up and shout across the room. *It wasn't my fault. I was hypnotized. He's always been able to hypnotize me.* AND THAT'S WHAT HE'S GOING TO DO TO THE PRIME MINISTER! She longed to make the Brains understand that she was not to blame.

But there was no time for that. Not a second to spare on her own selfish feelings. She had to work out if there was anything she could *do*.

Looking up at the Headmaster, she spoke in a small, tight voice. 'What have you done?'

'I have prepared the way,' he said calmly. 'My name and my description have been added to the list of people with security clearance for emergencies. The people who *must* be let in to see the Prime Minister, if they give the right password for the day. And I have learnt today's password – *Disraeli.* All I have to do now is travel to Downing Street. So you can stop trying to think of a way to interfere with my plans. There is nothing you can do now.'

He glanced around the room, to make sure that all the Brains had heard him and understood. Then he began to turn away, to go back up to the front of the room.

But, while he was speaking, Dinah had glimpsed a movement, over his shoulder. A quiet, stealthy movement up at the front. The first time she saw it, she could hardly believe her eyes, but there it was.

At the front of the room, next to the Saladin's main terminal and printer, was a rubbish chute with a flap across the opening. As Dinah watched, the flap was pushed up and a head emerged, followed by a body and a pair of legs. The figure crawled cautiously out, crept a little way across the room and ducked down behind the printer.

It was Lloyd.

Dinah had to use all her self-control to stop herself squealing with surprise. *I mustn't give him away,* she thought frantically. But what could she do? Already another head – Mandy's – was sticking out from under the flap. If the Headmaster turned round, he was sure to see the movements. And if he captured all the other members of S P L A T, that would be the end of everything.

Thinking quickly, Dinah reached out and grabbed at his sleeve, desperate to keep his attention on her.

'Look,' she said loudly, 'I don't just think your plans are wicked. I think they're stupid and inefficient. You've wasted all your energy planning this competition and setting up a gigantic computer program – and it will all be for nothing.'

'*What?*' Outraged, the Headmaster turned back to stare at her. 'You are talking nonsense.'

'No I'm not!' Dinah said. *Louder*, she thought. *I have to talk as loudly as I can, to drown any noises from the front.* She raised her voice until she was almost shouting and forced herself not to glance over his shoulder. 'You say you're going to take control of the Prime Minister's brain. And I'm sure you can do it. But what's the *point?* The Prime Minister's not all-powerful in this country.'

She could feel her voice giving out, beginning to croak with the strain of speaking so loudly and for a moment she wavered. Instantly, Bess picked up the argument. Had *she* seen the people crawling out of the rubbish chute as well?

'That's right!' she said, in a high, shrill tone. 'We're a *democracy*. The Prime Minister's not a dictator.'

Far away, at the front of the room, Ian and Ingrid and Harvey had all clambered out of the chute and hidden behind various cabinets. Somehow, without looking directly, Dinah was aware of them. And now she saw yet *another* head. Robert's! She was so pleased and relieved that she burst in as soon as Bess had finished, not waiting for the Headmaster to answer.

'*Please* change your mind. It's really not worth all the trouble, just for one measly Prime Minister and there must be lots of other ways to get power, if that's what you want. You could –'

'*Silence!*' The Headmaster was icy with anger. 'How dare you argue with me? You are only showing your own stupidity in failing to understand the full scope of my plans.'

'Tell us then!' yelled Bess.

'Yes!' shouted Dinah. *Tell us, and then you'll keep looking this way.*

'The Prime Minister is only a stepping stone,' the Headmaster said scornfully. 'Oh, I shan't have any trouble getting my own way with the Cabinet and the government. Not once I have been appointed the Prime Minister's valued adviser, present at all meetings.'

Present at all meetings. Dinah felt her face grow pale as she imagined it. The Headmaster looking round the Cabinet Room. Staring into the eyes of all the Cabinet Ministers and murmuring, 'You are feeling sleepy. Very, very sleepy . . .' The Headmaster in the House of Commons itself, gazing up and down the long benches with his huge green eyes, until the clamour of MPs' voices grew still and there was silence over the whole Chamber. Oh, he could do it, she had no doubt of that. She shuddered.

'But that is only the beginning,' the Headmaster said triumphantly. 'Because the Prime Minister's trusted adviser will travel all over the world, of course. To summit meetings and international conferences. I shall be able to meet all the major world leaders face to face. Or *eyeball to eyeball*, as people say now.' He smiled thinly and Dinah realized, with a sort of horror, that he was so exultant that he had actually made a joke.

'But you mean you're actually going to hypnotize all the world leaders and take over everything that's mad you can't mean it,' Camilla said desperately, 'how can you think you know best about the whole world –?'

'Of *course* I know best,' the Headmaster said scornfully. 'And soon everyone will realize that I do. Nothing will be able to stop me once I have taken control of the Prime

Minister's brain. And I shall have that within the next two hours.'

Ignoring Camilla's moan and Bess's white face and the gasps of the other Brains, he turned firmly away and began to stride up the room towards the main controls of the Saladin. Everything at that end of the room was still now. Dinah was sure that, if she had not seen the figures creeping about and hiding behind the cabinets, she would never have guessed that they were there. Certainly the Headmaster did not guess. He began to tap away at the main keyboard.

'We've got to stop him,' Camilla hissed across at Bess and Dinah, 'it would be terrible if he succeeded but is he telling the truth can he really do it –?'

'You saw what he did to me,' Dinah muttered miserably. 'He doesn't fail with many people – and what could those few do against all the rest?'

'– but that would be like the end of the world we've got to stop him somehow but I can't see –'

'Well,' whispered Bess timidly, 'why don't we start with that security list he's put himself on? If he leaves us here when he goes off, we could take his name *off* again – and add in a warning to show them their security has been broken. After all, *we* know how to get into the Prime Minister's computer as well as he does.'

'You're right!' Dinah hissed. She gave Bess a friendly grin. 'We'll try that if we get a chance.'

The Headmaster could not have heard what they were saying, but when he had finished what he was doing on the keyboard at the front, he looked up and spoke to the whole room.

'In a minute I shall leave you. But do not suppose that you will be able to interfere with my plans while I am gone.

Or that you will be able to use the lift to escape from the building. To do either of those things, you would need to use the Saladin – and I have set it on Automatic Booby Trap.'

For a moment, no one dared to speak. Then a nervous voice from the back of the room said, 'What's Automatic Booby Trap?'

The Headmaster smiled his thin, unpleasant smile. 'It is a wise precaution that I have built into the machine. Any attempt to use the Saladin now will short a special electric circuit and start a fire.' His smile grew even thinner and nastier. 'The fire will be in the lift, just to make sure that your escape is cut off. As you know, there are no stairs – no other way of getting down from here.'

'You mean,' the nervous voice said, 'that if we try to tamper with the Saladin – we'll all die?'

The Headmaster nodded. 'It would be slow and very painful. And no one would be able to save you, because all my staff have now gone home and no one else will guess that you are here.'

'That's monstrous,' shouted Camilla, 'do you really mean to say that you would burn all these children to death just because –?'

'*No one* will burn to death,' said the Headmaster firmly, 'because no one will dare to interfere with my plans. It would be senseless. You will all simply stay here until I have time to make further arrangements for you. There is a good stock of food in the store-rooms and the Saladin is programmed to provide you with regular meals in this room. You will all be perfectly safe. *As long as you obey my orders.*'

As he was speaking, Dinah became aware of a peculiar whirring noise outside the building. It grew louder and

282

louder, closer and closer, coming up from the ground. As the Headmaster finished talking, it was directly above them. Then the voice of the Super-Saladin sounded.

'Your Helicopter Is Overhead. Please Select Route Program And Press 'O' To Open Roof Doors.'

'Goodbye,' said the Headmaster. 'Next time I see you, we shall be living in a country that is being run *efficiently*. The beginning of a new, efficient world. All you have to do is wait. And I have given you something to help pass the time.'

He reached out and tapped at the Saladin's keyboard. Immediately, the huge panels of the ceiling slid apart, letting in a blast of warm air. For the first time, Dinah realized that they were at the very top of the building, with nothing above them except blue sky. Hundreds of feet up in the air.

In the very centre of the patch of blue sky above them, a small single-seater helicopter was hovering. It was completely empty. As they watched, a rope ladder snaked down from the helicopter and through a gap in the roof. The Headmaster began to climb it, glancing over his shoulder from time to time to make sure that none of the Brains had moved.

He's getting away, Dinah thought unhappily. *And there's nothing we can do.*

As he reached the helicopter and started to pull the rope ladder up after him, the roof panels slid together again, smoothly and quietly. Dinah had a final view of the helicopter turning in the direction of central London. Then the sky was hidden and the Brains were alone in the room.

We must do something. But before Dinah could speak the words aloud, things began to happen.

The first was up at the front of the room. As soon as the

283

Headmaster was safely out of the way, people darted out from behind the cabinets. Lloyd and Harvey. Ian and Mandy and Ingrid. Robert. Even that other boy who had been taken away.

'Fantastic!' said Camilla, 'if Robert's OK we can stop worrying and start trying to make some kind of plan . . .'

But her voice died away, in the very middle of what she was saying. Her face went blank and she sat down suddenly, her eyes fixed on the screen on her desk.

All round the room, the same thing was happening. Lots of the Brains had jumped up in fear and rage as the Headmaster explained about the Automatic Booby Trap. Now they were all sitting down meekly. Watching the green lines that began to snake their way across every screen in the room.

Oct –

'No I won't!' Dinah said out loud, standing stubbornly beside her chair. She couldn't look. She had to explain everything to Lloyd and Robert and the others. Try to make a plan –

284

Octo –

But all round her, on every side, green lines wriggled and arched and danced . . .

Octopus –

'No!' she said again. But this time she did not manage to sound so determined. After all, Lloyd and the others were already running down the room towards her. What *harm* could there be in just glancing at the lovely intricate curling lines that spiralled and sparkled and spun and . . .

Octopus – s – s – s – s!

Chapter 17

The Brains Fight Back

'No!'

Lloyd heard Dinah's shriek when he was half-way down the room. Before he had time to wonder what she meant, there was another shriek behind him, from Ingrid.

'Oh no! Not more octopuses!'

Octopuses! At the mere sound of the word, Lloyd felt himself filling with dark, speechless rage. So the Headmaster was doing it again, was he? Thinking he could treat people just like machines. Press the right button and they'll do what you want. Show them a few octopus patterns and they won't be any trouble. Well, he wasn't going to be treated like that! He screwed his eyes up so tightly that he could not see anything except prickles of light against the blackness of his eyelids.

'Ian!' he shouted. 'Mandy! Robert and Doug! Shut your eyes quickly and *don't open them*!' Then he thought fast. 'Ing, are you and Harvey all right?'

'*We're* OK,' Ingrid said scornfully. 'But we seem to be the only ones. The whole room's full of people gawping at octopuses. Pathetic!'

'Well, is there some way we can switch off the screens?' Lloyd turned towards Robert. 'Could you tell Ingrid how to turn the computer off?'

'Not safe,' Robert said firmly. 'You heard what the

287

Computer Director said before he left. Any interference with the computer will start a fire.'

'But there must be *something* we can do.' Lloyd thought even harder. 'Can we cover up the main screen? Is there any paper?'

'Gallons.' All of a sudden, Robert sounded much brisker and more cheerful. 'There's rolls and rolls of paper in the printer up the front. If Ingrid and Harvey stuck that all over the main screen, to hide the octopuses, then they could unplug all the little screens on the desks. That ought to be safe. It's not really interfering with the main computer.'

'Right,' said Lloyd. 'Hear that, Ingrid and Harvey? That's what you'll have to do. Cover the big screen first and then turn off the little ones. Got that? Ingrid! Harvey! What are you doing?'

'Don't be thick!' Ingrid's voice came from far up at the front. 'We didn't wait for you to tell us. We started as soon as Robert had the idea. We've nearly finished the big screen already.'

Lloyd bit back the cross answer that came to his lips. After all, if he annoyed Ingrid, they were all in trouble. Next to him he heard Ian chuckle.

'Horrible being dependent on those two, isn't it?' he drawled. 'Ingrid will really enjoy having us under her thumb.'

'Oh Ian, don't be *mean*!' Mandy said, on Lloyd's other side. 'We're jolly lucky that Ingrid and Harvey *aren't* addicted to the octopus patterns. If they had sat and watched them, like everyone else at the Computer Club, we'd all be fumbling around with our eyes shut now.'

'No we wouldn't,' Lloyd said bitterly. 'We'd all be standing like dummies in the Restraint Room. Like we were until Ingrid switched off *that* screen.'

As he finished speaking, Ingrid called from the front of the room. 'That's done! Now we'll do the little screens. Won't be long. Come on, Harvey.'

There was a sound of feet pattering down the room, stopping at every desk and then pattering on again at top speed. Mandy sighed anxiously.

'It's so awful not being able to *see*. Do you think I should take a peep? Just so we know how they're getting on?'

'No!' Lloyd's answer was fierce. But he knew what she meant. He was aching to open his own eyes. Just to get one more sight of those lovely swirling octopus patterns that he was missing. Those beautiful, twining . . .

No!

They had to defeat the Headmaster. *Somehow*. Otherwise he would take over the country and then the world. Nothing else mattered beside stopping that. Gritting his teeth, Lloyd screwed his eyes up even tighter and growled at the others. 'Don't you *dare* look until Ingrid and Harvey say we can.'

It seemed like another six or seven hours, but it could only have been a couple of minutes before Harvey called, 'It's all safe now. You can open your eyes.'

Lloyd unscrewed his, blinking in the brightness of the room. There was not an octopus to be seen. All round him, the little screens were blank and when he glanced over his shoulder he saw the thick cover of paper that Ingrid and Harvey had sellotaped over the main screen. They had made a good job of it.

On every side, Brains were rubbing their eyes and glancing round. Lloyd could tell from their horrified faces that they were just beginning to remember the frightful trap they were in. Some of the little ones had started to cry softly and the older ones were pale and tense. For a second, no one spoke and then a tall girl with long hair launched herself at Robert from the middle of the room.

'Oh Robert Robert thank goodness you're safe I've been so worried about you but did you hear the terrible things the Computer Director said how are we going to stop him – *what are we going to do?*'

As if she had pressed a switch, every head in the room turned in their direction. Big and small, old and young, all the Brains were staring at Robert and Lloyd as though they expected them to produce some marvellous plan. And the girl's question hung in the air, ringing in everyone's ear.

What are we going to do?

They had been freed from the octopuses, but the Headmaster was still flying across London in his helicopter, on his way to take over the Prime Minister's brain. And any attempt to use the computer to stop him or to escape from the building would start a fire. For a moment, Lloyd wondered whether they wouldn't all have been better off looking at the octopuses.

Then Dinah appeared beside him, so quietly that he did not notice her coming. She did not waste time saying how surprised she was to see him or asking how he got there. She just gave him a small, grateful smile and then turned to face the rest of the Brains, looking as calm as ever.

'Listen, everyone,' she said, in a steady, controlled voice, 'you don't need me to tell you what the choice is. You're all clever enough to work it out for yourselves. We can't escape from the building because we would need to use the computer to work the lift. So – we've got to decide. Are we going to sit back and wait for the country to be taken over? Or are we going to try and use the computer to warn the Downing Street security staff – even if it means burning to death?'

For a moment there was silence. Then a small girl, who was clutching a teddy bear, said timidly, 'I think we've *got* to do something. We can't just let him get away with it. It would be like the world coming to an end for everyone.' She stopped and swallowed hard before she added, 'Instead of just for us.'

'Right then, everyone,' Dinah said, in her inexpressive voice. 'We'd better vote. Who agrees with Bess that we should stop this evil plan – whatever happens to us afterwards?'

As she finished speaking, she put up her own hand, her thin arm looking very straight and steady. And one by one, all over the room, the other hands went up as the Brains voted with her. Some of them were crying and some of them looked frightened and sick, but they all voted to fight back against the Headmaster.

'What about you?' Dinah turned to the members of SPLAT. 'You ought to have a vote too.'

Lloyd had actually put his hand half-way up before his mind began to work properly. He had been so full of admiration for the Brains' bravery that he had not been *thinking*. Now he suddenly exploded.

'But we're *stupid*! *I'm* stupid. No one needs to burn to death!' He could see them all staring at him, and he hurried to explain, the words tumbling over themselves. 'Listen – the fire will start in the lift. Right? At the back of the room. Well we can all escape down the rubbish chute, the way the five of us came up. We've got ropes and most of us can get away before anyone *touches* the computer if we're quick. You don't need many people to stay and work it, do you?'

Dinah shook her head. 'I could do it. With one other person to watch me in case I made a mistake.' Her eyes were suddenly very bright.

'Well, I think you could escape as well,' Lloyd said. 'The rubbish chute will be on the opposite side of the building to the fire. If you're quick and you climb down fast you should have time.'

'Fantastic brilliant oh how marvellous to have something we can *do* I'll help to organize everyone to climb down where are the ropes –'

That was Robert's sister. But she was not just babbling. Even while she was talking, she had begun to organize the front rows of Brains to march towards the rubbish chute. And she had got Ian and Mandy knotting the ropes together to form a long string that would stretch all the way down the chute. Robert grinned at Lloyd.

'Don't let Camilla put you off. She only *sounds* thick. She'll get everyone out of here faster than anyone else could. And I'll stay and help Dinah change the information on the computer if she explains what she's doing. The rest of you can leave us here.'

'Not me,' Lloyd said. 'I can't go until I know we've stopped the Headmaster. But the others can.'

Ingrid tossed her head. 'Me and Harvey are staying. You might *need* us. Suppose you come across some more octopuses.'

Lloyd hesitated for a moment. Then he nodded. She was being sensible for once. 'OK. But that makes five of us left up here. We can't risk any more. Harvey, go and tell Ian and Mandy to go down with the others and leave the ropes for us.'

The room was already starting to look empty. A lot of the Brains were on their way down the rubbish chute and those who were left were crowded round the entrance waiting for their turn to squeeze under the flap. Dinah and Robert were huddled together at one of the desks, bent over a piece of paper, working out what they were going to do with the computer. Everyone was moving at a feverish pace. Lloyd shuddered slightly and hoped that it was not too late already. He did not know how long it would take a small helicopter to fly to the centre of London – but it could not be long.

Dinah glanced up as the last Brain wriggled under the flap. 'OK. I think we ought to start now. I'll do the first bit without switching on the screen, until I've got rid of the octopuses.'

Stretching out a finger, she pressed a key on the Saladin in front of her.

Immediately, the mechanical robot-voice rang through the empty room, startling them all.

'This Computer Is Booby-Trapped. Any Further Tampering Will Set Fire To The Building.'

'I think he meant it,' Robert murmured softly. 'Let's just hope it doesn't take too long.'

Without bothering to speak, Dinah nodded again and pressed another key and another. Lloyd looked nervously towards the lift doors. But nothing dramatic happened. There was no explosion, no instant burst of flame. What was it that the Headmaster had said? That it would be *slow and very painful*. Lloyd shuddered. Then his attention was drawn back to the computer. Dinah switched on the monitor.

'Let's just see what's running at the moment.'

For a second they all thought she had blundered, because what was on the screen was an octopus. But it was different from the usual twisting, swirling octopuses. This one was very still with all its tentacles stretched out straight, crossing

293

the screen diagonally and pointing at a tiny blob in the top right-hand corner. Behind the octopus, covering the screen like a sort of backcloth and moving all the time, as if it were unrolling, was a street map of London.

'What on earth –?' said Robert.

Lloyd and Dinah looked just as baffled, but Ingrid gave a loud squawk.

'Harvey – look! Oh Lloyd, you'll never guess what –'

But before she could finish her sentence, Lloyd smelt what he had been afraid of all the time. Scorching. Turning his head, he saw a small wisp of smoke curling under the lift doors.

'Be quiet, Ingrid!' he snapped. 'There's no time for chattering. Hurry up, Dinah.'

'But if you'd only *listen* –' protested Ingrid.

'Ssh!' hissed Lloyd. Really, she was hopeless. She had no idea of how desperate things were.

'But Lloyd,' Harvey joined in, 'if you'd only let us *tell* you –'

Lloyd nearly shouted at him. 'Don't you understand? *The lift is on fire.* If Robert and Dinah aren't very quick, we'll all burn to death. So don't distract them.'

Harvey looked unhappy and Ingrid sniffed and turned away, but they both stopped talking. Lloyd looked back to the screen and as he did so, Robert said, 'Found it! Well done, Dinah. Now you can get going.'

Across the screen spread a single sentence.

WHAT DO YOU WANT?

Dinah tapped the keys, typing in a reply, and for a moment Lloyd thought she had gone mad as the lines of print – question and answer – began to fill the screen.

KNOCK KNOCK

WHO'S THERE

OLGA

OLGA WHO?

Robert caught sight of his face and grinned. 'Password,' he murmured. 'Look, she's putting in the last line now.'

OLGA MAD IF I DON'T GET OFF THIS LOOP

Sure enough, as Dinah typed it in the joke vanished and a long catalogue appeared on the screen heading:

PRIME MINISTER

PERSONAL INFORMATION.

'That's what it was all about,' Robert said softly. 'The Junior Computer Brain Competition and *Octopus Dare* and

everyone being invited here. All so that your Headmaster could get at *that*.'

'Well, now *I'm* going to get at it,' Dinah said. She pressed the right key to select the list of:

PEOPLE TO BE ADMITTED TO PRIME
MINISTER TOP PRIORITY.

It was a fairly long list and she searched through it at feverish speed. Lloyd knew why she was hurrying so hard. A mist of smoke had drifted up in front of the lift doors and was slowly working its way down the room.

'There!' Dinah said at last. 'I've taken the Headmaster's name out. And I've replaced it with a warning – so that they know security has been breached when they look for him. That *should* fix him.'

'You mean you've done it?' Lloyd felt like cheering. 'We've defeated his plans?'

Dinah nodded. 'We've done everything we can.' But she did not look very happy. Lloyd peered at her, trying to ignore the crackling sounds that were coming from the lift.

'What's the matter, Di?'

'We-ell.' Dinah pulled a face. 'We've done all we can, but – suppose it's not enough? Suppose they don't bother to check the security list? The Headmaster's gone off to Number Ten Downing Street with today's password in his head and there's no way we can wipe *that* out. They might just let him in when he gives the right password. And then . . .' She let her voice die away and shrugged. 'Oh well, we'll just have to hope for the best. Like I said, there's nothing else we can do.'

She had stood up and was turning towards the rubbish chute when Ingrid suddenly exploded in a great yell.

'YES THERE IS, YOU STUPID IDIOTS!' she shouted. 'THERE *IS* SOMETHING ELSE WE CAN DO!!'

Chapter 18

The Last Octopus

Ingrid had gone completely red in the face with fury and her fists were clenched tight. 'You're all supposed to be older and cleverer and more sensible than me,' she panted, 'but you won't listen and now I expect it's too late and –'

'Ingrid!' Dinah caught her by the shoulders. 'If there's anything you can tell us – *anything* – then tell us. But please do it now, because there's almost no time left.'

They could all smell the scorching now, very strongly, and the doors of the lift were beginning to darken in the centre, as though the flames were eating a hole in them.

'It's – it's –' But Ingrid's rage had made her so breathless that she could not speak. She faced Dinah and struggled to gulp in enough air to say what she wanted to, but no sound came out.

'*I'll* tell you what she wants to say,' Harvey interrupted. 'We've been trying to tell people ever since we got into this tower. We saw that helicopter in the car park and it had an octopus picture on its control panel. Just like that octopus picture we saw on the screen just now, with the map of London behind it and –'

But Robert had already worked it out, in a flash. 'And we know that the Super-Saladin controls the helicopter, so perhaps *that* octopus picture is a diagram of how it does it. And perhaps *we* could get control of the helicopter and turn it back.'

Dinah looked at him very steadily for a second, her face white. Then she glanced across at the lift doors. As she did so, a small hole appeared in the centre of it. Flames licked through the hole, shockingly bright, reaching out towards the rest of the room.

'The rest of you had better go,' Dinah said quietly. 'I'm going to have a go at stopping the helicopter, but there's no point in everyone staying here.'

'Go on.' Lloyd jerked his head at the other three. 'I'm staying with Dinah.'

For a moment it looked as though Robert would argue, but instead he shepherded Ingrid and Harvey towards the rubbish chute as Dinah sat down in front of the keyboard again.

Lloyd looked nervously over his shoulder. He had no intention of letting Dinah stay on her own, but he hoped she would *hurry*. The far end of the room was completely filled with smoke now and the doorway of the lift was a bright square of flame.

'There we are,' Dinah said softly. 'There's the picture again.'

She made herself sit very still for a second, just studying it, gripping her two hands together to stop them trembling. It was no use being afraid. She had to concentrate on what she was doing.

As soon as she looked at the picture properly, she could see that Ingrid and Harvey were right. It was a diagram of how the Super-Saladin controlled the helicopter. The octopus's body represented the Super-Saladin and the tentacles were the lines of force going out to the helicopter – like radio waves going out to a remote controlled model plane. The map in the background showed where the helicopter was, above the ground. And it was – Dinah peered at the map and then gulped – it was almost above Downing Street. She had only about a minute left. Perhaps no more than thirty seconds.

Cautiously at first, but then faster and faster she began to press keys. Immediately she began, the octopus's tentacles started to move, answering the movements of the keys. And as the tentacles moved, so did the blob which represented the helicopter. Instead of travelling in a steady straight line across the map, it began to whirl and dance.

'It's like a sort of *Reverse Octopus Dare*,' murmured Lloyd. 'This time you're the octopus instead of the blob. And *you've* got the helicopter at *your* mercy.'

'Not properly at my mercy,' Dinah said, sounding flustered. She was struggling to make the tentacles turn the helicopter round and bring it back, but somehow she could not quite get a grip on it. And all the time she was aware of smoke billowing closer, starting to sting her eyes. 'I can flick the blob – the helicopter – about, but I can't get hold of it properly.'

'Well, flick it *down*,' Lloyd said fiercely. He could feel the warmth of the fire against his back. 'Make him crash. We haven't got time to hang about.'

'All right,' said Dinah. She reached out to do what he had suggested. And then it hit her. *Make him crash. Him.* It was not a game like *Octopus Dare* that she was playing. And the blob she had been playing with was not a blob. It was a helicopter. With a person inside. Feeling sick, she took her hands off the keyboard and stared down at them.

'*What's the matter?*' Lloyd almost screamed it at her. 'Di, we've got to *go*. You must finish it now.'

'I can't do it,' Dinah said stiffly. 'I'm sorry, but even if it is the Headmaster – *I can't kill him.*'

'Oh, for heaven's sake!' Lloyd shouted. 'If you dither any longer, he'll get to the Prime Minister and we'll burn to death.'

He reached over her shoulder, meaning to do it himself. To press a few keys and crash a helicopter. But as soon as he got within touching distance of the keyboard, he faltered and stopped.

'You see?' Dinah said miserably. '*You* can't, either. And anyway, think how dangerous it would be, crashing a helicopter in the middle of London.'

Lloyd coughed as the smoke caught the back of his throat. 'If only we could just get him *away*.'

'We can!' In a flash, Dinah saw it, with a great burst of relief. 'I won't flick him down – I'll flick him *up*, as far as I can. Right away. Then we must race down the rope, before it's too late. Ready?'

With her eyes watering so that she could hardly see and her ears full of the roaring of the flames, she reached for the keyboard.

Outside Number Ten Downing Street, a crowd of people had gathered to watch the strange sight up in the evening sky.

A small helicopter was tumbling head over heels, twirling round in a most extraordinary way. Was the pilot drunk? Had he gone mad?

The helicopter swooped down towards the earth. For a moment, the watchers had a glimpse of a cold, furious face. A face with huge, strange, sea-green eyes. It glared down at the crowd, the amazing eyes burning with unforgettable rage.

Then, just as suddenly as it had swooped, the helicopter soared upwards, as though someone had flicked it up and

thrown it. Up and up, further and further into the brilliance of the sunset, with the light glinting from its spotless glass dome.

Then it whirled away to the west and disappeared in the far distance.

Five minutes later, Lloyd jumped down from the dustbin and raced out of the underground car park, dragging Dinah after him. Smoke filled the air outside and they did not stop to see what was happening. They plunged straight across to the subway that led off Turk's Island and raced down the steps.

So it was not until they came out beside the station that

they looked back. They came up the steps and found all the Brains gathered in a huge crowd, gazing back across the motorway intersection. Ingrid and Harvey and Mandy were in the very front of the crowd and they pointed silently, until Lloyd and Dinah turned to see.

The Saracen Tower was a huge pillar of flame, three hundred feet high. Even from where they were standing, they could feel the heat of the flames and hear the noise of splintering glass and falling metal. The outside framework, which held the giant mirror panes, was glowing red hot as the mirrors shattered and showered to the ground.

For a moment Dinah could only think what a stunning sight it was. Then something occurred to her and a slow, relieved smile spread over her face.

'It really *is* the end of the Headmaster's plan,' she said softly. 'His whole scheme for running the country was stored on the Super-Saladin. In that building. Now it's gone.'

She heard a tiny snuffle at her elbow. Looking round, she saw Ingrid wipe her eyes.

'Whatever's the matter, Ing? You can't be sorry.'

'I'm *not* crying!' Ingrid said fiercely.

'No, of course you're not. But –'

'It's that lovely computer,' Ingrid burst out. 'That Super-Saladin. All burnt up.'

'But *Ingrid*!' Lloyd and Harvey and Ian and Mandy all said it together, turning to stare at her. 'You *hate* computers!'

'Not that one,' Ingrid said pathetically. 'How can you hate a computer when you've seen it cooking the dinner and treating Harvey like a packet of spaghetti? It was a lovely computer. *Funny*. And it could talk. I bet I could have got it to say *Down With The Headmaster*!'

303

Mandy put an arm round her. 'Never mind. Don't you remember all those SPLAT things we were going to do this holiday? The picnic and the camp and the visit to the Science Museum? We could still fit in a couple of them before the beginning of term.'

'Oh yes. Of course,' said Ingrid. But she did not look any more cheerful.

'And you can forget all about computers!' added Harvey.

'But computers are *fun!*' wailed Ingrid. She looked ready to burst into tears properly.

Lloyd and Dinah looked at each other.

'Do you think we could tell her now?' Lloyd murmured.

'I *think* so.' Dinah grinned. 'I think it would be safe.'

'What?' Ingrid looked up sharply. 'What are you two talking about?'

Lloyd chuckled. 'We didn't tell you before, because we thought you'd go up in a cloud of smoke, but Mr Meredith's starting a *permanent* Computer Club at school as soon as term begins. Every week.'

Ingrid glanced at Dinah, as though she could hardly believe it, and Dinah nodded. 'That's right. And if you join, I'll show you how to do things with the school computers. I don't suppose any of them can cook, but I *can* teach you how to make one of them say *Down with the Headmaster!*'

'WHOOPEE!' Ingrid's high, delighted shout screeched up into the night sky, making all the Brains laugh.

There was so much noise that only Lloyd and Dinah heard what Ian murmured as he glanced back at the blazing Saracen Tower.

'I wonder where he *did* come down . . .'